First published by Blasted Heath, 2014
copyright © 2014 Douglas Lindsay
This edition by Long Midnight Publishing 2017

www.douglaslindsay.com

ISBN: 978-1-54962-104-8

THE BLOOD THAT STAINS YOUR HANDS

DOUGLAS LINDSAY

LMP

1

There's a light on in the sitting room. Must have forgotten to turn it off. Close my eyes, stretch my legs, pull the duvet a little tighter on the right where the cold air is getting in.

No. I know I didn't leave the light on.

There are plenty of those nights. The nights that end with me collapsed in a heap, crawling to bed with no idea of the time, when I leave the light on or the television on or the fridge door open or forget to set my alarm or all of those things, and in the morning I wonder why it was that I didn't just step out the front door, walk down to the train station and fall in front of the overnight sleeper to Euston.

Last night wasn't one of those. It was a regular night. Worked late, bought a fish supper and a bottle of Coke Zero on the way home, watched some documentary on BBC4, went to bed, turning off the lights on the way.

I open my eyes again. Don't move. Look through the open bedroom door, at the closed door to the sitting room. The light shows around the edges. Attune my hearing to the night.

Silence. No wind outside, no cars in the vicinity, can't even hear the distant, low rumble of the M74.

Turn my head to look at the clock. 02:02. Fuck. Feel myself becoming more and more awake. These days I have no trouble getting to sleep, but often wake up in the middle of the night and I can never get back off.

I raise myself from the bed and look at the light. I want to ignore it. I can't hear anything, don't get the feeling that I'm being burgled. It's just a light. I start trying to tell myself that maybe I did leave it on, even though I know I didn't.

Fuck.

Feet over the side of the bed, sit there for a moment. Stretch. The air is cold, even though I haven't slept with the window open. Wearing a T-shirt and a pair of boxer shorts. Stand up, stretch again. Look at the light. Start to feel nervous.

Where are the nerves coming from? If I did believe it was a thief, I'd be straight in there. No nerves, wouldn't give a shit what happened. Not anymore. Nothing seems to matter anymore.

Jesus, pull yourself together, Hutton.

Walk through, across the hall, open the door to the sitting room.

The light is coming from the lamp on the small table. The room looks the same as it always does. The TV in the corner, the sofa where I conduct much of my life, watching sport, eating pizza, the small dining table big enough for two, the picture of Grace Kelly on the wall next to the door. The one that I ought to have taken down years ago.

There's a girl standing at the window, looking down on the street. For a second I wonder if it might be Rebecca, but this girl is too young, her hair too long. I didn't creep in, she should have heard me, but she doesn't turn.

I stand like that for a while, staring at the back of her head, then finally say, 'What are you looking at?'

She doesn't answer for a few moments, then she turns. I don't recognise her. She's young. Twelve, maybe. She's wearing a dress with a cardigan. The sleeves of the cardigan are too short. There's a timeless quality about her clothes.

'Just looking at the view,' she says.

'Do I know you?'

She shakes her head. 'No.'

She turns back and looks at the view again: the street five floors below, and the more or less identical block of houses across the road.

I walk over beside her and look down. The street is

quiet. A few cars parked as ever, none driving by. There's one person in sight. A man, directly across the road. He's talking, holding something in his hand. I can't hear what he's saying, but he's not looking up here. I can't see who he's talking to.

'What's that in his hand?' I ask.

'A Bible,' she says.

Maybe it is. Maybe it's a book. How can she possibly tell from up here that it's a Bible? I need my eyes tested, I know that. Putting it off. Not that I care about glasses, and the signs of encroaching middle age.

'How do you know it's a Bible?'

She doesn't reply. She's not there. I turn round to look at the room. She's gone. The light is off.

From the streetlights, I can make out the glint in Grace Kelly's lipstick. Turn back and look at the guy across the road.

A car approaches, slows as it passes him. The driver's watching him, possibly laughing at what he thinks is a drunk guy railing against the world in the middle of the night.

There was a young girl here a minute ago, wasn't there? That doesn't make sense. I turn again and look at the room. Dark. Silent.

Maybe not. It's the middle of the night. Maybe I was dreaming.

What was it I was dreaming about?

I walk back through to the bedroom and crawl under the duvet.

2

Things haven't been too bad since the night I stubbed out a cigarette on my arm.

You get your touchy-feely police officer. The one who wants to understand people. The one who thinks they can make a difference. Nip problems in the bud. The metaphorical arm around the shoulder, the calming word of advice.

There's not a huge amount of time for that kind of malarkey in these under-funded days of course, but there could be ten police officers to every crime and it wouldn't make any difference to me. Whatever the opposite of that asinine expression *touchy-feely* is, I'm it.

I do my job in the most pragmatic way possible. I deal with what's there before me. When a crime has been committed, and it lands on my desk, then I'll turn on the switch and get to work. I genuinely hate people who break the law, who take it into their own hands, who think they're above it, whose actions have a total disregard for others. Nevertheless, I never have any sympathy for the victims.

I never feel their pain. My heart does not go out to them. I do not empathise or sympathise. I don't try to understand what they're going through. The words *pull yourself together* stay tucked away, but they're not that far inside my head.

So I don't understand people and their problems and never think about them. For example, in this line of work one occasionally comes across someone – usually a teenager – who self-harms. I've always looked at them and wondered what the fuck they were thinking. It probably wouldn't have taken too much effort to find out, but I never tried.

But one night, alone in my sitting room in front of one of those atrocious Hollywood action movies, with an eighty-year-old Bruce Willis shooting people in the face in the blessed name of popcorn, America and entertainment, I stubbed a cigarette out on my arm. A fucking sobbing mess of depression, alcohol and cliché.

But I tell you what; that moment, that moment when I burned a fag into my skin and the pain shot up my arm, and I held it there until the burning tobacco fizzled out on the flesh, and the pain shot straight to my head, and I opened my mouth in a silent scream, I thought two things.

Firstly, it wasn't nearly as painful as getting your hand crushed by a pair of pliers or being tasered on your butt-naked erect penis.

And second... the second was the thing. The moment I realised why people do this shit. Why they burn themselves. Why they break their bones. Why they inflict pain. Because at that moment, I wasn't thinking about how fucked up I was; I wasn't thinking about screwing up my latest relationship, or how miserable my pathetic stupid life had become, and I wasn't thinking about the guilt I carried around from that forest all those years ago, or the on-going, never-ending stabbing guilt of being a total let down of a father. All I was thinking about was the stupid burn on my arm and the fact that it felt as though my flesh was on fire.

That'll be it, I thought. That's why you fucking stab yourself! I started laughing. Yep, hysterically. Was it the kind of laughter that turns to tears? Jesus, I don't know, I was already fucking crying before I started.

I lay there sobbing and laughing manically for God knows how long. Fell asleep at some point. Woke up the next morning at 11 a.m. It was still three days before I was due to return to work after my extended sick leave – as my doctor had declared me able – so I didn't have to run around, grabbing toast and diving into the shower. I just lay there, a dull throbbing in my arm, devoid of everything. Devoid of guilt, devoid of depression, devoid of fear. Empty.

I have neither laughed nor cried since. Nor, indeed, felt the need to stab myself with a cigarette.

The next time work brings me into contact with some poor fucker who's obviously been stabbing themselves in the eyeball with a fondue fork, I won't feel any sympathy for them, much beyond a vague curiosity about whether or not it worked. But at least I'll have a better understanding of why they did it in the first place.

Ha! Hutton, the humanist prick.

3

I'm talking to the guy who cleans the toilets.

Hmm, toilet vandalism. I'd been thinking the same thing since Ramsay passed on the case this morning. It's not something you get out of bed for, is it? No one joins the police so that they can investigate toilet vandalism. No one sits in class when they're fourteen and thinks, fuck me, I'd better stick in at this English and Maths shit so that I can investigate toilets when I'm older.

And the same would apply, you'd think, to the poor bastard who has to spend his life cleaning the toilets.

He's taken me on a quick tour of the vandalised area, and now we're standing outside the small building. The bottom end of Main Street. A cold morning, early November. Walking to work this morning – yep, I walked to work, so booyah! – there was that fabulous autumnal feel in the air. The one that makes you think that it was always like this when you were a kid, and it only seems to happen on about three mornings a year now. Reminds me of going to watch the Thistle on a cold day in Forfar.

Anyway, the scent of it has gone. Now it's just a regular cold morning in Scotland. A weak sun, a mournful suggestion of the loss of something that once was.

'How long's it been going on?'

So far the notebook has stayed in my pocket.

'How long has the vandalising of toilets been going on?' he asks.

'Yep.'

'I don't know,' he says, pointedly. 'Since the sack of Rome in 455?'

'Everyone loves a comedian.'

'What d'you want me to say, man? I started doing this job two years ago. Every one of the toilets on my route was already vandalised to some degree. I repair them, I clean them, people vandalise them. Every week. That's what happens. That's what people do.'

Sure, he's a bit lippy, but he's got a point.

'It's the equivalent of you catching a criminal and then the jury letting him off, allowing him to go and commit more crime. And doing it week after week.'

'That's pretty much how it works.'

'I bet it is. Perhaps we can work together to at least catch and prosecute the toilet vandals.'

'It's a fair cop,' I say. 'But why now?'

'Just had enough,' he says. 'A build up. Would be nice if you lot could do something.'

'So, you're the repair guy as well as the cleaner?'

'It's not exactly in my job description.'

'Why d'you do it then?'

'I don't know,' he says, but there's a wistfulness in his voice, rather than bitterness, or blind stupidity. There's something about this guy. You know, it's like that show, *Undercover Bosses*, or whatever, one of those shows where the chief executive goes and makes burgers. Or cleans the toilets. You form an impression of some guy who cleans toilets for a living and this guy isn't it. 'You clean the toilets. They look pretty good. You create a clean environment for people to use. I mean, is it world peace or a cure for cancer or scoring the goal that gets Scotland to the World Cup Finals? No. But day-to-day, you know, people's lives, it's nice to create somewhere where they can go to the toilet and not think, Jesus, this is a shit tip, I'm getting out of here as fast as I can. People have expectations of pubic toilets and I want them to be surprised when they come in. Like to do a good job. Then some bell-end defaces them, and I report it to the office and they stick it at number eight hundred on the list of eight hundred things that need to get done. No one gives a shit about the toilets. So I do. Just get on and take care of

8

things myself.'

'Fuck,' I find myself letting slip. There's something incredibly impressive about this guy.

'What?'

'Nothing. So, do you report the repairs, get them to pay you for the work and materials, that kind of thing?'

'Nope.'

'Must cost you.'

'Not so much. Money's not that big a deal. I just go home nights. Small place. Doing my Masters in English Lit.'

'Couldn't get a job after uni?'

'Worked for HSBC for a while. Split time between Hong Kong and London. Didn't like the travelling. All that corporate shit. Lunches and guys talking out the corporate end of their corporate arse, working until three in the morning on deals of absolutely no importance whatsoever to anyone. All that world, it's just emperor's new clothes. Wanted something simpler.'

'You're not serious.'

'That's what everyone says. You should hear my dad. But look, I provide a service. I make a small difference to a small number of people. I don't have to think about my work. Can let my mind wander. And yes, I know, there's some sort of OCD going on. If I walk into somewhere that's looking a bit dirty, I need to clean it. Don't know where that comes from, but I've got it. So I do it for a living. Albeit,' he adds, shaking his head, 'I don't actually need the living. Long term I'll probably end up in academia.'

He finishes his little justification, although there wasn't an ounce of self-satisfaction or affectedness in the tone, then glances at his watch.

'Look, Sergeant, I know there's not a lot you can do, short of setting up a massive surveillance operation, and I doubt the public are going to be happy about CCTV inside the toilet.' He laughs, I join him. 'Even then, if you caught them, they're probably twelve years old and all you can do

—
9

is report them to their parents, who themselves likely don't care. But if you could give it some thought and try to come up with something, I'd appreciate it.'

We shake hands. I turn and look around at the area. Cold and grey. How can you live here and not be depressed? I mean, fundamentally depressed, right down to the soles of your shoes.

'That house over there,' he says. 'The one standing on its own. Used to be the public toilet. Not many people know that.'

'They converted a public toilet into a house?'

'Yep. Weird, isn't it?'

'Not really a selling point,' I say. 'Converted public toilet.'

'No, but I'll tell you what's weirder. Estate agents will use "converted barn" as a selling point. Quite posh sounding, isn't it, in its way? Converted barn. Now, maybe the barn just had hay in it, but chances are it also had cows. Those cows would have been shitting up a storm. No matter how gross a public toilet can be, it's never going to be as bad as a barn. Yet, converted barn sounds pretty cool, converted public toilet... not so much.'

'Hmm. It's probably related to space, rather than hygiene. Barn suggests spaciousness, public toilet suggests dark and dingy squalor.'

'Suppose,' he says.

We both look at the converted public toilet for a while, and with a shrug he turns and heads off to the next toilet on his route. I stand at the bottom end of Main Street and look up at the sky. Tut-tut, looks like rain.

Jesus, where did that come from?

*

I pass DCI Taylor as I walk back into the office. He gives me the eyebrow as I slump back behind my desk. Look across at DI Morrow, who doesn't lift his head at my arrival.

The various files and photographs and reports that litter the desk are pretty much as they were an hour ago, just before I went out for my life-changing chat with the toilet cleaner. To my right I'm aware of DCI Taylor folding his arms. I look at the phone, knowing that I have several calls to make. Indeed, the act of interviewing the toilet guy was mostly one of phone-call avoidance. I'm back now and the phone is still there, looking at me, waiting for me to pick it up.

Sitting in silent judgement, it reminds me of my first wife.

Glance over at the recently installed coffee machine, something which they've done in an attempt to stop us all constantly trooping across the road to Costa. That, and I expect they're hoping it brings in some income which they can use to fund policing in this area, what with the government much closer to bankruptcy than anyone cares to admit.

From the coffee machine, I turn my glance round to Taylor as I'm aware he's still staring at me.

'You have a look about you,' he says.

'Just had an epiphany.'

Morrow looks up. Sure, you can ignore a guy when he sits down opposite you, but much tougher to disregard an epiphany announcement.

'Jesus,' mutters Taylor.

I shake my head, and stare off across the room, trying to capture what it is that talking to the toilet guy has made me realise. Though, was it even a realisation? There was just something about him. The simplicity of it. The ease with which he discussed his life. I don't think I've ever spoken to anyone who seemed so much at peace with how he lived. And he cleans toilets.

'Bored now,' says Taylor, when I take more than ten seconds to find the right words. 'Suicide, with a hint of potential murder, up in the public park. You might as well come along. If you can conjure up the right amount of poetry and drama, you can tell me about your dumb-ass epiphany on the way. We're walking, by the way. Nice day. Autumnal.'

Morrow watches us go and then once more bows his head to the paperwork.

4

We're at the bottom of the public park. Down by the large pond with three separate streams running into it. Came here a lot over the summer when I was off work. Sitting in amongst the trees. Getting used to things again. Thinking. Above us and behind us, through the trees, is the Old Kirk, the spire visible between the bare branches of the oaks.

Down here, set in the grass, is a plaque commemorating the Cambuslang Wark, a time when the local minister rallied the troops behind God. God, and all that. 1742, it says. Apparently thirty thousand people would gather in this place to listen. I used to sit on the bench here and try to imagine what that looked like.

We've come to get some perspective. There is a woman hanging by the neck from the footbridge at the top of the dip, where the footpath is taken high across the stream that runs through the gully.

There are a few of our lot around, including the pathologist, Balingol, waiting for the body to be cut down, something which is imminent. The area has been cordoned off, and already every inch photographed and examined. There are a few spectators at the edge of the cordon, and a couple of officers nearby trying to make sure that no cynical bastard is uploading the investigation and the cutting down of the poor deceased directly onto YouTube.

The woman is dressed in a light brown coat. The whole scene, horribly melancholic and grim, a sight to depress the crap out of even the most upbeat toilet cleaner, has the edge taken from it by the bizarre sight of the woman having a pair of large, feathered wings attached to the back of her coat. Clumsily attached, too, barely holding on.

We'd stood on the bridge looking down at the woman for a while, and now we've been down below, looking back up at her for some ten minutes.

'You ever come here?' asks Taylor, breaking a long silence.

'Yep. Nice walk, up the gully, round the top, back down to the football fields. Not long, but on a sunny day, it's all right.'

'A lot of people around?'

'The usual array of dog walkers and runners. You?'

He thinks about it for a while, eventually says, 'There was a mugging a few years ago, was up here for that. Guy was in a coma for a while. Haven't been since.'

'Hmm,' I say.

The water cooler chat of your average police officers. A guy in a coma is no more interesting than a guy buying a new pair of socks.

'The wings give the scene a peculiar quality,' I say.

'Know what you mean.'

He gives a quick wave of the hand to signal that it's time to bring in the body.

The stream beneath the bridge is swollen and unusually fast-flowing, so there will be no letting her down. They've decided to manoeuvre her to the side of the bridge, rather than haul her clumsily over the railing.

A police constable unties the knot around the top of the railing, while another grips the rope, taking the weight of the body. As it swings free, the first polis reaches down and the two of them start to move her along to their right. There are another two coppers on the bank at the end of the bridge, waiting to receive the body.

As it gets there, they reach out to grab it and haul it in, all the time aware that the pathologist, and the principal investigating officer – Taylor – are watching them, wanting as little impact on the corpse and her clothing as possible.

Unfortunately, the two guys at the side used to be lesser well-known members of the Marx Brothers. As they reach out to receive the body, one of them slips a little. He regains his footing, but in doing so knocks the other guy, who then falls down the bank, grabbing at grass and roots on his way, before ending up in the mass of branches and litter that is collected in the burn beneath the bridge. In trying to quickly recover from the slip, he puts his foot through the makeshift dam and plunges, waist deep, into the water.

A couple of our lot laugh. The distant audience are howling. Taylor and I glance at each other. We're a much tougher audience.

'Fucking idiots,' is all he says.

The body is safely brought to the side of the bridge and laid down on a prepared mat on the path. PC Gummo crawls to the side of the stream, and starts to scramble up the bank.

'Get them out the way,' says Taylor. 'Stay with Balingol while he takes his initial look. See if there's anything on her person. A note, or some ID. I'm going to go and speak to the crowd, then I'll probably head back.'

*

Back at the ranch with Taylor, flicking through notes.

'Balingol thinks she's been there since late last night, early this morning. On the face of it, it looks like suicide. Funny it wasn't spotted earlier, but it was dark until eight, I suppose. Must have been folk walked across the bridge and didn't notice.'

'It was misty,' says Taylor. 'Hangs in the basin some days. Look on Tumblr or Facebook or whatever, and you'll likely find people were posting pictures of it two hours before anyone reported it to us.'

Hey, he's not kidding. That shit happens.

'You've got a name?' he says.

'Maureen Henderson. Eighty-one years old. Three kids, widowed.'

'Recently?'

'Seems to have been a while.' Quick notebook check. 'One of the kids is in Hamilton, one in Canada, one in the US. And obviously, when I say kids... they're our age.'

He checks his computer, looks back at me. We have the telepathic, *who's going to deliver the bad news* conversation.

'No problem,' I say. 'I'll go now.'

'Take Constable Grant,' he says.

'Yep.'

Always better to have a female presence when delivering shit news. That's not official policy, mind. Just common sense. Most male police officers join up so they can legally hit people; as a result, when they're delivering bad news, it's not completely unknown for it to come out as something along the lines of, *'Your mum's dead. I'm going for a sandwich.'*

And it's always nice to spend some time alone in a car with Constable Grant. As time goes by, she's slowly recovering from the night she mistakenly ended up in bed with me. Not that I viewed it as a mistake, but you can see her point.

5

The daughter, Margaret Johnstone, has held it together pretty well. Under the circumstances. That your mother hung herself – or was murdered, which is just as shit – is a pretty brutal thing to hear out of the blue. Constable Grant has gone into the kitchen to make tea, leaving me in the high-ceilinged front room of the old Victorian house to talk about the deceased.

'Three weeks,' she says. 'That's terrible. It's just down the road. I was going to be seeing her this Sunday. We were going to church, then back to her place for lunch. John's away sailing. They're bringing the boat in this week.'

'Your husband?'

She nods. John Johnstone? Seriously? Perhaps his first name is Quentin or Ffarquhar and he prefers an abbreviation of his surname.

'Oh God.'

She takes a deep breath. Struggling. Maybe the middle-class upper lip isn't going to be as stiff as I thought. I glance at the door and hope that Grant gets a shift on.

'I was supposed to go on Sunday and I cancelled.' Another shake of the head. Not a lot to say to that one. Just something that's going to live with her. Cancelling what turns out to be the last time you'd ever see your mum. She's not getting that one back.

Keep her talking.

'You spoke to her?'

'Yes, yes.' Well, at least she didn't cancel the church trip by text. That would have been a killer. 'I called on Saturday evening to tell her I couldn't make it. She sounded upset, but then... she quite often... she could be difficult. Demanding.'

'Did you speak to her again?'

'I called her on Sunday evening. We spoke for about an hour. Maybe more.'

'And how did she sound?'

She shakes her head, stares at the ceiling.

'Just the same, you know, the same as always. Banging on about the church. She was a broken record...'

The voice starts to go, just as Constable Grant returns with a pot of tea and some biscuits on a plate. Oh happy day. I wonder why I didn't put up more of a telepathic struggle with Taylor.

'Thank you, Constable,' she says, managing to collect herself. She moves the coffee table a fraction of an inch as Grant sets down the tray. She pours three cups of tea. The liquid filling the mugs is the only sound in the room. Double glazing, nothing getting in from outside.

'What was the problem with the church?' I ask.

'Oh, God,' she says, 'if I start on that we'll be here until the middle of next year.'

She reaches forward and takes the tea. Has a large drink straight away, as if it's brandy. I lift my mug. It's steaming hot. She must have asbestos lips.

'Can you give us a two-minute outline?' I ask.

'I can try, though it'll be like giving a two-minute outline of the history of the Middle East.'

I take a sip of tea. Burn my lips, my tongue and the top of my mouth. Glance at Constable Grant.

*

Returned to the station and swapped Taylor for Grant. Now the two of us are on our way to see the minister. Driving, although it's not much further than the walk to the park where the body was discovered. Bob was playing when Taylor started up, but he must feel the need to talk as *Another Self Portrait* was quickly turned off.

Initial report from Balingol's lab threw up nothing new, no new marks on her body, no sign of a struggle. Mrs Johnstone told us enough to imply that her mother was prone to anger and depression and feeling sorry for herself. Not necessarily suicidal, but then she hadn't seen her for three weeks. So, at the moment, given the obvious lack of a struggle, suicide seems more of a favourite than murder.

No explanation for the wings. You could tell from the daughter that she just plain didn't believe it. It was such a bizarre thing that she sat there shaking her head and then moved the conversation on. Didn't know what to think about it, and so therefore didn't even try. Can't blame her.

We're on our way to the deceased's house, but have decided to stop off to see the minister beforehand. The Old Manse is up at the top of the town, about a mile away from where the body was found.

'You heard about the churches?' I asked.

'I know they amalgamated and no one was very happy,' he says. 'Read about it in the *Reformer*. What's the story? And remember, we'll be there in under a minute.'

'The Church of Scotland told the four churches they had to merge. Choose a minister out of the four, choose a building. Three of the ministers would go off and get other jobs, they'd sell the three spare buildings. Of course, everyone hates each other, so it's a total fucking bunfight.'

'When did this start?'

'Three years ago. Maybe four. She couldn't remember exactly when it all kicked off.'

'Jesus. We're lucky this is the first death. Might be time to start presuming the woman's been murdered.'

I laugh, but he's got a point.

'So, when did they choose, and which minister is it we're going to see?'

'Well, they chose several times. Every time they made a choice, someone would object and find a reason to overrule the decision and there would be another vote. It all got very nasty. They ended up with some absurd compromise where they used the building from St

Mungo's down by the golf course...'

'The 1950's carbuncle?'

'Yep. While consigning the other three regular, older, better-built and more church-like buildings to the scrap heap. However, they decided to hang on to the Old Kirk up the hill so they can use its halls, and sell St Stephen's at the bottom of the Main Street and Halfway Church on the way out of town.'

He stops at a junction. A funeral cortege is going slowly by, and we pull up just in time to see the hearse, followed by the black limo containing the relatives of the dead. There are four people in the car. Two women wearing hats, and a guy in a suit – they're not talking – and in the middle of them a young lad wearing a shirt and tie but no jacket. They can't have been able to find anything for him to wear. Hope the little blighter doesn't have to go and stand by a graveside for half an hour.

The faces of the bereaved drive hauntingly by, one by one, the same silent expression on every countenance. So much of life is a façade. Not this, however. This is the real melancholy of death laid bare.

'Must have been young,' I say.

'What?'

'The funeral. Everyone looks so... sad. So much sorrow. You don't get that so much with an older, more natural death. Look at them.'

There are cars going by, a few with teenagers driving, four or five to a car, as if the cortege had suddenly decided to confirm my thought.

The melancholy envelops us for a moment. Settles over the car, like a sudden fall of snow, and then melts away as the final car passes by and Taylor pulls across the road.

'So what happened to the other congregations? Did they launch an insurrection? The Scottish equivalent of the Arab spring?'

'It didn't get that far, although she hinted at things being pretty ugly. In the end the Old Kirk and the Halfway congregations caved, and moved to St Mungo's. However, all along the St Stephen's people maintained that they owned their building, so they told the Church of Scotland that it could go and take a fuck to itself.'

'That the official biblical term?'

'Indeed. They went to court over it. The paperwork was all a bit vague, but eventually St Stephen's won. So they broke away from the other three and the Church of Scotland itself, and set up as an independent. The minister stayed as was, and his flock gathered round.'

He pulls up outside the Old Manse, kills the engine.

'Right,' he says, 'that makes sense. I thought there were still people going in and out of that place on a Sunday morning. And this guy, he was minister where?'

'He's new. That was one of the eventual compromises. They couldn't agree on it, so the other three buggered off. One of them retired up to the Highlands, one of them got a gig in Northern Ireland, the other's off walking in Nepal, some shit like that.'

*

'Call me Brian.'

Taylor gives him a short stare, has no intention, I know, of calling him fucking Brian.

'You'd already heard about Mrs Henderson?'

He looks troubled.

'Yes. News travels quickly, I'm afraid. At least, when it's this kind of news.'

Brian, the minister, can't be more than thirty-five. Not wearing a dog collar. I don't know if these people are supposed to wear them all the time, but I expect they're allowed to slum it when they're in their own home.

'Who told you?'

'Penny Jardine. She's been good friends with Maureen's friend, Kelda, for many years now, and they both kn—'

'OK,' says Taylor, cutting him off before he launches into some tortured connection involving Penny's mother's auntie's daughter's husband's sister's third cousin. 'Mrs

Henderson was at church on Sunday?'

'Yes. Every week.'

Suddenly the words are more clipped. Obviously he'd thought he could be conversational, and now that he's discovered the opposite, he's flicked the switch.

'That hadn't changed with the merger?'

'Not as far as I know. She was a member of the Old Kirk, was always in attendance. Once the final decision had been taken, then she started coming to St Mungo's. Never missed a step.'

'Was she happy?'

'Quite the reverse,' he says.

'Had she spoken to you about it?'

'On many, many occasions.'

'What was her principal bone of contention?'

'Hard to know where to start.'

'Just throw them out there. The order doesn't matter.'

He makes a small throwaway hand gesture, which in other circumstances might have indicated that there were so many there was no point starting, but then he realises he's talking to the police and gets on with it anyway.

'She didn't like the building at St Mungo's, couldn't understand how you could elect to go there over the Old Kirk. Hated that all the money from the Old Kirk ended up being spent on St Mungo's. Hated that no one at the Old Kirk put up enough of a fight. She thought that the people at St Stephen's were prepared for a dirtier fight, and didn't like that no one at the Old Kirk would match them. Hated that ultimately St Stephen's got to keep their weekly services when the Old Kirk didn't.'

'What about Halfway?'

'She considered it a small church, with a small congregation, and therefore not worthy of particular consideration.'

'Sounds like she might have made some enemies in that time?' I throw in.

'No doubt she did,' says Brian, the minister. 'She did not suffer fools, nor adhere to much notion of Christian forgiveness and understanding.'

'Had anything happened recently to make matters worse? Had she said anything to you that might indicate that she'd had enough? That she was so fed up with it all, so miserable, that she might commit suicide?'

He stares at the floor in that slightly affected way that people do when they're talking to us coppers. Thinking things through, not giving the first answer that comes into their head.

'She must have been murdered,' he says finally, looking up.

Jesus.

Manage to keep that ejaculation to myself.

'Why do you say that?' asks Taylor calmly, as the vicar threatens to toss our straightforward, snappy wrap-up suicide in the bin.

'She was so full of fight. Listen, she was never in a position to actually influence the vote or influence the way this was carried out. She wasn't a church elder. She was on no committees. She was an outsider to the politics, but she loved her church. She loved the Old Kirk. I really think she'd been there every single Sunday since she'd been born, and I cannot believe for a moment that she would give up the fight quite in this way.'

He looks between the two of us. Neither Taylor nor I immediately jump in, so he adds, 'She must have been murdered.'

'Everything about her death looks like suicide,' says Taylor.

'That's what these people do, isn't it?' he says.

'What people?'

'They fake suicides to cover up a murder.'

'Who does that?' asks Taylor.

'You see it on the TV all the time.'

'You mean like on *NCIS* and *Lewis*?'

The minister looks slightly sheepish at the direction the conversation has taken, which is at least some measure of self-awareness.

'And *Poirot*,' he adds, although he does it with almost comic timing. Funny guy. Cannot even remotely get a handle on him.

'You know how many fake suicide/murders I've seen in my thirty years in the police service?' asks Taylor.

'Nevertheless,' says Brian, 'you're here to get my opinion and to find out what I know, and I really do genuinely believe that Maureen would never, ever have killed herself.'

'And the wings, you heard about them?' asks Taylor.

He nods, but doesn't venture anything further.

'Any ideas?'

He sits back and makes a general, all-encompassing hand gesture. 'Given the church connection, it's easy to imagine that it was meant as an angel metaphor. Difficult, however, to think that anyone had that view of her. She certainly did not think that of herself. Perhaps her killer was being ironic.'

Irony and metaphor. Jesus.

The door opens. An older woman, wearing a pinny, for all the world with the word *housekeeper* tattooed on her forehead, smiles benignly upon us all.

'A cup of tea?' she asks.

6

Poirot. That's what the guy said, that was his reference for the potentially strange death, and possible suicide of this old woman. And in its way, *Poirot* is what it feels like.

Day-to-day police work is so often carried out at ground level. Poor people trying to get richer; drunks disturbing the peace and abusing the family; clubs and bars tipping out at 3 a.m.; drug addicts doing anything to score; the desperate and the down-on-their-luck fighting for their one and only chance. All of them trying to catch up.

The people they're trying to catch, the middle classes with their own sets of problems, don't cross our paths so much. Sure, there's the sleazy world of white collar crimes, the fraud and embezzlement, there's domestic abuse and child abuse in every level of society, there's the occasional argument over a hedge, sporadic kerb crawling busts, but it's largely on a different level and they make up a small percentage of what we have to do. Consequently, the shitty domestic stuff aside, when we're sucked into their world, it feels like you're stepping onto the set of *Midsomer Murders* or *Murder She Wrote*. All safe and cosy, with slightly eccentric music playing and passions running like lava beneath the genteel world of amateur dramatics or the village cricket team or the local church.

And here we are, on a Tuesday that could have been any given Tuesday, with junkies and whores and child beaters and doped-up, fucked-off teenagers, and instead we're plunged into the world of Miss Fucking Marple.

I'm sitting in the pub. On my own. I don't know where I am at the moment. Somewhere in between, that's all. In between the last thing and the next thing. And I don't mean cases. Should go home and watch the football, get me out of this place.

Spent summer last year on suspension after banjoing that arsehole, DI Leander. Spent summer this year on sick leave after coming off worst in the investigation into the Plague of Crows, whoever she or he was. Had my moments of thinking that I wouldn't be back after that. Given that I'd been injured on duty, I could have walked off into the sunset with a decent pay-off, no one would have mourned my passing and, shortly afterwards, few would've even remembered that I'd been there in the first place.

Ended up lying on a floor crying my eyes out, having stubbed a cigarette butt into my arm. What a dick. Think that was the low point, but since then I've just levelled out into nothingness. Total, fucking, God-awful nothingness.

Yet every time I contemplate leaving, I can't think of what it is I'd be doing instead. This has been my life now for sixteen years. It seems utterly depressing that I can't think of anything else to do with myself, but I can't. So three days after lying on the floor, a total train wreck of a whacked-out psychotic, I returned to work.

Yes, madam, you're safe to walk the streets with me on the case.

Shouldn't have slept with my psychiatrist, but however much I shouldn't have slept with her, it doesn't suck the toes of how much she shouldn't have slept with me. That didn't end well either. Afterwards, we saw each other twice professionally, then we made some incredibly unprofessional agreement that she would sign off on my well-being, and we could go about the business of never seeing each other again. Like ever.

If I kill someone in the course of my duties, and there's an investigation into why I was allowed back, she's going to look pretty fucking bad.

Had a brief relationship just after returning to work. Met a girl, had some sex; soon enough, she was my ex. How many times could I sing that to myself? She was working downstairs in records, some shit like that. I never even bothered finding out.

After the whole Plague of Crows bullshit, and my five-month absence, I suppose there must have been some talk about me. All those who'd been at the station when it happened would have known that I was a worthless, wasted, alcoholic fucktard, a sideshow curiosity, a walking car crash. However, those few who arrived in the time I was on sick leave were bound to be curious. Especially the women.

No, seriously. I'm not talking myself up, or any shit like that, but really, you find out some guy you've never met before has had sex with a bunch of women in the same workplace, you're going to be curious, no matter the amount of bad things you hear about him. It's human nature. Curious as to what the attraction is. Curious to know why so many women ended up with this unattractive, deadbeat arsehole.

Then I came back to work, and I looked like this. Hadn't touched a drink for three days – ha! three fucking days! – eyes were clear, had lost some weight, and I had that look about me. Lost. Haunted. Alone. Filled with melancholy, yet not pathetic. Not desperate. Looking like the last thing I wanted was help from anyone. Strong, yet consumed by remorse, consumed by the past, weighed down by something so great it was hard for others to imagine what it might be.

If you could bottle that look for men, each and every one of us would be sleeping with a different woman every night. Women love that shit. They want to know. They want to help, precisely because they can tell I don't want to be helped.

Of course, back at the station this only worked with the newbies. The women there that knew me, well they might have recognised the look, but on the other hand, they also knew that I was beyond repair, utterly unreliable, and as likely at the crunch to be unpleasantly not worth it as I was to be enigmatically melancholic.

27

So they all steered clear, and the new girl had a free hand. She spoke to me at the coffee machine a couple of times. Maybe she planned it, I don't know. People plan these things. How does anyone ever know if a little coincidence is what it seems? Not that it mattered in this case. She wasn't a psychotic knife-wielder after all. She was just curious, wondering whether or not she should be attracted, and presumably not caring that she might be joining a list.

Went out for dinner one night. Back to my place. Fucked her. She was good. Been around. At some point I had the thought that I was getting added to her list, rather than the other way round. Which was fine, as it meant there was little chance of anyone's bunny taking a bath in boiling water.

We got on all right, although at no point did I feel my emotions get off my own one-yard line. Didn't care. It was just what was happening at that point.

The third time we had sex – third time in a week – she asked me if I wanted to do anal. That was unusual. I said no. She said she loved it, so don't think I'd be taking advantage of her or anything. I said, no really, I don't want to. I might have used the word *minging*. Think I was a bit drunk. We moved on, finished having sex, but that was the changing of the tide.

I wondered if she gauged a man by whether or not he wanted to have anal sex. Funny way to gauge, but each to their own. And that was the last time we saw each other out of work. So, actually the tide didn't just change, it turned in a moment and said, 'fuck this, I'm off,' disappearing out to the horizon.

There have been one or two others since then, although no one from the station. Don't think there's anyone left that there'd be any point in even trying. Mrs Lownes possibly. She's pretty fit, and actually older than me. But I believe there's a Mr Lownes, and she seems to have one of those comfortable, normal lives that some people have. The kind of lives where you have a house and a couple of kids and regular jobs, and life passes by without ever having casual sex with a fucked-up dickhead at the office.

Despite my total paucity of spirit, every now and again something edges through. The occasional strong feeling pushes its way to the surface. Of course, it's never joy, never excitement, and by God it's never expectation.

Anger. That's it. Always at other people, always at moments of total insignificance. Walking to the shops. Sitting in a queue of traffic. Overhearing people on the street, thinking, 'Jesus, you sound like such a dick. Shut up!' In supermarkets. I get angry in supermarkets. You're walking around with your little list in your head, you make for the frozen onions or the pasta or the grapes or the shower gel or the whatever the fuck, and fifty per cent of the time there's someone standing right in front of the pasta or the frozen onions or the grapes, studying them, trying to decide precisely which packet to buy, and you stand there, and you know that if the person is over eighty, chances are you'll be standing like that for quarter of an hour, waiting for them to choose between linguine and cannavaro.

But the thing is, of course, it's not as though you're ever standing there that long. It's not fifteen minutes, is it? Tops it'll be thirty seconds, and more than likely it'll be less than five. Yet, less than five seconds is all it takes. Such a minor inconvenience, such a base annoyance at others.

The thought flashes through my brain, an instant image, of stepping forward, planting my fist in the back of their head, shouting, 'Get out the fucking way, you stupid fuck!' Comes out of nowhere. The image. The feeling. Like a snap of the fingers.

So far, on the plus side of this malign affliction of my character, I haven't actually done it. And I hope, if I ever finally snap and lash out at someone, it's for something far more fundamentally deserving than taking a while to choose between blue or green milk.

*

There's a peculiar feeling about searching through the things in the house of a pensioner. Nowadays so much searching and background checking is done on computers, and endless trawling through Twitter and Facebook and the rest of them. Suddenly, when you have to investigate the personal effects of an old person, it's like going back to the 1950s.

All right, keep your toupee on old man, yes I know there are plenty of old geezers who use the internet. But line up a hundred teenagers and ask them how many have never used the internet, and you'll come away with a big fat zero. The over-70s? You're looking at thirty to forty per cent, and Maureen Henderson was one of them.

Wednesday morning. Woke with a start, woke with the awareness of having been talking to someone, but the memory of it was gone in an instant.

In to work, and then back out with Morrow. We spend a morning at Maureen's home, rooting through her things. There's still been nothing definite to indicate that she might have had her suicide thrust unwillingly upon her, the words of the minister aside, but going through the dusty old sideboards and the small desk, and the kitchen drawers crammed full of stuff, it's evident she was no stranger to a protest letter. There are, at any rate, a lot of defensive replies.

Between us, Morrow and I have so far accumulated about fifteen names of people who'd had to write to her defending their position. Some of them were blunt, and some of them quite wonderfully offensive, but you get the feeling that was in response to the tone of Maureen's original.

This is confirmed when Morrow finds an envelope where the sender was returning Maureen's robust screed of outrage. Maureen's letter had used the expression "fuck-brained twattery" in the first sentence, and had become gradually more vitriolic from there.

The more we look, the more we find. On those

---

occasions when you stumble across something at the start of the search, you wonder if that might be it for the duration. However, this is the search that keeps on giving. Old Mrs Henderson was as involved in the church and its amalgamation as someone who wasn't technically involved in it could have been.

A full list of all members of the four congregations and their voting intentions, colour-coded depending on how definite she considered the information; files on all those she considered the main players in the piece, full of newspaper clippings and gossip, lots of gossip; confirmation of all those letters we assumed she sent, with a folder containing photocopies of her outgoing correspondence.

At some point, I catch Morrow staring out the front window at the grey November morning. The street outside is deserted.

'All right?' I ask.

He turns.

'Sure beans,' he says. I must remember never to say *sure beans*. Like, ever. 'Just taking a break. Tell you what, sir, if they do decide she was murdered, we've got about fifty suspects.'

'Ain't that the truth,' I mutter.

7

'Well, we've got one thing going for us,' says Taylor.

Sitting in his office, a quick recap on the kind of thing we've found. Morrow and I have three barrel loads of paper waiting on our desks, a brilliant afternoon ahead of us, making a list of the most likely.

'If she was murdered,' he continues, 'whoever did it had no idea she'd left all that shit at her house.'

'Maybe,' I say. 'Could be they knew about it, extracted anything related to themselves, and left all the other shit hoping there'd be a variety of other people implicated.'

'Fair point' he says. 'Any hint of that?'

Shake my head. Glance at Morrow, who joins me.

'Well, gentlemen, you know what to do.'

Taylor's phone goes, and he makes a small gesture towards the door. Morrow and I rise to head on our way.

'Yep,' says Taylor, lifting the phone. He pauses, catches my eye as I get to the door, indicating that we should wait. Morrow and I move back into the office, spectators to the phone call.

It's not the greatest spectator sport.

'You watch the Celtic last night?' asks Morrow, his voice low.

I nod. Did I watch the Celtic last night? Jesus. Got in the from pub, had a crappy pizza – and really, Dr Oetker, whoever the fuck you are, eating your pizzas in front of the TV perfectly replicates eating a crappy pizza in front of the TV, not eating with some fit bird in a fucking Italian piazza – and two bottles of Stella Artois – yep, I gave into the advertising on that one as well – and then I fell asleep when it was still mind-numbingly 0-0 with Celtic playing ten at the back at home, and missed the inevitable sending off and defensive capitulation.

'Shite,' he says.

I nod again.

'You're fucking kidding?' says Taylor, but not in a *big fucking wow!* kind of a way, just a low mutter, the tired policeman's tone. The tone that says *this isn't going to make anything any easier.*

'And you couldn't have spotted that any earlier?... Whatever...'

Another short pause, and then he hangs up without saying goodbye.

'Balingol,' he says.

Morrow and I both take a further step back into the office. Never a good sign when any detective says *you're fucking kidding* to the pathologist. He stares at us for a moment, and we wait for the announcement.

'Right, gentlemen,' he begins, 'seems we might have a murder investigation on our hands.'

I smile. Of course we do. Morrow glances over his shoulder, as though there might be someone from the *Daily Mail* lurking behind the nearest desk.

'There are significant traces of a sleeping drug in her blood.'

'Maybe she was an insomniac.'

'Maybe she was, Sergeant. Or maybe she was drugged so she wouldn't struggle. What did you find in the drugs cabinet?'

'Nothing interesting, I don't think,' I say. 'We've got it all in a bag.'

'Go through it, anything that isn't off the shelf at Tesco, take down to Balingol and get him to have a look.'

'Will do,' says Morrow.

'It's not really a surprise, though,' I say. 'I mean, the fact that she was doped up. It doesn't feel like it really warrants you saying, *you're fucking kidding me.*'

Taylor glances at his computer screen as another email pings in, then turns back, the expression of distaste never having left his face.

'She'd had sex in the previous twenty-four hours,' he says.

Morrow looks vaguely disturbed by the thought of octogenarian sex. I can't help laughing.

'Good on her,' I say. 'At least she was still getting some.'

He gives me the look.

'It wasn't me,' I add quickly.

'Funny,' he says. 'Something else to think about as you go through her correspondence. I'll go and speak to the daughter, now that she's had a day to think about it. She might have remembered something, might have some idea who her mother was...' and he lets the sentence go, as he can't bring himself to mention any sort of word for sex in relation to a dead eighty-one-year-old.

Morrow and I return to our desks. They're usually laden with shit on any given day, but today, what with the sum total of Maureen's life added to them, they look even more of a disaster zone.

'That's just gross,' says Morrow, sitting down.

'What d'you expect people to do? Forget that sex exists? A couple of old folk getting it on, Jesus man, good on them. As long as, you know, they don't post pictures online.'

Morrow barks out a laugh, and I join him. A couple of schoolboys.

'But how do they even do it?'

'Fuck, I don't know,' I say. 'Viagra and lube, I suppose.'

'Jesus,' says Morrow, making some sort of low, distasteful sound, as though he's bitten into the old persons' sex equivalent of junk food.

Taylor emerges from his office on his way to interview the grieving, guilt-ridden daughter, probably passing Superintendent Connor's office on the way to deliver the good news about the potential investigation upgrade.

'And you might want to factor in,' he says, slowing as he passes our desk, 'that Balingol says the quality of the sperm they found in her vagina suggests her lover was in his early twenties, possibly even a teenager.'

He delivers this alarming added detail with a complete lack of inflection, and then heads on his way. Morrow and I stare at each other across the divide of Maureen Henderson's personal files and correspondence, and slowly his look of distaste transfers itself.

There's something about old people having sex. You know, it's, I don't know, like pandas having sex or something. It's kind of cute, as long as you don't think about the actuality of it. But the old person/teenager combo... That there is all bad. On every level.

'What were you saying?' he says eventually. My face is blank. 'That,' he continues, 'is gross, and don't try to imply otherwise.'

I wasn't going to.

'Sure beans,' I find myself saying.

8

DI Dorritt comes to speak to me at some point in the late afternoon. Already beyond regular home time. Not that I ever leave when I should. It's not that I'm wedded to my work, but seriously, what the fuck have I got to go home to?

'Going to need you tomorrow morning, Tom,' he says.

Dorritt and I are getting on better now. It's weird. It's as though he felt sorry for me after I nearly died in the spring. Why would he do that? I guess I still lack empathy. I don't give a shit about him – nor, indeed, about myself – so why should he?

Morrow is already gone, having reduced the immeasurable list of those against whom Maureen held a grudge to something in the region of twenty. He has a B list of another forty-one names. I'm compiling similar lists, then we'll crosscheck.

'Working on the suicide slash murder up at the Old Kirk,' I say. 'I'll need to check with Taylor. What's up?'

'Need a few hands for the paper storage bust in Halfway.'

'Sure,' I say. 'I'll speak to Taylor.'

'Cool,' he says. 'Thanks. I'm just looking for feet on the ground. We've got the paperwork covered, just need bodies. Shouldn't be more than an hour and a half.'

I nod. He pauses as if there's something else he wants to say, then turns back into his office. Maybe he's been told to include me in his team as often as possible to aid my recovery. It's reasonable that they probably think I need to recover.

Taylor emerges from his office and snaps his fingers at

me. Snaps his fingers. I jump up like the obedient little poodle.

'Connor's office,' he says. 'He wants to speak to us about Maureen.'

We walk quickly down the short corridor. The door to Connor's office is no more than twenty yards away, although fortunately he rarely emerges, so we don't see too much of him.

'DI Dorritt ask you about the raid tomorrow morning?' Taylor says as he knocks on the door. A sharp 'enter' comes from within.

'Yep.'

'It's fine,' he says. 'They need the bodies. I'll take care of this for the morning.'

'Thank you, sir.'

We go in and sit down. Connor lifts his head from whatever paperwork he's studying. Financing, probably. He's your classic, modern-day superintendent. His days will be filled with paperwork, finagling budgets and moving people around to fill holes and questioning whether we can get away with using cheaper toilet paper. The management of doing more with less. Crime will cross his desk in the same way as a report on vehicular repair expenditure.

'Update,' he says, by way of introduction. God, he's so warm. Touching really. I just want to reach out and hug him.

Taylor and I haven't spoken for a few hours, and I immediately start wondering whether or not I want to pass on everything I was going to tell him in front of the superintendent.

'Balingol has completed the autopsy,' says Taylor. 'He now believes there are possible signs of Mrs Henderson having been restrained, which could tie in with her potentially being forced to take the sleeping tablets. However, he does concede that it's also possible it occurred during coitus.'

I do wonder if he could have said that without actually

saying it.

'I spoke to the daughter and she seemed genuinely surprised at the notion that her mother might have been having sexual relations. I wondered about not mentioning the age of the lover, but of course there was always the possibility of her having some young guy that hung around, that the daughter presumed helped her with the shopping or some such. Anyway, she claimed not to know of any young men in her mother's life, and I think was appalled enough at the suggestion that she'll strike it from her mind as most definitely untrue.'

As soon as Taylor finishes talking, Connor slides his chin over in my direction and nods it by way of instructing me that it's my turn. He seems to be able to move his chin without moving the rest of his head. I wonder if he's ever considered going on *Britain's Got Talent.*

Picking up on his demeanour while Taylor was talking, I decide that the superintendent has us in here so that he can do the talking, not the other way round. He has an instruction to pass on to us, and has no interest in what we're bringing to him.

'Nothing,' I say.

I get a side-glance from Taylor, but I'm pretty sure he'll have the measure of the boss.

'Fine,' says Connor, then he leans forward on his elbows. 'I've been speaking to one or two of the members of the congregation.'

As soon as he says that he raises his hands to silence any objection that might be coming. Obviously wary of stepping on his investigating officers' toes. 'Listen,' he continues, 'I've been attending the church for the past year now, since we came down from Aberdeen.'

'You knew this woman?' asks Taylor. His tone is a bit snippy, perhaps because Connor never mentioned this when Taylor spoke to him earlier.

'There are several hundred members of the congregation,' says Connor. 'I don't know everyone.'

'She appears to have put herself about a bit,' I say.

They both give me a look for the interjection, Connor more so because of my implied disbelief.

'Obviously, I mean,' I say, 'she wrote to a lot of people, had plenty to say. Not, you know, that she had sex... with... you know, a lot of them.'

'Are you finished?' snaps Connor.

Another glance at Taylor, then I turn back to the superintendent and lower my eyes. Time to acknowledge the authority of the supposed alpha male.

'I wasn't aware of Mrs Henderson, nor of her proclivity for writing letters of complaint as I was never in receipt of such. It would appear from my friends that those who did receive them tended not to discuss the matter as so many found the letters, and Mrs Henderson herself, so utterly distasteful.'

'You would've thought she might've found you a worthwhile recipient of one of her angry missives,' I chip in. Don't know what's got into me today. I usually sit before Connor in depressed and oppressed silence. Perhaps today I'm seeing him as disingenuous, whereas usually I just see him as dull and jobsworthy.

There's something about disingenuousness. Barefaced lying and thuggery and crack dealing and murder, the kind of things we come across in this job, you get used to. You understand it. But the artifice of disingenuousness pisses me off. And it's always a guy in a suit.

'I can assure you, Sergeant Hutton, that I had no contact with that woman.'

Hmm. The Bill Clinton defence. That usually works.

I hold his eye for a moment, then once again lower my gaze to the desk. It's a reasonable point, of course, since we've already found the folder of all Maureen's outgoing correspondence on the church business, and there were no letters to Connor.

'Gentlemen, the church has been through enough trouble in the past year without this getting out. There's been a horrible amount of infighting, and the congregation has just melted away. The last thing we need is an implication that one of our Christian family has murdered another.'

'You want us to brush it under the carpet?' says Taylor. Nice edge to the voice. I approve.

'Of course not,' he snaps back. 'If this is a murder investigation, then it's a murder investigation, and that's how it's going to be. The last thing we need, however, is a scandal around the town and around the church if all we're dealing with is a suicide of a mentally deranged old woman. It's the firm opinion of many of the people to whom I've spoken that she was showing clear signs of senility. Perhaps no one suspected she might commit suicide, but how can any of us even begin to understand what a woman in her condition might do? She was clearly unbalanced, and I wouldn't even be surprised if what we discover in the end is that she was doing this to implicate someone else. All part of her mischief-making.'

Taylor has gradually eased himself back in his seat, the tension leaving him.

'What do you want us to do?' he asks, his voice now having lost its edge. Disappointing.

'I want you to hold onto your hats,' says Connor. Fuck's sake. 'I want you to not get carried away and think this is your new big case, something to help salvage the reputations you've both flushed down the toilet in the last two years. Until such times as you have absolute proof that Mrs. Henderson was murdered, you will deal with this case as a suicide. You will ask questions as though it was a suicide, you will treat it as a suicide, you will go to bed tonight believing it was a suicide, and if the press come asking, you will tell them you are dealing with a suicide. Do I make myself clear, gentlemen?'

Oh yes, you make yourself clear.

You're a wanker.

9

Another night in the pub. This time, at least, Taylor has joined me for a while. I have my vodka tonic, he has his pint. Two miserable old middle-aged sad sacks chewing the fat and grumbling about the world.

'We could do with finding the lover,' he says. 'Maybe he's not involved, but there might've been some pillow talk.'

'You ever go to church?' I ask.

'When I was a kid,' he says. 'Sunday school, all of that.'

'When'd you stop?'

'Don't remember. Teenage years some time. When they stopped making me. You?'

'Not really,' I say. 'I mean, I've been in the odd church, but never did Sunday school or any of that shit.'

'You're going this Sunday,' he says.

'To church?'

'Indeed.'

'Oh, good. You coming? Will we sit incongruously together at the back? If we wear work clothes, they'll probably think we're Jehovah's come to steal their congregation.'

He smiles after taking a long drink from his pint. I've already got the feeling that he's only staying for one. I can't believe that he's got much more to go home to than I do, but he seems more at peace with it.

I wish I could be at peace. There's probably some nineteenth century German philosophical shit about achieving that when you're dead. Or maybe that's biblical shit.

'One of us is going to St Mungo's, the other to St

Stephen's. We're going to blend in.'

'Undercover?'

'Not necessarily. If you get talking, I'm not looking for you to pretend that you're someone you're not.'

'Well that's my Sunday morning sorted,' I say.

'Like you were doing something else.'

'Sleeping off the night before. Three hours, is it, something like that?'

'The service? An hour. It's all very civilised, the Church of Scotland. They don't expect much for your membership, although murdering a fellow congregational member is probably off limits.'

I drain my glass and mutter, 'Fuck,' just because I can. Glance over at the bar. Taylor looks at his watch.

'Got a lot of interviewing to do tomorrow,' he says. 'You, me and Morrow, splitting it up. Need to get around as many of the parishioners as possible from all four of the original churches.'

'You're saying I should go home, have a cup of tea and a biscuit, watch some crappy TV documentary and get an early night?'

He downs his pint and sets the empty glass on the table, then smiles in his paternal way.

'Maybe you should do an Open University course or something. Study philosophy, some shit like that. It'd be good for you.'

What the fuck?

'Really, no,' I say. 'Fair enough if you don't want me turning up at work in the morning, breathing fumes of fire all over these whiter than white church-going bastards, but don't go... Jesus... philosophy? Seriously? It's a fucking shit world, full of sadness and loneliness and melancholy. Then you die. Period.'

Getting a bit annoyed, which is stupid. He means well.

'I know,' he says, 'yet people get by. They enjoy themselves. They find the little things. People get jobs, people fall in love.'

He's about to turn into Julie Andrews.

'Thistle are in the Premier League,' he continues. 'The Scotland team's getting itself together. There are always new women to sleep with, even you haven't gone through them all. Crime's down, believe it or not. Serious crime, even the petty shit. Economy's on the mend. Exam grades are up, university results are up, there's less teenage pregnancy, there's talk of a new Scottish enlighten—'

'Most of that's shit,' I say, finally cutting him off. 'We know crime isn't down, it's just reported less because people are so disaffected with us, which is fair enough because we've been cut back so far we are total shit. There may be the odd positive economic indicator, but the country's in trillions of pounds of debt, which one day soon is going to bite us all on the arse and we're going to be totally fucked. Thistle are getting gubbed most weeks, Scotland are still shit, and the only reason there's been a drop in teenage pregnancy is because of online porn.'

He's been smiling at my rebuttal, but at that last one he laughs out loud.

'Seriously? Only you, Hutton. How do you work that out?'

'Firstly,' I say, turning and looking at the bar, because I don't care what he says, I'm having another one, 'there's lots of talk about the malign effect of porn on teenage girls. But I bet there are thousands of teenage boys scared to show themselves naked to a girl, because all they see are those monster porn guys with fifteen-inch erections who make them feel incredibly deficient in the cock department, and so they sit in total inadequacy in their rooms watching porn, rather than getting out there, getting girls pregnant.'

'Hmm… has someone done a study on that?'

'And secondly…'

'Here we go,' he says, and now he gets to his feet.

'The ones who are having sex have learned how to do it from the porn channels, so there are all these kids who are about to ejaculate inside the girl, then at the last second they withdraw and the girl's thinking, what's with that,

that's incredibly sensible, then the kid starts pulling his pudding furiously beside the girl's head and she's like, what the fuck are you doing, and he says, I'm going to cum all over your face, and she's like, NO YOU'RE FUCKING NOT, and then blam, he does it anyway, and she's like, what the actual fuck, you moron, and he's like, that's what happens! That's what you're supposed to do! This is how you have sex! I've seen it on triple-fucking-X! And it's fucked up, man, and a bit mental, but on the plus side... nobody ever got pregnant from snorting semen.'

Taylor is laughing and shaking his head as he walks out. I watch him go and then turn and look at the bar.

Vodka tonic, bag of peanuts.

10

There's a small house attached to the halls beside the Old Kirk, and in the house lives the church officer. Kind of the gatekeeper figure, you know, if this was some kind of epic, Arthurian quest. But since it's just a bleak little house attached to the halls of a church that's on the verge of becoming an ex-church at the top end of town, gatekeeper might be a little too grand a title.

Mary Buttler, early fifties, I'd say, and an air of common sense about her. The husband answered the door, didn't invite me in. She came and stood on the doorstep for a while, then offered to show me round the church.

Across the small car park, through the padlocked iron gates to the approach path to the church. We pass the centuries-old head stones. Three locks on the church door.

'Get much trouble up here?' I ask. 'Graffiti, kids getting drunk in the graveyard, that kind of thing?'

Spent a couple of hours this morning on Dorritt's paper bust up the road. Not far, in fact, from the fourth church in our current little disaster. Didn't have much to do with the operation. I was there to add to the numbers as we were trying to impose ourselves. Everything came off well. Must admit, overall Dorritt impressed me in a way I wasn't expecting. Smooth, clinical, carried the whole thing off with competence. Lacking in the kind of panache that I bring to a procedure, you might say, but no one got shot, none of the suspected criminals even tried to leg it. They were impressed with the show of force.

Me? I got some fresh air and didn't have to do any paperwork.

'Comes and goes,' she says. 'We thought there might be

more once the church stopped getting used full time, but there's still enough going on round here. There's the occasional wedding or a memorial service and, of course, the halls are used all week round for one thing or another.'

She fiddles with the locks, takes her time to open, and then we walk into the church. She hits the light switches inside the door. A short entrance hall leading to a corridor running the width of the church. Doors at either end open into the nave, with stairs at one end leading, presumably, to more seating above. The gods.

She turns to her right along the corridor, then opens the door to the nave of the church, ushering me in first. It's large, painted in pastel colours, the natural light in the room entering through stained glass windows.

'Would you like the lights on in here?' she asks.

'No, it's fine.'

I stare up for a moment, and then walk slowly down the aisle. Each row of seats is split into three, with two aisles creating a centre phalanx of seating. I walk into the body of the church, and then take a seat. Long, old-fashioned pews, with thin red cushioning. I sit and stare up at the chancel. The pulpit, set low down, the lectern with a large Bible open on top, a long table, the baptismal font, seating for the choir behind, organ pipes, although the organ is not situated next to them, and then at the back, a high, and pretty damned impressive, stained glass window. Twenty feet tall maybe. Maybe more. Beneath are two pots of red flowers.

The silence is almost ear-splitting. I don't speak for a while. Mary Buttler sits across the narrow aisle in another pew. She doesn't look at me, and I don't look at her. I stare up at Jesus in the window. Suddenly I feel that I could sit here all day. I can't sit alone in silence in my own home for more than thirty seconds. I need noise, I need distraction. But this. This is a silence you can crawl into and surround yourself with. Let it envelope you, and shield you from everything outside. And everything that's inside as well.

No wonder people come here. It doesn't matter whether

you believe that the guy up there was the son of God or just some geezer who had a way with words. That's not what it's about. And no wonder fewer and fewer people are coming. No one sits in silence anymore. We all need noise. We all need music and chatter and videos and movies and TV shows and the internet and Facebook and friends and the sound of our phone pinging with an update on something that we haven't had an update on for upwards of three minutes.

I don't think there's anything on earth, or otherwise, that could convince me to believe that Jesus was the son of God, or that religion wasn't just invented as a means to control the population, but I could be converted to sitting in this kind of silence.

No idea how long we sit there, but I realise when I start to think about creating a little shrine in my own home where I could go and sit and meditate while sitting cross-legged beneath the picture of the Thistle side that beat Celtic in the '71 League Cup final, that I'm coming out the other side of my brief moment of awakening.

'You ever come in here and just sit?' I ask.

'Every day,' she says, smiling.

'It's beautiful,' I say. 'Doesn't look like it's under-used.'

'It was in good order before the merger,' she says. 'The church was well enough off, had a lot of money bequeathed to us.'

I think of a comment someone has made in the last couple of days, that this was the posh church of the four, the congregation that everyone else viewed as the snobs. Perhaps that's all it was. Jealous of their money. Another deadly sin to add to the list of un-Christian behaviour that is mounting by the day.

Was jealousy one of the deadly sins? God knows. Sounds like it ought to have been. Typically, when trying to remember the seven of them, my thoughts have nothing to do with religion, going straight to the movie *Se7en* with Brad Pitt, before quickly giving up and heading off to check that I can still remember the names of *The*

Magnificent Seven.

'Since the merger, all the money's been spent by that lot down the road. God knows what they've done with it. A couple of pews and a kitchen cupboard. If you ask me, someone's got his hand in the cookie jar. This whole business... Well, it's got a long way to go, that's all.'

I glance over at her. There's nothing on her face. No resentment. Perhaps sitting in here every day helps with that kind of thought process.

'We'll do our best, but inevitably this place will start to go, deteriorate, you know, and then someone will say, why are we spending the money keeping it going when we rarely use it? And then there'll be some argument, but most of the people who feel passionate about it, good people from around here, they've already given up. And then it'll be sold. And that will be that...'

Her voice trails off, a melancholic quality to it. I've been looking at her as she spoke. The whole time she's been staring up at the window at the back of the church.

'This place was originally selected?' I ask. I know this stuff.

She smiles, affords me a brief glance.

'Well, you'd like to think that everyone had seen some sense right at the beginning, but to be honest, we had the biggest congregation so we had the highest number of votes. So we won. Unfortunately, in trying to be corporate, the various church positions were handed round, and that cunt from down the road got the position as property convenor.'

In all I end up spending over an hour in the company of Mrs Buttler. That's the only time she swears. A bluntly effective denunciation of the man who remains property convenor at St Mungo's. Perhaps I should try that. Only swearing every now and again, so that it's really effective and powerful when I do it.

I can add that to the list of aspirational items that I'll never get around to.

'Excuse my language,' she says.

'It's fine.'

'He came up here and picked this place apart with a toothcomb. The nerve of the man, as if St Mungo's is perfect. Every little.... every single little thing he could think to say about the building. Everything. The long list of expenditure that was needed to meet health and safety this, and health and safety that. We'd already passed all that stuff! And then he found the rot in the roof of the halls.'

She shakes her head. Her gaze has dropped and she's staring at the floor. She's not sounding so sanguine and peaceful anymore.

'This is Paul Cartwright you're talking about?'

She snorts. I didn't even need to ask. Every time this guy's name is mentioned you know you're going to get some sort of reaction.

'And just look at what they've done down there,' she says. 'They twisted the vote, said that we couldn't use the Old Kirk because of the amount of money that'd be required, and then they've gone and spent all our money, *our* money, repairing their church.'

Another shake of the head.

I look back at the stained glass Jesus looking down on us from the rear of the church.

'I'm sorry, Sergeant, I shouldn't be getting annoyed. Take a look around if you like, I'll just wait here for you to finish. We can talk further over a cup of tea.'

I get up and walk down to the front. The pulpit is set low, and I'm tempted to climb the few stairs up there and stand and look down over the rows of empty pews. I'd probably do it if she wasn't here. Instead I stand at the lectern and look at the open Bible.

Revelation 9.

And the shapes of the locusts were like unto horses prepared unto battle; and on their heads were as it were crowns like gold, and their faces were as the faces of men. And they had hair as the hair of women, and their teeth were as the teeth of lions...

OK, so let's get this straight. We've got locusts that look like horses, with women's hair, men's faces and lion's teeth. Well, that makes sense. No doubt there's some of that metaphor going on in there.

I glance up and contemplate reading some of this shit out, but if I did that I'd probably end up sliding into Sean Connery. Mrs Buttler looks upset enough as it is, what with me getting the conversation round to Paul Cartwright. It's not going to be helped by my saying, 'And the name of the shtar ish called Wormwood: and the third part of the watersh became wormwood; and many men died of the watersh, and they too had blackened fingersh and blackened tonguesh.'

11

My original intention had been to get around as many parishioners as possible, a broad spectrum, and then if there were any that I thought needed adding to the list, to seek them out tomorrow. However, it seems pretty obvious that I really need to speak to this Cartwright character to find out if he's as much of a bell-end as everyone implies. Given that I tend to have a low view of pretty much everybody, it's a fair bet that I'm going to dislike him even without him being as awful as they all say, but let's not let that stand in the way.

He's an architect, and a quick phone call to his office tells me that he's at a project site in Largs all day. Won't be back in the office until Monday. I weigh the odds, two hours on a round trip to Largs to interview one person – and not a very long interview included – or spend that time on four of five people in the area? Contemplate calling Taylor, then decide that I need to speak to Cartwright regardless. Largs it is, and at least the drive won't take as long as it used to back when I was a kid, hitting the coast for the ferry to Millport.

The project site is on the hill looking down over the town, the Clyde and Great Cumbrae out in the firth. A beautiful view from up here, even on a crappy day like this. This is at the point where the river has opened wide, and Cumbrae sits in the middle, with the low hills of Bute beyond, and behind Bute the hills of Arran and the hook of the mainland, as the Mull of Kintyre dips south, forever awash to the sound of Paul McCartney. To the right, the mountains of Argyll, although today they are obscured.

The board at the entrance to the construction site

promises *a beautiful development of exceptional four and five bedroomed homes in a stunning location*. I pull into the small car park beside the temporary office, take a moment to stand looking at the view, and then walk inside.

There's a woman sitting behind a desk, a few seats, and everywhere lavish brochures, shiny with pictures of the view, artist's impressions of the houses, and polished off with an air of desperation.

The receptionist is young and beautiful. Not much make-up, long hair tied back, a meticulously uneven fringe, dark-rimmed glasses. Looks as though she doesn't realise she's as attractive as she is, which is unusual these days.

I know, I'm terribly old-fashioned – or, if you prefer, a sexist dinosaur – but when I see someone this good-looking behind a desk, I always think, Jesus, darling, you are way too gorgeous to be doing this. At the very least, go out with a footballer. Spend all his money.

She smiles.

Here's a top tip. I know she's just smiling because that's what she's supposed to do. She's paid to be nice. Receptionists are the whores of the business world. Wait a minute, I probably ought to re-word that. Anyway, you know what I'm trying to say. They're kind of paid to be nice, it's their job. So, of course she smiled at me. But here, at last, is the top tip. Ignore that shit. Ignore the fact that she would have smiled at the Shoe Bomber if he'd walked in. Ignore it all, and just imagine that she's smiling at me because she wants to. She doesn't have to. It's a smile born of pure attraction. She's young, and she recognises an experienced guy with that look about him. The look of wisdom, mixed with a melancholic other-worldliness.

'Good afternoon,' she says. Nice voice. Goes well with the rest of her.

I turn and glance over my shoulder. Sitting at that desk of hers, she has a great view, out of two large windows, of the Clyde and Cumbrae and the rest of it.

'Nice place to spend your days,' I say.

'Thanks,' she says. 'It's better when the sun shines.'

'That was three weeks ago on Saturday, wasn't it?'

She smiles again. That there is a great smile. From nowhere I suddenly get a sense of dreadful middle-age, and a wish that I was at least twenty years younger so that there was some worthwhile reason to be flirting with her. Yes, I feel myself lurching uncontrollably towards flirtation.

And just like that, it transpires that my flirtation isn't uncontrolled, and it leaves in a snap of the fingers.

'Would it be possible to speak to Mr Cartwright?' I ask.

She holds my gaze for a moment, glances at her computer screen – currently showing the building company's home page – then turns back with a questioning look.

'Mr Cartwright?'

'The architect. I was told he was on-site today.'

'Of course,' she says. 'Mr Cartwright. I'll just put a call out to the site manager. Who shall I say is here?'

This is the point where, if I hadn't already given up, I'd likely lose the girl.

'Detective Sergeant Hutton,' I say, dipping my hand into my jacket pocket and showing my ID.

'Of course,' she says again, with another smile, as though they'd been expecting me.

*

As we talk we look down over the view. The cloud has shifted in the last ten minutes, and the ever-changing landscape looks a little brighter. There's a ferry in the middle of the channel, making the short trip between Largs and the Cumbrae slip.

'I'm getting one of the properties myself,' he says. 'Won't live in it for another ten years yet, but Jean and I will come down here when I retire. Already a member of the golf club, aiming to get my handicap into single figures by this time next year.'

He's already talking a lot, and I haven't even asked him anything.

'You could move now, couldn't you?' I say. 'Pretty short commute up to Glasgow these days.'

'Look at that,' he says, and he throws his hands over the vista. 'I'd never get anything done. No, no, I'm aiming to retire here, when I'll have time to sit in the conservatory and watch the ferry. Back and forth, back and forth. You should see it on stormy days. Like a week last Thursday. Why was it you wanted to see me?'

This guy is smooth.

'The suicide of Mrs Henderson. Did you know her?'

'Bah!' he barks. Yep, I think bah! just about covers the weird noise that he ejaculates. 'Crazy old bitch. Never spoke to her, never wrote to her, never had anything to do with her. She wrote to me often enough.'

'How many times?' I ask.

Being in possession of all the crazy old woman's correspondence, I already know the answer.

'Seventeen,' he says, which is bang on.

I give him a glance.

'Can you believe it?' he adds.

'That seems a lot,' I say. 'Also seems odd that you can remember the exact number.'

'Got a head for detail,' he says. 'Jean says I'm on the spectrum, you know, that I've got no empathy, don't understand people or how my actions impact on them. And that I've got this extraordinary awareness and recall of detail. She's right about that, at least. Seventeen. At least she'd stopped.'

That, too, I know. She'd finally given up on him, for some reason, if not most other people.

'What made her so keen to write to you?'

He takes a deep breath, but it's an ostentatious breathing in of the autumnal sea air, a gesture to indicate just how fucking great it is to even think about living in this spot where he's designed an elegant scrotum of enchanting homes for rich people.

'I pissed her off. I pissed them all off, all those ruddy wankers up the hill.'

He barks out another laugh, then shoves his hands in his pockets. Lord of the fucking manor.

'Listen, Sergeant, don't go thinking that there's anything Christian about the running of the church. It's politics, pure and simple. Sunday morning, hymns, prayers and the sermon, yes, yes, religion. Christianity. The essence of what we are, kneeling before Jesus and before God. Trusting in him, believing in him. But the rest of it, it's all political. I'm not going to apologise because I recognised that and they didn't, because I had a war room and they didn't.'

'A war room?' Nice.

'Yes, Sergeant, a ruddy war room. You must do it yourselves, when you have a big investigation.'

'I guess we do.'

'Every organisation that succeeds needs one. A war room, where men sit down and plot and plan, down to the merest detail. If there's something you can take control of, you work out how to do it. You own it. If something's out of your hands, you establish how to minimalize it, or how to fight it. That's what we did. We had a war room, and what did they do? They walked into the merger and thought everything would be fine. Well, more ruddy fool them. I'm not going to apologise for my due diligence towards my church when they weren't prepared to do the same for themselves.'

Weirdly, I don't dislike this bloke anything like as much as I thought I would. One might not associate a war room with the church – apart from, you know, all those wars that have been fought in the name of Christianity through the centuries – but it's hard to fault him. Most of human interaction is a game; he played it, and they didn't. No wonder they all hate him.

'I spoke to someone from the Old Kirk in the last couple of days who called you a cunt.'

I thought that might get the laugh barking out again, but he just continues to stare contemptuously out over the sea and the islands and the hills.

'You know,' he says eventually, 'Mrs Henderson might have been an appalling irritant to me, and to many of us, but if the Old Kirk had had her as part of their team from the start, things might have turned out differently. Instead, they chose to never use her particular talents. She was always the outsider, always the irritating old woman who wouldn't shut up, who wouldn't accept defeat. I admired her. I won't say I'm not glad she's dead, but I admired her all the same.'

'You think she killed herself?'

'Didn't she?' he says, looking round, surprise in his voice. 'You think she was murdered?'

'I didn't say that,' I lie. Shut up, you dick. Have never lost the tendency to say too much. Some women find it endearing.

He gauges me for a moment and then turns back to his precious view, which I'm starting to believe he thinks he owns.

'So you're not questioning me as part of a murder investigation, then?'

'No,' I say. 'We're just following up on Mrs Henderson, to establish her state of mind before she died.'

'She was ruddy miserable,' he says, 'but I doubt that's so different from how she spent her last eighty-odd years.'

'Why did she stop writing to you?' I ask. 'She was still bugging plenty of other people.'

He looks imperiously over his land and his sea.

'God knows, Sergeant,' he says. 'Maybe she was beginning to see sense.'

*

Driving home I have a brief interlude of road rage. In my head I don't consider it road rage though. It's just rage to me, regular rage, the same kind of thing resulting from impatience that I'm liable to feel in the supermarket or watching TV when there are too many adverts. Road rage has a specificity to it that I don't feel is appropriate.

Nothing more than the usual, stuck behind a slow-moving vehicle. A Peugeot 206 or something. I can see the sprouting of grey hair above the driver's seat headrest. An old woman driving, the kind who I would test every couple of years after the age of seventy, so we could get the licence off them and make the roads safer. Not that my ensuing actions are liable to make any road safer.

Try to control it for a while, then I start to go. Drive up really close behind her. She's doing thirty-four in a sixty zone. No long straights, too many cars coming from the other direction, no chance to overtake. My presence close to her rear end is enough to make her slow down even more. As her speed drops below thirty I have a brief contemplation of pulling her over, producing my ID and telling her I'm an unmarked traffic cop, and booking her for driving liable to cause an accident. The thought is brief indeed.

Instead I lean on the horn, then start jabbing it repeatedly. My head is exploding with instant, uncontrollable fury, the kind of fury you can unleash from behind a wheel.

'Fucking move!' I'm screaming at her. 'Jesus! Would you just fucking move!'

Punching the horn. Punching the horn so hard it hurts. Spittle flying onto the plastic of the centre of the steering wheel.

We approach a parking place. She slows down even more, then pulls in. I don't turn and stare at her, just gun the accelerator. Ultimately, of course, I'm not in a rush. I've no intention of thrashing the speed limit into non-existence. Within about a hundred yards, I hit a thirty zone, and I slow right down and am now driving more slowly than I was previously. A red Škoda catches me and sits in behind. Bang on thirty miles an hour.

My rage passes. I forget that I was angry. I forget about

the old woman, and do not wonder how long she sits in the parking area recovering her equilibrium.

12

'How's this?' I say. Taylor's office, me and Morrow, coffee and doughnuts. Yes, coffee and doughnuts. We're all Americans now, as the Muppet Blair said. 'There's a correlation between the sleeping drug and the semen, but not directly with the death. Someone drugged her and raped her. Maureen, unable to cope, killed herself.'

'Hmm...' begins Taylor. 'Not bad. I know, just because a woman is raped, doesn't mean she's going to commit suicide, and you'd think that an older woman might be able to handle the situation better than someone much younger, but then... what do any of the three of us dicks know?'

'I'll check it out,' says Morrow. 'Speak to some people. Rates of rape amongst the over-60s, the victims' psychology. Like you say, everyone's different, but there might be some sort of pattern of behaviour.'

'Have we established her whereabouts on her final evening?'

Shake of the head from Morrow and me.

'OK, well that's something we really need to find out. Did she go anywhere, did anyone come to her house, did she have any clubs or other regular Monday evening activity?'

'On it,' I say.

'I've been hearing a lot about Paul Cartwright,' says Taylor. 'We need to get along to see him.'

'Me too,' says Morrow. 'There's a general feeling that he's a nasty piece of work.'

'Interviewed him yesterday afternoon,' I say.

'Good man,' says Taylor. 'How was that?'

'There's something about him,' I say. 'I can see why

everyone hates him, and I can see why his church won out in the end. Very focussed. He set out to achieve something, and he did it. People in his church will have been pleased, those in the others pissed off. What are you going to do?'

'He know Mrs Henderson?'

'Just from the letters, which he was happy to talk about. Recalled every one…'

'Quite a few people said he has a freakish memory.'

'Yep, happy to admit it. Before this is out I think we'll be talking to him again, and I think there's a lot to learn from him, if we can work out how to get him to say the right things… but I don't think he had anything to do with her death. Not directly, at any rate.'

'OK, we'll leave him for the moment, but keep tabs on him. Once we get to second interviews, that's when people start to think, hang on a second, isn't this something more than a suicide enquiry?'

'And Cartwright's the kind of dude that Connor will be hanging with. Written all over him.'

'Well, I'm sure you were your usual discreet self,' says Taylor.

Morrow even laughs at that. Fucking hilarious.

'The fact is,' continues Taylor, 'we've yet to come up with proof of anything suspicious, so we have to continue to be careful. The superintendent is going to be shutting us down first opportunity he gets, so no mention of a murder investigation until such times as we know for definite.'

A couple of raised eyebrows dispatched across the table, and Morrow and I take the signal to leave.

*

I find myself back at the Old Kirk. No reason. I just felt drawn here for the silence. I parked in the small area between the church and the halls, noticed that the gates were unlocked. I'd been intending knocking on the gatekeeper's door and asking in some sort of small voice if she wouldn't mind me sitting in the church again. I wasn't going to have a reason. There was a fair possibility that in fact I was going to sit in the car park for ten minutes, not get out of the car, and then drive off.

Do I have a pathological fear that she might think I'm contemplating turning to God, or do I have a pathological fear that I am actually turning to God?

Neither, really. I want the silence, that's all. I'm just as happy to share it with Mrs Buttler.

So I walked in through the front door of the church. She turned at my footsteps as I entered the nave, and now we're back in a not dissimilar position to where we were yesterday. Her sitting at the end of a row, me directly across the aisle at the end of the adjacent row. I get the smell of her today, something I didn't notice yesterday. A light fragrance.

Neither of us has spoken. Not sure how long we've been sitting here. Ten minutes? Fifteen?

If God is everywhere, then is this place any closer to God than anywhere else? Does the silence and the art and the Bible and depictions of Jesus make it any closer to God than a forest or a field or a supermarket or a studio basement flat with no windows, rats in the walls and a soiled mattress lying in the middle of the floor?

I lower my eyes from Jesus in blue above the chancel. I'm thinking about God now. Stupid bastard. How many times have I asked the question in the past? If there's a God, why did my dad get killed by a drunk driver when I was two and a half? Why's the bastard who killed my dad still alive today?

How many times? I asked it enough to not need to ask it anymore. To not even consider God.

'You believe all this stuff?' I ask, my voice cutting uneasily into the bright light of early afternoon.

'How do you mean?' she says. Glances round at me.

'Historians these days,' I say, 'they know. They know how it worked out. There were hundreds of religions in the Middle East two thousand years ago, and Christianity was just one of them. St Paul was better organised than everyone else, managed to drag Christianity's head above the parapet, and eventually it flourished. It was like Hitler emerging from the shambles of post-WWI German politics. It wasn't like he was the divine leader or anything, he just played the game better, persevered, played his cards at the right moment...'

'You're comparing Hitler to Jesus?' she says curiously, although she's smiling.

'Actually, I think I was comparing him to Paul.'

'Oh, OK, that's fine.'

We laugh. Together. Like some sort of version of normal conversation. It's been so long.

'I just mean, it's kind of clear how Christianity got started, and how it managed to flourish, and how the books of the Bible were chosen, et cetera. It was all just politics. Which, you know, is why this church merger business wasn't so un-Christian after all. This is how it works. People have self-interest, they work to protect and extend that self-interest. In this way, Jesus was just a product that Paul was selling, and he was good at his job. Nowadays he'd be working for Apple.'

'Unless,' she says, turning away and looking back down the body of the church, 'Jesus is the true son of God, and then he would undoubtedly have risen, regardless of whether or not Paul had been a good salesman. Perhaps, in fact, it was God who made Paul a good salesman on the road to Damascus.'

'A fair point,' I say. 'But that's what I'm asking. In the face of the evidence and the plethora of historians and books and documentaries, which do you believe?'

'Can't you believe both? That God delivered Jesus to us, and then used St Paul to extend His message?'

'But all those Bible stories that are just made up or cribbed from other religions. The virgin birth and the wise men and all that?'

Notice how I'm not swearing in church.

Notice how I'm not mature enough to do that without

thinking I should be earning some kudos. From somebody!

'You believe what you choose to believe, Sergeant. One cannot argue with faith. I will say, however, that I have never truly believed. I have prayed and I have come to this church all my life, but I've never truly believed. But that's not what it's about. I would say, in fact, that it doesn't matter one bit. It's community, that's all. About being there for people, having a set of values, sharing those values, helping others, giving of yourself, and hopefully receiving too.'

'Do you need God for that? I mean, do you need the church for that?'

She finally turns and looks at me again.

'People need a focus, that's all. The church gives them a focus. We preach understanding and compassion. It does no harm.'

'The crusades weren't so hot.'

She smiles at that, rather than whacks me over the head with the nearest heavy object.

'What was it you wanted to talk to me about?' she says after a few moments.

I turn away and stare off into the far distance.

'Nothing,' I say. 'Sorry. Just felt like I needed the silence.'

She smiles. I can feel her smile, although I'm not looking at her.

The silence is like a wall, rising up, surrounding us. Slowly melting, folding in at the sides, closing in at the top. Blanking everything else out. Enveloping us.

God, what am I on?

My phone beeps, cutting through the wall.

She glances over as I take it from my pocket, embarrassed.

'You should switch that off when you come in here,' she says, unnecessarily.

'Sorry.'

'I mean, not just during a service. If you're coming in for peace and quiet, you're not going to get it if you leave your phone on.'

I read the text.

21 Burns Street. Now.

Rare for Taylor to invest anything with a note of urgency.

'Got to go,' I say.

She watches me as I get to my feet.

'I come into the church most days at this time,' she says. 'You know, if you think you can find what you're looking for in here.'

'Thank you. When's the next time the church will be used for a service?'

She gives it some thought, lets her eyes express doubt.

'There's a wedding in three or four months. But then, I expect Maureen would have wanted to have a memorial service here, so that might happen shortly. I suppose you'll need to release the body first.'

I don't think that's going to be happening any time soon, unless Connor pulls rank and shuts us all down.

I nod. She smiles and I leave.

13

It's a small bathroom, so not a huge amount of room for our lot. Three at a time maybe. I stick my head over the back of one of the SOCOs, catch a quick look at the pasty teenager lying in cold bathwater turned bloody red, then go back through to the lad's bedroom.

Taylor is in here; the mother is downstairs with a couple of constables, if she hasn't already been taken off somewhere else.

Tommy Kane was seventeen and he's not coming back. Dead as a badger.

'You have this guy on your list?' asks Taylor.

'You mean, anything to do with the church business? Maureen and that?'

'Yes,' says Taylor, irritably, as if I ought to know what's going on inside his head.

'No. You think they're related?'

He looks up from where he's been rifling through some music magazines, gives me a glance. His annoyance seems to dissipate, and then he shrugs.

'Fair point, Sergeant. Who knows? But you know as well as I do, this town is a small place. Months go by without anything ever happening. Ever. Two apparent suicides a few days apart, especially when the first is a woman known to have had sex with a young man, possibly a youth, and the second is of a youth...'

'No way,' I say, shaking my head.

'No way what?'

'No way Maureen had sex with this kid.'

'You heard it from Balingol,' says Taylor. 'She had sex with a young man.'

'Yeah, I know, but a twenty-five-year-old or something.'

'For someone who'd have sex with a packet of biscuits, you can be terribly prudish and old-fashioned sometimes, Sergeant.' He lets out a big sigh, as if talking to a child, then he gives a slight wave of the hand. 'We'll know once Balingol's had a look at him.'

'Did he have anything to do with the church?'

'He helped out at the Sunday school down at St Mungo's,' says Taylor, 'so that at least puts them in the same ball park.'

I look round the room at the standard teenage walls. Posters of bands and half-naked women. Hey, nice one of Emily Blunt's breasts, wonder what movie that's from. I'll need to check it out. Iron Maiden. Judas Priest. Natalie Portman, topless but with a conveniently positioned arm. A Green Bay Packers pendant. A Neymar picture. Fucking Neymar, the cheating, diving little cunt. Dylan. Good lad, he's got a poster of Bob, circa 1962. Some concert ticket stubs. Some football ticket stubs. Rangers. So, he's the one.

'He taught at the Sunday school?' I ask.

'Given his age, I don't think he was enrolled as a student,' says Taylor pointedly. As he speaks, he's looking through a drawer, tossing some porn mags onto the bed. I glance over. Commercial, off-the-shelf porn mags. Very mundane, in these internet days. I turn back to the walls.

'The walls don't look like the walls of a Sunday school teacher.'

'Maybe not,' says Taylor, 'but he's a teenager in the third millennium. What would you expect? Posters of Jesus?'

'Suppose.'

Taylor straightens up, gives another quick look around.

'See what you can find. I'm off to speak to people. Try not to spend too much time looking at naked women.'

'I'm on the job,' I say, with irritation.

He looks at me blankly.

'Try not to spend too much time looking at naked women.'

*

An hour in the room of a dead teenage boy. One long, depressing hour.

It takes me back to the awfulness of it. The awfulness of being a teenager. Jesus. There's just so much shit. Sure, you might think, I'd love to be a teenager again. There are so many possibilities, the world is your clichéd fucking oyster. But if you do ever think like that, what you're really thinking is, I wish I could be me now, an adult, transported back to my teenage years, before I fucked up my life.

No one really wants to be a teenager again. What you want to be is an adult who happens to be seventeen years old, an adult who hasn't yet committed himself to all the mistakes that he's made (and would inevitably remake, if given the chance).

And yet teenagers grow up. They escape those god-awful years. At least, they should do. They hopefully do. If all goes to plan. If they make sure they don't end up lying in a bath of their own blood. And every life has so much promise. Even the ones that start off shitty and depressing, they still have the opportunity to get out, escape, fly into the world and create something for themselves.

But not this kid. Not Tommy. Tommy is dead. All these higher exam past papers are for nothing. And the football and the girls and the music and the few scattered books on eastern philosophy, and the DVDs of Chinese war epics, and the posters, and Call of Duty. All for nought, because he's dead in a bath.

Almost doesn't matter whether or not he committed suicide. Murder, suicide, accident (it wasn't an accident!), whatever way, it's just sad.

I could look through the room in about ten minutes. I spend much of the hour sitting on the bed staring at the walls. Not looking at anything in particular. Just tired, filled with an unusual melancholy.

There are different types of melancholy, and this isn't one of the good ones. This is one of those that says, I just want to get out of here, I want to go home, I want to drink. I probably also want some female company. Little chance of getting that.

A constable sticks her nose into the room at some point. Webb, maybe, not sure of her name. She's new.

'Everything all right, sir?' she asks, at the sight of her sergeant staring idly into space.

'Yes, thank you. Has the body been removed?'

'Yes, sir,' she says. 'The SOCOs are finished in the bathroom.'

'OK, thanks. I'm nearly done here.'

She waits to see if the lead investigating officer on the premises is going to add anything else, and when I don't, she takes her leave. Thereafter I get on with it and wrap things up quickly, finding nothing of interest to the investigation in the process.

*

I meet Taylor in the pub. Unusually, it's his suggestion. Pub rather than the office. It is after six, so I suppose that legitimises it in some way. As if, as police officers, we need legitimisation.

A pint each. Just after six seems a little too early for vodka tonic.

'Suicide note?' he asks, as I settle down and push his pint across the table.

'Left under his pillow for the investigating officer? I'm afraid not. How about you?'

'The mother's in bits, getting little out of her for the moment. She was away the last couple of days visiting her sister. Somewhere in the Borders. Moffat, that was it. Left the lad on his own. First time she'd ever gone away overnight and left him. Thought he was ready for it. He seemed happy when she left. She thought he might get some of his friends over, but was sure there'd be nothing bad. Said he was a good kid.'

'Father?'

'Long gone. Hasn't been in touch in ten years or something. We can look at the kid's e-mails, see if he's had contact that she doesn't know about.'

'He went to church on Sunday?' I ask.

'Seems to have done. Nothing unusual. Did his Sunday school gig, came home, ate a sandwich, spent his Sunday afternoon watching football, spent his Sunday evening watching American football. She didn't see him much apart from dinner.'

'Monday? Tuesday?'

'Kid was at school. She saw him last on Wednesday morning. Dropped him at the school gate, which she didn't usually do, and that was that.'

'So she was around for Monday evening, when it's possible that young Tommy and old Maureen got together...'

'And had sex,' says Taylor, finishing the sentence for me.

'And now they're both dead. Did you mention the possibility to the mum, ask if he went out anywhere?'

Taylor actually smiles at that, but I don't join him. There are no smiles from me tonight.

'Too early for that. If we had no other way of finding out, then sure, we'd have to ask. But we've got a guaranteed answer coming from Balingol, so why upset anyone with that kind of question? We'll have the results in the morning, then we can get our shit together and get on with it. If the kid and Maureen did it, we can ask the mum where she thinks he was and who he was with.'

'Of course, even if it turns out they had sex, doesn't mean they were both murdered. Maybe, in fact, it makes it even less likely. Perhaps he raped her, then she killed herself because of the shame and he killed himself because of... well, that would be shame too, I guess.'

'Yep, you're right,' says Taylor, in between large gulps. This is a man who, once more, isn't staying. 'However, if there's evidence of the same sleeping drug, that might be a different bag of bananas.'

He downs the pint and lays the empty glass on the table.

'Let's regroup in the morning. I've got a date.'

I look at him quizzically, then find myself saying, 'No, you fucking don't!'

'Why, thank you for the confidence boost, Sergeant. I will take that forward into the evening, and if I have cause to ask myself what exactly it is that she sees in me over the dinner table, I will remember those kind words and feel even shitter that I do already.'

*

Can't fight it this evening. It's a night for going home and staring into the abyss. The death of young Tommy has really hit me for some reason. For some reason? It's kind of obvious why any teenager's death would affect anyone, yet you need to learn to be immune in this job. Of course you do. There's so much shit, so much sadness. We only see people at their worst, when they're at their lowest, or when they're at their most venal or abusive or most unpleasant.

As soon as it starts getting to you, you're done. Really. You have to be able to switch this stuff off, leave it at the desk, go home and get on with your life. If you can't, you're fucked. Life is just so sad. There are many jobs which involve working at the coal face of that sadness, and this is one of them.

But I don't want to take Tommy's death home with me. Tommy the teenager, only a year or two older than my eldest; Tommy who never saw his father, and me who so very rarely sees my kids.

I should stop drinking, go home and at least pick up the phone. Call my kids, listen to them. Of course, they're liable to grunt three or four words at me, if they can even be bothered coming to the phone, but it can be enough sometimes. It would do tonight, it's all I need. Maybe they'd even open up, and if they didn't I'd at least get a bit more from their mother.

But I don't stop drinking. Can't. I sit with one hand on the glass, and my mind sliding into the alcohol. It has the same effect as sitting in silence at the church; so much more destructive, yet so easy to sink into, to embrace, to cling to.

Can't go home alone tonight. Haven't felt this shit since the cigarette in the arm. Tonight would be another night for that. Having done it once, the thought is there to do it again. It's like anything. The first time is the breaking down of the wall.

But I don't want to lie curled up in a ball on my carpet, tears flowing for my fucked-up life, for all my faults, for my embarrassment, for my pain. I don't want to be angrily, desperately, mundanely stubbing the cigarette out on my arm like some teenage loser who can't handle the hormones.

I stumble out of the bar at just after eleven. My car is there, a testament to my initial intention to have only one drink, but at least I'm sensible enough tonight not to drive. I get a taxi into the centre of Glasgow, all of fifteen minutes at this time of the evening, and head for Hope Street. Bound to be a club or two that's just getting going, where I can show my face and pick up whatever's available. Maybe I can play on that moody, melancholic, been-there-done-that thing I like to think I've got going on.

As it is, I don't have to bother. I find her even before I get inside the first club I come to. She's drunk, might have already thrown up, I'm not sure. Twenty maybe, if I'm being kind to myself.

There's been a bit of a stramash, the usual club tipping out on a Friday night kind of thing. A couple of rozzers hanging around, trying not to get too involved. In these kinds of situations, you're trying to avoid too much paperwork. There's a guy being dragged off by his mates, still shouting abuse over his shoulder. Then there's the girl, the object of his abuse, in her red dress that barely covers her arse, leaning against a wall, crying, shouting at the wall, words that are aimed at whatever his name is.

There really isn't much to the dress. Not even sure you could call it a dress. More of a handkerchief really. Strapless, held up by God knows what, a wonderful amount of cleavage on display, great breasts, gorgeous legs.

Tricky situation. I just need to play it right.

I lean back against the wall next to her.

'Fuckers,' I say. I don't look at her.

She stops shouting abuse for a moment and looks round at me. She wipes her hand across her mouth, presumably taking away the vomit. I look at the ground.

I don't say anything else. Certainly I'm not enquiring about her. She turns away, but can't help looking back at me. I look drunk, lost, pathetic. I'm not even acting. I am drunk, lost and pathetic.

I take a packet of fags out, but drop the lighter, the fag and the packet in one carefully useless moment. 'Fuck,' I say, then make an abject effort to bend down for them, but quickly give up, with another expletive thrown out into the chill November night.

She bends down to get them for me. I stare down at her, get a wonderfully clear view of her breasts as they tumble out of the dress. Up to this point I'd just been thinking that I needed the company, on some purely practical level of emotional necessity. The sight of her in the dress, and those gorgeous breasts, goes straight to my groin.

I look away in plenty of time as she straightens up, sorts herself out with a very inelegant movement, and offers me the fags.

'You want us tae light one for you?'

I look at her as though I hadn't even noticed she's there.

'Wha'?' I say. I sound confused. A bit helpless.

She lights the cigarette for me and puts it into my

mouth.

Result.

Get a slight taste of vomit from the end of the fag, but I don't care.

Twenty minutes later I'm back at her place, she's grinding her pussy into me and those gorgeous breasts are in my mouth.

14

Bad start. Slept in. Not much, but enough. Didn't have time to get home, muddled into work in yesterday's clothes, stinking of who knows what.

Slump down behind my desk. 08:57. Morrow looks up, stares at me for a moment, smiles awkwardly.

'Rough night, sir?'

'I need coffee,' I say.

The plus side of hooking up with whatever her name was – and, no, I never did find out – is that I'm not as hungover as there was the potential for me to be if I'd gone on drinking. Look over at the coffee machine. Jesus, even walking that far seems like an effort.

Taylor appears at my desk. Must have been waiting for me to come in; had been hoping he'd be out, that I'd not see him until later on in the morning.

'Walk with me, Sergeant,' he says.

I glance at Morrow, who looks back at his desk, then I follow Taylor out into the corridor. He stops when he thinks we're out of earshot of the office. I stop beside him and he noticeably takes another step away from me.

'Go home, sort yourself out. Shave, have a shower, clean your teeth. Get something to eat. Change your clothes. Don't take too long about it, but don't come back before you're in a fit state, and don't come back looking like that. I've been cutting you slack long enough, Sergeant. All right, you made it in before nine, and you haven't had the chance to fuck up, but you don't come into work looking and smelling like you do, so go home. Come back in and mean it. I've had Connor hold off from disciplinary proceedings against you for long enough, but if this happens again I'll happily start them off myself.'

He starts to walk by me.

'Sorry, sir...'

'Don't want to hear it.'

And he's gone.

I don't turn to watch him go. Drop my head to look at the floor. Sgt Harrison approaches along the corridor. She sees Taylor disappear round the corner, slows as she comes alongside me.

'You all right, Tom?' she says.

I look up. Smell like shit. Look like shit. Clothes like shit. Eyes like shit. Breath like shit.

'Been better.'

She hesitates, but there's not a lot else to say, then she's on her way. I look back down at the floor, and then, with my eyes on my shoes, I walk down the stairs and out the front door.

*

I find Taylor standing next to Balingol, looking down at three small bones in a metal dish. Neither of them is speaking, neither of them acknowledges my arrival. I glance at the detective and the doctor, and then follow their lead and stare meaningfully at the bones. Wonder how long I need to do this before I can ask what it is we're looking at.

Got my act together. Walked to the pub, collected my car, drove home – might still have been over the limit, although perhaps not, because of the earlier than expected cessation of alcohol consumption – shaved, had a shower, brushed my teeth, drank two litres of water, had a bowl of granola, drank a cup of coffee and two glasses of orange juice, took the time to iron a shirt, polished my shoes, suit on, walked back in. Found that Taylor had gone out, and got one of the constables to give me a lift down here.

'Ribs from a rat,' says Balingol.

I gather from Taylor's lack of reaction that this

information is aimed at me rather than him.

'Where'd you find them?' I ask.

'Inserted in young Master Kane's throat.'

I glance at the two of them, but they're both still studying the bones.

'OK,' I say tentatively. Feel, in some way, like I'm being examined to see if I've recovered from being out of my face last night.

'You have anything else?' I ask.

'Of course,' says Balingol. 'We can confirm that Mrs Henderson had relations with this young man. The lad was also drugged with the same sleeping tablets as the first victim, and then presumably someone else slashed his wrists. We cannot rule out, however, that he slashed them himself before the sedative had completely kicked in, but that wouldn't explain the ribs at the back of the throat.'

'Feels like someone was leaving a message,' says Taylor.

I nod. That makes sense.

'What does it say?' I ask.

Taylor finally looks up from the bones.

'That's what we're trying to figure out, standing here looking at them. Any ideas?'

I look back at the bones. From somewhere the image of Maureen hanging from the bridge comes into my head.

'Might, in some way, be related to Maureen having wings on her back. That looked like a regulation suicide apart from the wings; this looks like a regulation suicide apart from the freaky, weird bones in the throat. Maybe there's some connection.'

Taylor nods as I speak.

'Hmm,' he says. 'You can look into that later.'

'Ribs and angel's wings,' I say. 'Does have that biblical vibe.'

'You're right.'

He nods again, straightens up.

'Right, Doc, we should be getting along. Anything else to tell us?'

'One more thing. Mrs Henderson used Tesco's own lube to smooth the act of love-making.'

We stare at him for a moment.

'Thanks for that image,' says Taylor.

'Tesco do their own lube?' I ask.

'Yes,' says Balingol, 'they do. Not, you know, in the way that they do their own bread, making it on the premises, but they have their own brand-name lube.'

Fuck.

'Isn't it possible,' I say, clutching at some sort of straw, because the thought of young Tommy and old Maureen coupling in inter-generational sex is just too grotesque for me, 'that someone extracted Tommy's semen and injected it into old Maureen with a turkey baster? You know, to make it look like they had sex.'

I get a glance from Taylor, but then he gives the question some level of validation by turning to see what Balingol has to say. Balingol smiles in that slightly weird way of his.

'Not bad, Sergeant, but no, I'm afraid not. There was clear evidence of penile insertion, and since the young lad's penis remains intact, for the moment you should work on the basis that the two of them had intercourse.'

And let's just celebrate the fact that there's no video.

Oh God, what if there is?

*

We find the minister at the chancel of the nave of St Mungo's church. Me and Taylor. The gatekeeper let us into the church, saying we'd find the minister in the vestry, but he's out in the main body of the building, looking at the Bible which is open on the lectern.

St Mungo's was built in the 1950s, and looks every inch what you'd expect. A dump. Just walking in you wonder how on earth a group of presumably educated people could choose to come here every Sunday rather than the church up the road.

Paul Cartwright must have done one hell of a job. There's the guy you want on your side when you've got some negotiating to do. If we'd had him in 1936, Hitler would have become a sausage salesman and happily handed ninety per cent of Germany over to France and Poland.

The sun is shining outside, yet still this place seems cloaked in a clawing, Stygian murkiness. For the moment I feel like I have my head in the right place. Sure, in general I'm all over the damned shop, up and down and sideways, but that means there are moments of focus and competence. And I'd been having one now, until I walked in here. This place is enough to suck the life out of anyone.

'Detective,' says the vicar, looking up. 'I thought you might come.'

'You've heard about Tommy Kane?'

'Yes,' he says. 'Another suicide. It's almost too much to bear.'

Now that I'm in this place, I can understand it if that's what it was. Coming here every Sunday morning, I'd want to kill myself as well. Of course, in calling it another suicide he's contradicting himself from the other day, when he seemed certain we were in Murderland.

The minister approaches us, and now the three of us stand at the end of the aisle, beside the chancel, and take in the surroundings and the moment. Taylor looks up at the windows behind the pulpit. Dark glass, enhancing the mood.

'How well did you know Tommy?'

The vicar shakes his head, a prelude to being positive, as it happens.

'Very. He was one of our bright young things. The average age of the congregation keeps growing, of course, same across the country in every church. And as the older generation die off they are not replaced, and so we come to situations like we find here where congregations have to merge. It's rare these days that we find teenagers so committed to the church. Tommy was a jewel.'

'You told us the other day you felt sure that Mrs Henderson must have been murdered. You don't think the same about Tommy?'

The minister lowers his head, doesn't look Taylor in the eye.

'That was just... that was foolish,' he says. 'Just the emotion of the day. I do rather regret those words, Chief Inspector, and would be grateful if I could, as it were, have them back.'

Oh, they're out there, chum. Just because you're wearing a dog collar, doesn't mean you're in charge of the time machine eraser button.

Hmm. Time machine eraser button. God, could I use one of those.

'Why did you say it when you did?'

'Heat of the moment, I suppose.'

'What moment?' says Taylor, leaving him wriggling on the line. 'You must regularly have to deal with the death of parishioners, you just said so yourself. You'd already heard news of her death, you'd had plenty of time to become accustomed to the fact of what had happened. There was no moment. We were fairly certain, up to the time we spoke to you, that Mrs Henderson had committed suicide, then you had us believing and suspecting otherwise. You changed the course of the investigation. You cannot, now, casually withdraw the remark.'

The fellow looks surprised. Good on Taylor, even if he is being slightly disingenuous, not taking any of his shit, just because he's got the whole Man of God thing going on. Probably thinks himself above this kind of interrogation.

'I don't know what to say,' says the vicar. 'My initial reaction was one of such disbelief that I could not accept Maureen would do such a thing to herself. It seemed clear to me. Yet, with the passing of time, the acceptance of much sadness, I realise that I was hasty. I should not have been so bold in my assertions, and I genuinely did not mean to lead you down any specific path in your investigation. In the cold light of day, and at some distance, I now feel sure that I was wrong.'

Neither Taylor nor I give him an easy escape from that. We do the taciturn cop routine, stare him out, wait to see if he's going to say anything else. You know, it's fair enough, people change their minds. And anyway, we've now got a lot more to go on to suggest there has been murder committed than the word of this clown. Nevertheless, never good to just let people off with talking shit.

'So,' he says after a few moments. 'I should probably be getting on.'

'Can you think of anything in your acquaintance with the two of them that might have pointed to them wanting to end their own lives?'

He looks slightly taken aback by the question, as though the very thought of them committing suicide – even though he's admitted that's what he thinks happened – is utterly unbelievable.

'I cannot think,' is all he says.

'Was there any connection at all between the two of them?' I ask, as I feel I've been standing here, somewhat superfluous to proceedings.

'How do you mean?' he asks.

'Did they know each other? Had they sat on the same committee, or had she helped at Sunday school, or had he done anything for her in relation to the church?'

'I really couldn't say,' says the vicar.

'Yes, you can say,' I reply sharply. 'Either you know something or you don't.'

He swallows, glances at Taylor, then back to me.

'I don't,' he says.

*

'You were a bit harsh on him there,' says Taylor. 'Good though, it worked.'

'You started it!'

'What?'

'You were harsh first,' I say.

'I wasn't harsh. I was thorough and professional. You were harsh.'

'Whatever.'

15

Sitting in the canteen eating a mince pie. Not good for the waistline at my age. The line *who ate all the mince pies?* was first spoken for a reason. I have a box of them at home, which means that I'll likely have one with a cup of tea when I get in – if I don't go to the pub, and after last night, I'm really not going to the pub – and then probably have one later on, when I'm doing my best not to touch alcohol and flicking through endless channels of shit TV.

The box I've got at home is labelled Christmas mince pies, and they have a use by date of the end of November. Well, that's not a Christmas mince pie, is it, for fuck's sake? That's a fucking autumn mince pie, that's what that is. Or, you know, it's just a mince pie. Christmas needn't come into it. If I was rich, like those pointless rich people who have pointless wealth and can afford to do pointless shit with their money – like buying an apartment in Monaco that they use one weekend a year, or buying a round of drinks in an exclusive London club that ends up costing £100k, or buying their kid a horse, even though they don't have a kid – I'd get a lawyer on to them. Why say something's for Christmas when at the same time you're defining that it's a requirement of the food that it be consumed weeks and weeks before Christmas?

I know, stupid thing to get annoyed about. Like slow drivers and people taking too long staring at a shelf in the supermarket.

I take my last bite of mince pie and feel a certain self-loathing for having eaten it at all.

The seat opposite me is pulled out and DI Gostkowski sits down. DI Gostkowski, with whom I had a brief fling earlier in the year. A low point for both of us. Well, certainly, for her it was. She could do a lot better than me. It was only a low point for me in that I was feeling low at the time. Having said that, not a lot has changed in that department.

'How are things, Tom?' she asks.

We haven't worked together since I got back. Indeed, we've barely spoken, just the occasional nod as we pass each other in a corridor.

'Much as they usually are,' I say. 'How are you?'

She dumped me, that was how it went. So there's that inevitable stiffness of conversation. The dumper and the dumpee. Technically, of course, we'd just been fuck buddies, so there shouldn't have been any actual dumping, but in reality, when it came to it, I didn't want to stop and she'd had enough. So she dumped me. As a fuck buddy.

'Good,' she says. 'You looked a bit rough this morning. Who was she?'

I hold her gaze for a moment and then laugh.

'Just, you know.... didn't know her name.'

'Was she worth it?'

I take a sip of tea. Still too hot, even though I've already finished off the two hundred and seventy-five calories of the mince pie. Candour bubbles its way to the surface.

'You know,' I begin, then look up at her again and let myself fall into her eyes, 'it did the job. I wanted to go home, I wanted to... God, what am I trying to say...? I didn't want to kill myself. I don't want to die. Not yet. I don't think so. Not yet. Some time soon. But last night, my head was right there, right there waiting to explode, and if I hadn't gone out and got drunk and found some girl throwing up on the street who was ready to be taken home and fucked, well I was going home on my own and I was going to take a knife, and I was going to slash the fuck out of... I don't know... my arms, my legs. I don't know. Then I was going to throw up and fall asleep in my own puke and blood, and I was going to wake up, if I actually ever woke up, at six a.m. feeling like utter, total fucking death.'

She doesn't say anything to that. I wonder if she sat down thinking she'd have a couple of minutes idle chatter. I wonder why she sat down at all.

'So, I never got her name, and I know I couldn't find her house again, but yes, she was worth it. She got me through the night.'

'Have you spoken to anyone yet?'

I'm about to ask what she means, but I know what she means and she knows I know.

'No.'

'What happened with the doctor? Dr Sutcliffe?'

'Shagged her,' I say bluntly. 'Thereafter it didn't work out so well.'

She smiles ruefully, but the smile dies quickly.

'What is it you're not talking about, Tom?'

'Don't,' I say. 'I can't.'

We stare across the narrow canteen table. I'd been doing fine today. I mean, it's not like a great fucking day or anything, but I'd got my shit together enough to be able to get through it. Enough to be able to contemplate a night sitting alone at home watching lousy TV that was going to end with me going to bed well before midnight and without any alcohol tripping through my system.

'The alcohol,' she says, not picking up on the fact that I desperately want her to stop talking, or else, choosing to ignore it, 'is one thing. You're in the west of Scotland. Ninety per cent of people in Glasgow with a problem exacerbate it by adding alcohol to the list. The sex addiction is much more suggestive—'

'I don't have a sex addiction!'

A little too loudly. There were probably about six women in here with whom I've slept who heard that. I lean forward and lower my voice.

'I don't have a sex addiction.'

'How many women have you slept with this year?'

'What does that matter? I'm a man. I'm not currently married. And yes, fucking boo hoo, I'm lonely. I need the company, and, yes, yes, I admit, having fucked up several marriages, I'm a bit of a commitment-phobe. So, what's the answer? Casual sex, that's what.'

'There's a gap, and it's a pretty big one,' she says, 'between casual sex, and you, who would have sex with every single woman you ever meet.'

'That's...' I start to say, but then cut it off. I can't say that's not true. I'd be lying.

'You're forty-five...'

'Six.'

'You're forty-six,' she says. 'You ought to be at a stage where women are people, not just sex objects. You've worked with them, and worked for them, you've seen them as victims and as criminals, you've been married to them, and soon enough your daughter's going to be one of them. Women can be all things in life, just the same as men can be all things. Women aren't just there to have sex with.'

An intense look across the table. The narrow table. Her lips look great. Those are lips that have been everywhere on me. She's wearing a white blouse, open at the neck. My eyes start to drift.

I close them.

Jesus, stop it! It's not about her lips! It's not about her blouse! She's trying to talk to you!

'You need help, Tom,' she says.

Deep breath. I open my eyes. She's right. Jesus, of course she's right.

'Hey, guys, this is too funny, shouldn't laugh 'n' all, but you just can't help it sometimes.'

Morrow lays his tray on the table, sits down next to Gostkowski. God, here comes someone with even less empathy than I have. Even I'd have spotted that there were two people sitting in a giant bubble of fucking emotional tension.

He takes a spoonful of chicken, rice and plastic sauce then talks through it.

'Young Tommy,' he says, and he's smiling, 'was partial to granny porn. We got into his school locker, and there were, like, serious magazines in there. I mean, you know, it's pertinent to the investigation 'n' all, but it's too funny, man. You should see this stuff.'

Gostkowski gives him a glance, turns back to me, gives me one of those think-about-what-I-said looks, then gets to her feet.

'I'll leave you boys to your investigation.'

I watch her go. Morrow takes another mouthful.

'Man, and you know, I mean these days grannies can be anything, can't they? I mean, you get, like, thirty-year-old grannies, so actually granny porn needn't be all that bad. But young Tom, he liked 'em old. Old and wrinkly. And you should see some of this shit, man. Those grannies will do anything. Anything!'

16

Sunday morning. Church. Taylor is at St Mungo's. He chose that one as Connor would be there and he wouldn't want to risk his loose cannon of a Detective Sergeant anywhere near the superintendent. So, I get to come to St Stephen's at the bottom end of Main Street. The church that went rogue.

Not so far from the immaculately fragrant public toilets.

The fourth church, the small one at Halfway, on the road out of town, has already been sold off. It's currently being converted into a house, in a kind of *Grand Designs* affair. Taylor had a look round, spoke to the new owners, decided there was nothing doing of interest to us.

Morrow's already had the job of speaking to those from the St Stephen's congregation to whom Maureen had dispatched her missives in the past couple of years. Those had rather tailed off in recent months, however, with St Stephen's unilateral declaration of independence.

Maureen was obviously cheesed off when she discovered that the congregation owned the building and were therefore in a position to make the move, while those at the Old Kirk were wedded to the greater church. However, grumbling about that aside, it seems there might be little else for St Stephen's to contribute to the story. They've gone their own way, and perhaps there's reason for others to be resentful of them, but seemingly little reason for that resentment to go both ways.

St Stephen's are like the man in an unhappy marriage, beset with unhappy teenagers and an unhappy, miserable home life. The parents split up, the mum is left at home with the kids, while the dad gets a job working in Boston or Singapore or Ouagadougou, buggers off on his own and gets to live the life of the merry bachelor, leaving the stresses, strains and aggro behind.

That's almost me in my marriage, without the moving to Singapore part.

So Maureen and some others at the Old Kirk were left bitter and resentful, while St Stephen's happily gets on with its life, a lone wolf among churches.

The word is that it's all the minister's doing, and I can see it now, sitting here, listening to the sermon. We've sung some songs, he's done his little bit for the kids – and there are lots of kids – there have been readings from the Bible, and I couldn't help but notice that one of the blokes seemed to affect a bit of a Sean Connery, and now the Reverend Jones is onto his sermon.

He's talking about God.

Usually I'd have switched off by now and would be letting my mind wander to get me through to the end. And yes, Detective Inspector Gostkowski, it's not entirely unlikely that I'd be thinking about having sex. That usual fantasy of mine, lying back on a sofa, one woman sitting on my face, another watching us, masturbating, before coming over and taking my aching erection into her mouth.

Church. We're talking about church.

I probably shouldn't be thinking stuff like that in church, should I? There's bound to be a commandment covering that. Because there weren't just ten commandments, you know. I think I learned that on *QI*. There were like fifty or something. Or fifteen. Can't remember exactly. But one of them was pretty much guaranteed to be along the lines of, when you're in the house of the Lord, thou shalt not fantasize about having sex with more than one woman at a time.

Anyway, I don't even need to let my head disappear into the usual clouds to get me through the sermon. This guy is good. I mean, he's still talking about God as if he actually exists, and he talks about Heaven as though it's an actual place where people end up, so you know, the subject matter is bonkers, but he knows how to hold an audience.

It's a bit like listening to Hitler. What he's saying is nuts, but you can't help but admire the delivery.

Usually on Sunday mornings I have other things to do, like lie in bed, or crawl to the bathroom to vomit, but if I didn't, I can think of worse things than coming to listen to this fellow. This guy is charisma in a dog collar.

He almost has me believing that if I devote my day and my life to helping others, and think not of myself, that I will sleep more easily at night. Weird.

However, like all these people, like all leaders whose attraction is based on charisma, there's something about him. Something that doesn't quite click. I wonder how many don't like him, how many people decided to switch to the amalgamated churches.

And yet the attendance here belies the feeling about the church in general that we've been picking up the last few days. This place is almost full. And the notices that are read out at the start, and that are also printed at the back of the order of service, list all sorts of other services and events around the church. A Sunday evening service. A Wednesday morning service for young mothers. The Church Guild meeting. The Bible Group. The Sunday school. The monthly Sunday school outing. The church trip to York Minster. Choir practice. And that choir at the back isn't the usual collection of octogenarians, slowly dying off as the years pass. There are teenagers in there.

Coming to this place is like hoofing it back to the 1930s.

The service ends with a call to arms, or at any rate, a call to a cup of tea in the halls at the back. I have my orders. And where else am I going to go this afternoon?

Well, I'm going to sit in a pub and watch Dundee United versus Kilmarnock, that's what. Dundee United versus Kilmarnock. Booyah! What choice have I got in this empty, unrelentingly miserable life? Sit in the pub watching lousy football – with Newcastle United versus West Ham to follow! – or sit at home and chew my leg off.

Nobody would sooner chew his leg off than anything. Not really.

*

The coffee is provided by Costa. Really. They have someone from Costa serving hot drinks at the back. I guess the church picks up the tab. I wonder if anyone just pitches up after the service to grab a latte. It's the kind of thing that people do.

The hall is pretty busy, and there are people grabbing a coffee and going to stand outside. Lovely autumnal afternoon, slight chill in the air, but just the right amount of chill. Beautiful day.

The minister is doing the rounds. Not sure if I'm going to talk to him here. Playing it by ear. We'll come and have a chat with him in the next day or two.

I stand on the periphery, taking in the scene, but it's not long before someone comes to talk to me. These church people have an eye for the newbie. There's a stranger in town, so they want to talk to him, and establish whether he's passing through or whether there's an opportunity to absorb him into the collective. Sure, the Church of Scotland aren't Scientologists, they're not going to get psychotic on me or try to plant a chip in my ass, but it's similar.

'Hi,' she says.

See, they know who they're dealing with. They sent over an attractive woman in her thirties as their envoy. Attractive women in their thirties are my kryptonite.

No, really. Even more than all those other attractive women. Still got the body, but not stupidly young, not inexperienced, less likely to be hurt by my commitment-phobia, more likely to be attracted to my seeming indifference and that strange melancholic quality.

Hey, it is what it is.

'I'm Philo Stewart. I run the Bible study group with my husband on a Saturday evening. How are you?'

Bible study group on a Saturday evening? Holy shit. Never realised this place was such a party town.

And Philo? Hmm. The fuck kind of name is that? Short for Philippa, maybe? Shit, a, that'll be it. Jesus, poor bastard.

I hope all that runs through my head without getting anywhere near my face, but my history in that respect ain't so great.

As she speaks she indicates a fellow in a shirt and tie in deep conversation with a couple of old women. He's not looking over.

Unlike some, I see marriage making the woman even more attractive.

'Very well, thanks. Great coffee,' I add. Bibble babble.

'Yes, isn't it? It's only been going a few weeks, but it's a great idea.'

'Seems kind of odd. I presumed there'd be tea and biscuits made by old women with blue hair rinse, wearing tweed.'

She glances around her, presumably checking that none of that lot are listening – she needn't worry as most of them will be deaf – then smiles as she turns back.

'Well... it was like that until fairly recently. But with this whole merger thing... You know, sorry, I didn't get your name? Are you new to the area?'

Rats. It was all going so well. A decent cup of coffee, kryptonite-lady, and there she was, starting to burble on about the merger, which was why I'd come. And she's just caught herself in the act, and stopped her tongue before it picked up a head of steam.

As discussed with Taylor, there's no point in pretending to be something I'm not. No point in being undercover. It's a small town, with every chance of stumbling across someone that we know, or someone that we've arrested.

'Detective Sergeant Hutton,' I say.

The cloud crosses her face. Such a shame.

'You're working?'

'Not really. I mean, I'm not here to interview anyone, nothing like that, but equally I'm not here because of religious reasons. Just... my boss wanted me to check things out.'

'Related to the suicide of that old woman?'

'Yes.'

'Or was it murder?'

I smile but don't answer. She seems to relax a little, glances around the busy room of churchgoers. She gives me a look that seems a little conspiratorial. Bang on, that's what we need.

'You think someone here might have had something to do with her death?'

'Not really.'

'OK... so why the visit?'

'Covering all angles,' I say.

'Due diligence?'

'Nicely put.'

She smiles. Naturally I smile back. Grateful that I didn't drink anything last night, so consequently don't look like three kinds of shit this morning.

'So,' I say, because I might as well run with this to see where it gets me, 'you know everyone here? Is there anyone who, if you suddenly heard they'd been arrested for the murder of old Mrs Henderson, you wouldn't automatically think, holy shit, I didn't see that coming? You know, someone who'd have you nodding sagely and saying to your husband who runs the Bible group, *I said, didn't I? I said he had the cold eyes of a killer.*'

There's the smile again.

'*I* run the Bible group, and my husband helps,' she says.

I nod, but leave the conversational stick in her hands.

'Not here,' she says. She glances around the room, turns back, shaking her head. 'It's not like I'm going to say to you, oh yes, old Mr Crackjaw, he'd been banging old Maureen for years and wanted her dead. Just... I think we've talked enough. We're in the phone book. Top end of Glenvale Road. Give me a call, and maybe you could come to the house.'

I nod, stop myself saying anything which implies that I like the fact she's inviting me on a date.

'Would you like me to introduce you to the minister?'

What the Hell. 'Thank you.'

*

In the office of the Reverend Jones. Unfortunate name for a vicar. I keep thinking of Jim Jones, and all those poor fuckers he had put to the sword in Guyana. Maybe that's just me. There are probably hundreds of Reverend Joneses around the world who have never been responsible for the deaths of nine hundred people.

Like this guy.

'But you didn't know right from the off that you'd be able to break away? You were in the mix for the amalgamation at the start?'

He considers this for a while as he lightly plays with the teaspoon in his saucer.

'I think I always knew. I know what you will likely think, that I didn't actually know, not in the way in which I was in possession of the facts. But I knew. We never really got involved with the project, not in the manner in which the others did. They fought it out between themselves while we remained on the periphery. I think they believed that we were trying to be above it, that we would bide our time and then produce some Machiavellian masterstroke, borne of artifice and deceit, to win the contest. Church of the Year 2013. Ha! It wasn't for us. No, I think we always knew that something would come up, that the Lord would help us in whatever way he saw fit.'

'It was the Lord who brought you the coffee franchise?' I ask.

Yes, that's big of me, isn't? Trying to be cooler than this guy.

'Some of our people aren't happy,' he says, 'but just wait until the Sunday morning when they come in and see the Reebok Church of St Stephen sign above the door. Then there'll be trouble.'

He delivers the line ruefully, and with perfect comic timing, so that just for a second he sucks me in.

'Funny,' I say. And it was. Add this guy to the list of people I was expecting to hate, and who are proving to be much more engaging.

'We won't get that far, but we have to look at different things. Congregations everywhere are going through the floor. It's how the town ended up in this awful situation in the first place. But what you can't do, what doesn't work, is trying to reinvent your product. They had a praise band up the road there for a while. A praise band? Nobody wants to see drums and guitars in church. It's wrong. Our core beliefs and traditions have to remain as they have for hundreds of years. That's who we are. We need to attract people using the sense of community, and with the message of God's love. We have to say to people, this is where you can come for help. This is where you can come to get away. Switch off your mobile phone. Leave the Blackberry at home.'

'Most people left the Blackberry in the shop...'

He holds up a hand.

'You're right,' he says, although I'm not sure what he's agreeing with. I was just making a glib comment, but that's pretty much what I always do. 'You didn't come here to hear the speech I gave the church session. You wanted to talk about Maureen.'

This fellow is smooth. And I'm not even getting the vibe that he's too smooth. He's got a way about him. If he hadn't found God, he'd make a perfect politician. Good thing we're not in America, or he'd have done both.

'Did you know her? Had you ever talked to her? Did she ever come to St Stephen's?'

He laughs.

'She was a life-long hater of St Stephen's,' he says, the

smile slowly leaving his face. 'That's how it is around here, and in most towns with more than one church. People think that the great rivalry in towns in the west of Scotland is between the Protestant and Catholic churches. In reality, they have little to do with each other, and the real rivalry is in-house. There's been long-standing enmity and antagonism between the four churches for decades. It's how it's always been. How on earth the Church of Scotland expected it to be sorted out satisfactorily, no one knows.'

'What should they have done?'

'Let nature take its course. Let the churches pay their own way. Let them stand or fall by the amount of people they attract. If they can't get the people, they fold.'

'Which is ultimately what you're attempting here.'

'Indeed.'

'Would St Stephen's have broken off on its own if it hadn't been for you?'

He takes a moment with that, but I'm not picking up on anything from the guy. No artifice, no question-avoidance. He's happy to talk.

'It *could* have happened. Whether it would or not, I doubt.'

'And what happens when you go?'

A sigh and a parting of the hands gesture.

'That's for the future,' he says. 'I doubt any of us can say.'

'You haven't put anything in place yet.'

'One thing at a time, Sergeant Hutton,' he says. 'One thing at a time.'

17

I stand outside the church for a few moments. Check my watch. Just after one. The Dundee United-Kilmarnock game that everyone's been talking about will just have started. I look along the deserted stretch of Main Street and contemplate heading for the pub.

A bright, autumnal afternoon. Will be dark in just over three hours. There's something in the air, something more than the smell of wood smoke coming from the houses along Church Avenue.

There are one or two cars parked outside the church gates, but most people are long gone. I stood around having coffee until people were leaving, then went and had my fifteen-minute audience with his Holiness, the Reverend Jones; the only people left now, those clearing up the detritus of another riotous morning at the kirk.

I'm not going to the pub. Don't want to sit down. Don't want to be inside. For once in my stupid, wasted life, I can appreciate a pleasant afternoon.

Still standing inside the church gate, I take out my phone and dial home. My old home. The one I was kicked out of.

Peggy answers.

'Hey,' I say.

'Hello, Sergeant,' she says.

Immediately I feel some relief. She only ever calls me Sergeant when she's feeling reasonably benevolent towards me. I'd have got 'Thomas' or complete silence if I'd done anything recently to piss her off. As it is, I just haven't done anything at all recently.

'Everything all right?'

'Rebecca's pregnant and Andy's in prison for killing his maths teacher. But other than that, sure.'

Funny. And I wish she wouldn't make jokes about Rebecca being pregnant. Jokes like that have a way of biting you on the arse. On the other hand, I wouldn't mind if Andy murdered his maths teacher. Seriously, the guy's a dick.

'You OK?' I ask, ignoring the comedy shock tactics.

'Same old, same old. How about you?'

'Just been to church,' I say.

She laughs.

'No, really.'

'Is that the name of your new pub?'

Yeah, well, it's not like I don't deserve it.

'Andy in? I thought I might be able to drag him up the park to play football.'

'Seriously?'

I don't blame her for that tone either. When you're as rank awful a father as I've been, there's always a reason to question my actions. When was the last time Andy and I played football in the park? Two years? Three? Five? He's fourteen now, maybe the idea is a complete anathema to him. Perhaps the only chance of playing him at football is to get an Xbox and go on-line. Even then, I'd likely have to pretend to be someone else.

'I… I mean, I know he's probably too old for that kind of thing. It's just a nice afternoon, and I wondered… that's all. I'm just trying not to be an arsehole.'

My voice has flattened out as I speak. Just trying not to be an arsehole. There's a personal mission statement. I could have it stamped on my forehead, if not for the fact that there are plenty of times when I don't make that particular effort.

'No, I'm sure he'd love to,' she says, her voice softening. 'He might still have said no, of course, but then he's fourteen. He's out, though. Over at the new kid's, the one who just joined the school a fortnight ago.'

'Ah, OK.'

'Sorry. And Rebecca and I are just about to head to my mum's.'

And that'll be that. Maybe the next time I think of one my kids – in nine months or so – they might be available.

Another couple of minutes, then we hang up. Nothing promised, nothing else suggested. The merest civility is just about all we aspire to these days.

'Excuse me.'

I look round. And down. There's a kid standing next to me. A girl, twelve years old maybe, long hair, a dress and a cardigan. The sleeves of the cardigan are too short.

Where have I seen her before?

'Yes?'

'You should look at this.'

She holds out a small book. Thin. The title of it is written in small print on a plain, faded black cover. The Book of Daniel. I take the book from the kid, and immediately think of standing in the Old Kirk a few days ago, reading the large Bible. What had that been opened at? Not Daniel. Revelations.

I open the book, flick randomly through it in the way that you do. Not stopping to read anything. The type is small, and I guess you would call it a book, but there are only thirty pages. There are a few illustrations, of great beasts and apocalyptic visions.

'Why?' is the only word that comes into my head as I look up.

The kid is gone. Like, completely gone. I step through the gate and look along Church, up Oak Avenue, out onto Main Street. No sign of the kid, no sign of a car driving off.

I turn back and look round at the church and at the bright November afternoon. The small book weighs heavily in my hands.

18

'A kid?'

'Yes.'

'A mysterious kid, out of nowhere?'

'Yes.'

'Offering you the Book of Daniel?'

'Yes.'

'Jesus, Sergeant. Did he look anything like Damien?'

'It was a girl. Think I've seen her before, but... just not sure, you know, where. When. Or how, even.'

We're sitting in Taylor's office. Monday morning. We have coffee. From the coffee machine, not from one of the coffee giants in the vicinity. Although, presumably one of the coffee giants actually operates the coffee machine. It just doesn't have any branding on it.

If I was a coffeemeister I'd be able to tell whether this was Starbucks, Nero, Costa or Scotrail, but I'm just a guy. It's only recently that I've expanded my knowledge beyond telling the difference between an Americano and a mocha-frocha-vanilla cappuccino.

'Describe her.'

'It's... I remember standing next to her, and I remember the moment she gave me the book, I just don't entirely remember what she looked like.'

'So a strange, un-placeable girl gave you one of those Old Testament apocalyptic books. Well, that's.... ominous. Had you seen the kid during the service?'

'Don't think so. But... you know, it was pretty busy, man. The place was jumping. Not quite standing room only, but I sat at the back and there were only a few spare seats. Upstairs looked like it was heaving 'n' all.'

'Hmm,' he says. Takes a sip of latte. I mean, here we are, grown men. He's got his latte, and I've got my bog-standard milk, no sugar.

'St Mungo's was dead,' he says. 'And not because there was no one there. It wasn't empty, there were a couple of hundred folk, I suppose. Space for plenty more, but still enough to create some sort of atmosphere. And, of course, they'd lost two of them with Maureen and young Tommy. Particularly Tommy, it'd be the kind of thing that's really going to drag a place down. Yet, there was something more.'

'Like the life had been sucked out of it.'

He nods.

'And St Stephen's was the exact opposite. Like the life had been injected back into it. Like they're the vampire, sucking the life from the other three.'

'Maybe that's it,' he says. 'The forced union of the churches has really screwed up the three that had to go through with it. Even those who won the fight over the building, it still rankles with them. They're still having to share their home with the opposition, and they had to listen to the others when it came to choosing a minister. But St Stephen's… they escaped. They're free to do what they want.'

'Who knows how it'll work out in the long run,' I say, 'but for now they're having a party.'

'God, it's a right shitstorm in a biscuit factory, isn't it? Did you know about any of this stuff?'

'Nah,' I say. 'Like we said before, I'd heard they'd amalgamated, but didn't think anything about it. Thought it'd all be a very straightforward procedure. Turns out it was like trying to reform Yugoslavia.'

He smiles and nods.

'That, Sergeant, is a very good analogy.'

'Was Connor there?' I ask, quickly getting the subject off Yugoslavia, having been stupid enough to bring it up in the first place.

'Oh, yes. I'd given him the heads up that I'd be going,

just so there was no Lee Van Cleef stare-down across the church, but we avoided each other all the same.'

'Post-match cup of tea?'

'Yes,' he said. 'But nothing like your high-end beverage operation. A few women with large pots of PG tips and Nescafe Gold Blend... D'you still get Nescafe Gold Blend?'

'Fucked if I know.'

'Me neither. Anyway, it was plastic coffee, a few bourbons and some custard crèmes.'

'We had muffins. Blueberry. Raspberry and white chocolate. Double chocolate chunks. Vanilla. I think it was vanilla.'

'Yeah, if we're still on this next week, we can swap.'

'Shit.'

'What?'

'Another week of church...'

He takes a drink, lays his cup down and looks outside at the grey mid-morning.

'If you'd rather be on your domestic abuse cases, petty drug crimes and failed car theft, I'm sure there will be plenty of them to keep you busy.'

Another week of these serious-looking dudes in suits and shoes, with all their pious shit, I think I might be just about ready to go back to the usual petty drug crimes, no matter how shitty all that stuff is.

The image of the girl in a dress and the short sleeves of her cardigan, the thin book in her hands, flashes across my mind. I eject the thought, lift my coffee.

*

Our lives are dictated by food and drink. Mostly drink. It's automatic. Want a coffee? Cup of tea? Would you like to go for a drink?

Here I am, having escaped a slow day at work to come and speak to Philo Stewart, the woman who runs the Bible group with her husband. One of those big old detached houses up the top end of Glenvale Road. Not too far from the Old Kirk in fact. I suppose church allegiances, like football team allegiances, will be dictated by much more than geography.

I'm standing at the bay window of the lounge. From here I can see the houses across the road, a little of the hills in the distance. They've probably got a better view over the town, and the sprawling south side of Glasgow, from their bedroom upstairs.

Bedroom. Hmm…

Stop being such a dick, Sergeant.

The door is pushed open behind me. Mrs Stewart enters the room clutching a small tray containing two mugs of tea, and what looks suspiciously like a plate of home-made flapjacks. About five each.

'That's a lot of flapjacks,' I say, as she places the tray on a small table.

She smiles as she takes a seat.

'Brain freeze,' she says. 'I put one each, and then I thought, well that looks a bit mean, so I put two each, and I thought, that might seem terribly proscriptive. So I panicked.'

She giggles.

I sit down opposite her. Have that familiar feeling – attraction, desire, an awareness of the inevitability of infatuation – accompanied by its negative pal, depression at the thought of here we go again. Someone else for me to lust after. Someone else to make an idiot of myself over. She's married, she's involved with a church which is, in some way at least, under our investigation. This has so many ways it can end badly, it could be a Middle Eastern democracy.

She's wearing a V-necked sweater, thin cotton, which rests lightly on her breasts, accentuating their shape. And jeans. She's wearing jeans.

'No children?' I say, a thought that I regret to admit came to me as I had been looking at her thighs, and as soon as it's out of my mouth, I could shoot myself in the face. Never, ever, ask a woman – especially one in her thirties – if she has children. Who knows what sadness lurks millimetres beneath the surface?

'Only been married a couple of years,' she says. 'Thought we'd enjoy the peace for a little while longer, then start trying in a year or two.'

See, right there, even though that was harmless enough, that's more information than I wanted to hear or that she wanted to tell me.

'Sorry,' I say, 'ridiculously rude of me to ask.'

'That's OK, but you're right. You got lucky this time, Sergeant, but in general it's the conversational equivalent of pulling the pin on a grenade.'

She smiles again as she leans forward and lifts one of the mugs, indicating for me to do the same. I hold her gaze, get swallowed up by it – and there it is, flashing through my brain, the image of her naked, sitting on top of me, me deep inside her – and it's gone, and I drop my gaze, lift the mug and a flapjack, then say, 'All right, tell me about old Mr Crackjaw, or his equivalent,' and bite into the biscuit. If you can call a flapjack a biscuit. I mean, it's not a cake.

Traybake?

She reaches forward and lifts a flapjack. The smile is still on her lips. I look at the V in her V-necked sweater, look at the first curve of her breast, look away as she straightens up, watch as she puts the flapjack to her lips and takes the tiniest bite.

'We're relatively new here. A couple of years. Arrived just as the whole thing had started off.'

'Where were you before?'

'Working for the Red Cross. I'd been in DRC, Afghanistan, Somalia, a little time in northern China. Heilongjiang province.'

'Shit.'

You don't get much of that kind of thing around here.

'DRC?' I ask.

'Congo,' she says.

'Of course.' Feel stupid. Provincial.

'Met Tony in Kabul. You know what these places are like. Everybody's having sex with everyone else.'

'Yeah. I was in Bosnia for a time, mid-90s.'

'Crap,' she says, 'no way. I've heard that was all kinds of a shitstorm. You'll have to tell me about it.'

I wouldn't like to see my face at the moment. I suspect a shadow is passing across it. A dark one at that, one that threatens to block out the light from the window.

'Some other time,' I manage.

'Of course,' she says quickly, and makes a small gesture with her eyes to apologise for intruding into whatever private grief was apparent from that there shadow. 'Anyway, over time we found that we generally were having sex with each other and no one else, and then I got posted to Syria, just as all that was kicking off. Went there for a few weeks, Tony got a job back here, asked me to come with him, and you know... I just thought, even then, you could see it. You could see that Syria was a country that was just going to get slowly fucked. Sorry. Shouldn't have said that.'

'That's OK.'

'So, I took him up on his offer. Tony. I mean, that sounds almost like it was a business deal. I didn't mean...' and she completes the sentence by waving a casual hand.

That's OK, I think. You don't have to explain. You're sitting with someone who you find far more attractive than your husband, and you're finding it a bit awkward. Could happen to anyone.

'And the church?'

'Tony joined. I came with him. I'd grown up with it, and it was one of the things that took me abroad in the first place. Seemed natural to join once we were here. And, as it turned out, all that time in Somalia, Syria, Afghanistan and the Congo had been good preparation.'

I laugh. Have been making my way through the flapjack as she talked, now down it with some tea. Make discreet dabs at the corner of my mouth in case there are any oats attached.

'Tell me about it.'

'It was ugly. Political factions everywhere, splinter groups, people meeting in each other's houses to plot and connive. Incredibly messy. I don't know, maybe it was because of our background, but Tony and I used to say to each other, someone's going to die over this. When there's this much anger, this much resentment and this much passion, someone usually dies.'

'And it was Maureen.'

'I don't know. That part just seems kind of odd. I mean, she was a horrible old witch. Really nasty. Used to write all sorts of letters to people.'

'We have copies.'

Go on, tell her everything, why don't you?

'But why now? Believe it or not, things have settled down. St Stephen's broke away, the other three came to whatever accommodation finally worked for them. If someone was going to kill her, you'd have thought they'd have done it a year ago.'

'She was still sending letters. She hadn't given up.'

She shrugs. 'Well, maybe that's it. It just seems not of its time. I wouldn't have been surprised a year ago. Now, well I'm sure I know a lot less than you about it, but I'm more inclined to think she probably killed herself.'

'You know a kid named Tommy Kane?'

She nods. Finishes off her flapjack, takes a sip of tea.

'I know *of* him. I heard what happened. But I don't think I'd ever spoken to him. It's not possible their suicides are connected, is it? That'd just be too weird.'

Have to be careful. I've fallen for her. Right here. Well, not right here, it was during the first minute standing at the church hall yesterday. The dangerous thing is, she feels like someone to talk to. Someone on the inside off whom I can bounce ideas. That's what I want her to be. The person off whom I bounce ideas, while we're chatting over a post-coital cigarette.

But what do I know about her? Nothing. Even all that

Red Cross stuff. She could be making that shit up. That's what people do. They lie. Maybe she's trying to impress me, because she's sitting here thinking the exact same things that I'm thinking. Or maybe she's telling the truth, the slight flirtatiousness about her is nothing more than her being pleasant, and this attraction is entirely one way. Wouldn't be the first time.

I manage to stop myself telling her that Maureen and Tommy had had sex, even though it'd be a great way of introducing sex into the conversation. Actually, given the context, not so great. Perhaps, ultimately, that's the reason I don't mention it.

'Investigations are continuing,' I say. 'I know this might be awkward for you, but is there anything you feel able to mention? Anyone who ever openly voiced anger at Maureen for the letters she wrote…?'

'That would be everyone, pretty much.'

'Anyone who looked like they might take it beyond anger? Anyone, any thing, out of the ordinary? I guess, at any time over the last two years, but more pertinently the last week or two.'

She takes her time, then eventually shrugs.

'Sorry, I don't think so. Things have really settled down with us now. We're detached from the mess. David – Rev Jones – is really throwing everything into getting St Stephen's up and running as a single entity, making sure it thrives in the community. He's doing some good stuff. It feels like… you know, I know more about what's going on in Syria now, because of the news, than what's going on down at St Mungo's.'

'You ever get people coming from St Mungo's to your place? Defectors?'

'Been a couple, I think. Not many. David's not trying to be in competition. He wants to get people back, get people that haven't thought about coming before. He's reaching out to the community, not to the opposition.'

I stay for another twenty-five minutes. We talk about the churches, talk about her time in the Red Cross. She senses enough to not ask me about my time abroad. She has nothing else to tell me that's of any relevance to the investigation. Eventually I tear myself away. It's not until I'm almost back at the station that I realise she'd invited me over, saying she couldn't talk at the church yesterday because she had things to tell me in private when she didn't really have anything particularly sensitive to say at all.

*

'You getting anywhere with the angel's wings and the rat's ribs in the throat?' asks Taylor.

Morrow and I look up. I know we've both tried, although it's been pretty half-hearted on my part. Shake of the head from me. 'Sorry, sir,' from Morrow.

'Yeah,' says Taylor, nodding. 'Me neither. Need to ask some church freak, just not anyone from around here.'

I laugh and shake my head as I turn back to looking through Maureen's paperwork. The endless search.

'What?' says Taylor.

'Basically we need a Bible scholar, but you describe them as a church freak. Funny, that's all.'

'Humph,' he mutters, turning away.

Could have asked Philo Stewart. Wanted to ask. Kept my mouth shut. Taylor stops a couple of yards away, turns back.

'One of the two of you find a Bible scholar and find out if there's any connection between an angel's wings and the ribs of a rat, will you?'

Mock salute. He loves that. He turns. I look at Morrow.

'Yes, sir,' says Morrow.

19

8.31 p.m. Sitting down to dinner. Stopped off at Tesco, bought a meal for two for ten pounds. In all likelihood I will eat all of it. Cottage pie. Vegetables. New York cheesecake. A bottle of South African Sauvignon Blanc.

I probably won't eat both pieces of cheesecake.

Worked until just after seven. Not much doing on the double suicide/murder/whatever case. Busied myself with a couple of alcohol-related assault cases. Can't get enough of them. Neither of the alleged perpetrators seemed in the least repentant.

One blames alcohol for everything, but I think these two would have been up for the fight regardless, contrition be damned.

First mouthful of cottage pie. Cooked to perfection. Ha! Well, heated up to perfection at any rate. Got Bob playing in the background, not too loud. *Tempest.* I love his voice now. I love the snarling, croaking wreck that it's turned into. Yes, his throat must be completely fucked, but it's magnificent all the same. Seriously, who would you rather hear sing *Make You Feel My Love*, Bob with his other-worldly growl, or simpering Adele, bursting into tears at the drop of a hat?

Adele, you say? Well, fuck you.

So, I've got Sauvignon Blanc, I've got cottage pie, the cheesecake awaits, Bob's on the CD player. What else?

There's the small book, the one I ignored last night, before me. I decided I would look at it over dinner. It feels like work, which is why I'm sitting at the table instead of slumped before the TV. The book that was given to me by the strange little girl. Perhaps strange isn't quite right. She didn't appear strange at the time. Yet I'm sure I've seen her somewhere before, and she becomes strange in my imagination.

The Book of Daniel. I know nothing of the Book of Daniel. Taylor said he thought it was one of the apocalyptic ones, but that was all he knew. One of the apocalyptic ones... That'll be a fucking laugh-riot then. Only one way to find out. The Book of Daniel it is. Right, what have we got? I open the book, turn to Chapter 1, Verse 1. *In the third year of the reign of Jehoiakim king of Judah came Nebuchadnezzar king of Babylon unto Jerusalem and besieged it.*

OK, not a bad start. War, straight from the off. No messing around, no drawing your audience in by making them care about the characters. Doesn't look like there are going to be any comedy sidekicks.

And the Lord gave Jehoiakim king of Judah into his hand, with part of the vessels of the house of God: which he carried into the land of Shinar to the house of his god; and he brought the vessels into the treasure house of his god.

Have to re-read that one a couple of times, and still not sure what it means. That's the trouble with the Bible. You start reading it with the best intentions, but before you know it you come across a paragraph that just makes you think, what the fuck?

And the king spake unto Ashpenaz the master of his eunuchs, that he should bring certain of the children of Israel, and of the king's seed, and of the princes;

Children in whom was no blemish, but well favoured, and skilful in all wisdom, and cunning in knowledge, and understanding science, and such as had ability in them to stand in the king's palace, and whom they might teach the learning and the tongue of the Chaldeans.

All right, I'm bored. I mean, if Maureen had written this to some geezer at the church I'd feel compelled to read it. But this? Because some crazy kid hands me a copy outside church?

And the king appointed them a daily provision of the king's meat, and of the wine which he drank: so nourishing them three years, that at the end thereof they might stand before the king.

Now he's giving the kids wine? Nice. I bet these freaks don't talk about this in church. Hey kids, get the fuck boozed up. It's cool, this shit's in the Bible!

Close the book, push it away. The king's seed... Batshit crazy, fucked-up shit.

An apocalyptic book of the Bible. A strange kid in a cardigan that fitted her last year. A minister who reminded me of Hitler. Four churches. Two suicides, more likely murder. Extreme cross-generational sex. Hate mail. An architect, the genius behind the 1950s shit-tip winning the selection war against the more attractive Victorian building. And another man's wife, who used to work in war zones, and now lives in my town. Not to mention the beautiful silence of sitting in that old Victorian building up the road, accompanied by the woman who sits there with me.

I left Philo Stewart with the old familiar phrase, *if you think of anything else*. Usually I don't care if they call, or if I do, I'll hope it's something of significance. This time, I hope she calls about anything. To remind me to tie my shoelaces, to tell me to get my car serviced before winter kicks in. Anything. Just call.

But then, it hardly matters, because I'm going to call her.

The cottage pie comes and goes. I work my way through the bottle of wine. The CD comes to an end, and then automatically kicks back to the start. Bob croaks on. I finish the wine. I eat a piece of cheesecake. I try to think about the case, but all I think about is Philo Stewart.

*

I wake in the night, troubled by something. I was talking to someone, I'm sure I was.

Who was I talking to? Talking in my sleep. Must have been talking in my sleep. Was there someone else here?

Lie awake in the night, staring at the ceiling, feeling cold, listening to the occasional car on the road outside.

20

Tuesday morning. Me and Morrow, at our desks, working away like good little soldiers. Filling in paperwork. Digital paperwork, that is. Completing reports. There's a new system, which pretty much goes without saying. There's always a new system. Computer systems are like football managers. There's always another one just around the corner, and no one ever seems to realise that the best thing to do is to pull an Alex Ferguson and leave the same thing in place for as long as possible.

Budgets seem to disappear when it comes to funding police on the streets or serious crime units, but when it comes to computer systems, the government is ever willing to be taken to the cleaners by large commercial organisations who push their new hardware that will revolutionise policing or health care or border control or whatever.

So we've had another new system to learn in the last couple of months. Another new password to remember. There are, naturally, teething problems that haven't been sorted out yet. The last system never got over its teething problems before it was binned. Now, because we've got the new system to make things easier, they've cut some support staff. We have to do more of our own paperwork as it's all so much easier.

In all, we have very little time for policing. This is how government-funded jobs now work. More with less. That doesn't make any kind of sense, not in reality. You can't do more with less, unless you were fucking around before. But no one's been fucking around for years.

More with less is just management wank, that's all. And

it's inherently insulting. It's saying, you have the capacity to work much harder than you have been doing. You have the capacity to do everything you've been doing up until now, plus all this other shit, plus getting to grips with a new computer system every two months.

My thoughts on how big a bunch of wankers these people are, are always at their most virulent when I'm attempting to update something on the new system and it's not letting me, keeps throwing me back a stage and making me start all over again.

It's a good thing I'm so cool and even-tempered, *or I'd fucking throw this dumb-ass stupid fucking piece of computing shit out of the fucking window.*

Calm. Calm.

Taylor appears, stands beside our desks.

'What up, diggity dawgs?' he says.

We look at him. The slight smile leaves his face and he waves away the flippancy and, frankly, absurdity of that line.

'Got laid last night, then?' I say. Morrow can only aspire to that level of humorous contempt of one's superior officer.

'Not saying,' says Taylor.

'You don't have to.'

'Moving on,' he says bluntly, and you can see that now he's let that little bit of good humour at last night's successful campaign out into the world, he can relax, stop smiling, and get back to normal. 'Either of you any further forward?'

We both shake our heads.

'Sorry, sir,' says Morrow. 'Spent the last hour on here trying to upload one report.'

'Ditto.'

He nods, stares at our computers.

'I suppose they'll work out the glitches over the coming years,' he says. 'It might be up and running properly before it's replaced. Look, just been in with Connor.' He hesitates, shakes his head. 'We need more than we've got. We all know how this looks, but it's been four days since the last murder, death, suicide with bones in his throat, whatever you want to call it, and we've nothing definite. Sure, the church thing is a nest of vipers, but really... That in itself isn't a crime. It's not for us to judge these people. If we've nothing else, Connor's looking for us to wrap it up for the time being, release the bodies.'

'What? That's shit! I mean, seriously, that's just shit.'

'Yes, it is, Sergeant. But what do we have? Beyond the fact that everyone on earth hated Maureen, we have no suspects and no motive. There's no specific connection to the sleeping pills used, we've no witnesses to either crime.'

'But they were still murdered!'

Getting annoyed, although of course, my annoyance is at Connor, not Taylor.

'Yes. More than likely they were. Which is why we're going to continue the investigation. For the moment, however, we have to be seen to play along with the politics. The superintendent wants to let the church mourn, so we'll let it mourn. It doesn't mean we throw in the towel, but we need to take a step back and, at least, let the corpses go. We know he's a politician, not a policeman, and he's thinking about the politics.'

'Fuck.'

Taylor gives me a look for that, but he's probably standing there thinking *fuck* himself. Morrow, for his part, is not yet at a pay grade which requires him to think *fuck* or otherwise.

'Gentlemen, if there's nothing else, I'm going to give the release order on the stiffs. We cool?'

Nods from Morrow and me, and off goes Taylor to let the bodies of the deceased out into the world to meet their fate, burned or buried.

*

Inevitable then, that once the bodies were gone, there'd be some more information come to light. But then, it's a fair bet that Balingol had managed to extract everything he was going to, and it wasn't as though we could ask either of them further questions.

Morrow is off out to investigate the third break-in at a newsagents on Rutherglen Main Street in a week. I am, no word of a lie, still trying to file the report that I was trying to file four hours earlier. Four fucking hours. I'm determined to see this thing through to the end, and when I'm done, I'm going to detail everything about this excruciating experience, then e-mail the Chief Constable, the Superintendent, the First Minister, the Prime Minister, the Justice Secretary in both Holyrood and Westminster, and every other bastard I can think of, just to let them know how shitty a piece of utter shittiness this shitty computer system is.

That should get me the promotion I've been after for so long.

Sgt Harrison sits opposite me, lays a neatly folded copy of the local paper down on the desk.

'Sergeant,' she says.

'Sergeant,' I reply, nodding.

'Might have something for you,' she says.

I lay down my computer angst and smile.

'You've realised you're not a lesbian?'

'Fuck you, Sergeant,' she says, showing me the middle finger.

'I just like to check every now and again.'

'Just in case I've been cured?'

Smiles all round. It's almost flirtatious, but it's obviously not going anywhere. If we actually spent any time together, she'd be my gay friend and I'd be her straight friend. As it is, our paths cross only occasionally in the office.

'I was looking through the small ads in the local rag.'

'Looking for love?' I ask.

'Well, since we have a blunt conversation going on here, Sergeant, yes I was. Looking, in fact, to have sex.'

I hold up my hand at getting too close to the truth

through glibness, and stop myself asking if she manages to get a lot of sex via the *Rutherglen Reformer*.

'Anyway, I saw this.'

She tosses the paper over, folded open at the personal ads section. One of them has been circled.

Octopussy. Specialises in instruction for teen boys.
Good rates. Octopussy will make you into a man.
Suite 437, G72 etc etc

I read it several times. Once would have been enough. Too much, in fact. Once read, it can't be unread. Finally I look up.

'You think… I mean, this has nothing to do with James Bond?'

'I think this has nothing to do with James Bond,' she says. 'And there are all sorts of things that it could actually refer to, but you know, it's just a thought. The 'octo' part of it could be short for octogenarian, that's all. Seems weird that around here you'd have a woman in her 80s offering teenagers sexual instruction, but I think it'd be weirder to have a James Bond-level of villainy.'

Long, exhaled breath. Rub of the eyes. Can I allow myself to be distracted from my mission to file one stupid fucking report on this stupid fucking computer system?

'I don't know where it gets you,' she says. 'Maybe that ad was placed by your suicide/murder victim, maybe the kid answered it, maybe they had sex. It just supplies the method by which they met, not a lot else.'

'You're right, but it's more than we've been working on the last few days. Thanks.'

I tap the paper. Harrison starts to get up.

'D'you need this back?' I ask.

'Slim pickings,' she says, with a shake of the head.

'Well, if you're ever desperate,' I say, and she rolls her eyes and off she goes.

That's probably sexual harassment these days. In fact, no probably about it. It is sexual harassment. She's cool with it, though, all part of the game. The politically correct brigade would be as annoyed at her as they are at me.

Shit, must go on that diversity course. Keep forgetting. It's part of my objectives.

*

Get the necessary paperwork, make my way along to Mail Boxes Etc. in Rutherglen. The girl on the counter is naturally suspicious, which is really the appropriate attitude with the police. Can't blame anyone who regards us with suspicion.

I look in the box. It's empty. That was kind of what I'd been expecting. If it was weird that Tommy Kane had answered the ad, it was going to be double weird to find he wasn't alone, and this end of Glasgow just isn't a double weird kind of a place.

The necessary paperwork, which I have in my hand, also happens to allow me access to information on the owner of Box 437. Suite 437 as it had been rather grandiosely referred to in the advert.

The girl on the counter hands over the necessary documentation without a word. She's looking at her hands. There's a stiffness about her, an awkwardness about the whole exchange, that we find quite often in this job. People don't like speaking to the police, so they cover their discomfiture with rudeness.

Whatever.

The name Maureen Henderson leaps off the page.

'I'll need a copy of that,' I say.

She lifts her eyes, only briefly engages mine, and then turns away to the photocopy machine.

Hmm. Another reason people are awkward with the police is when they're hiding something. She's probably got drugs in her handbag. That'd be the usual kind of thing.

She hands over the paperwork. I smile.

'Thanks for your help.'

She looks through me as if I am an agent of Sauron. I leave.

21

'Octopussy?'

Taylor slowly lifts his head. Morrow and I are standing in his office. Morrow has been smiling since I filled him in on the details. Obviously, for the younger police officer, this kind of thing is the equivalent of working in A&E when someone comes in with a Barbie doll inserted in their penis.

'It's definitely her. Seems logical to assume this was how he found her.'

He stares at me, then at Morrow.

'Stop smiling,' he says.

'Yes, boss,' says Morrow, although he doesn't.

'I mean,' says Taylor, 'apart from the James Bond thing, it's a pretty vulgar name, isn't it? Is it obvious from just the name that it's an eighty-year-old offering sex? Really?'

'True enough,' I say. 'I just put the word into the urban dictionary. It has a variety of meanings, none of which relate to old people sex.'

'I don't want to know what those definitions are. But it does beg the question, how would anyone replying to the advert know that this was an eighty-year-old offering sex, rather than one of those other definitions you're talking about?'

Morrow laughs.

'I'm loving this,' he says.

It's refreshing not to be the immature one in the room.

'Don't know. Maybe it's just one of those things that are known around here. In the way that people know stuff. Communities know stuff. They know where to go dogging, they know when pampas grass in a garden means the owners are swingers, rather than that there just happens to be pampas grass growing in the garden.'

'Yeah, *maybe* doesn't really cut it. You,' he says, pointing at Morrow, 'stop grinning, and I mean, really, stop grinning, you're pissing me off.'

He nails the tone. Morrow quits grinning.

'Thank you. Now that you've sorted your face out, go and do the usual internet search. It's what we invariably end up doing these days.' Internet and alcohol, the two main drivers of crime. 'See if Maureen had an online presence of some sort.'

'She didn't have a computer,' says Morrow.

'True enough,' I say. 'Her house was like going back to the 1950s.'

'Did she have a library card?'

Glance at Morrow. Morrow nods.

'There you have it,' says Taylor.

'You think she ran some kind of porn school from the library?' I say.

'Funny. There's that internet café down in Rutherglen, isn't there? Or she could've taken the train into the city. Constable, try and find her online; Sergeant, identify places she could have used the internet, go to those places and see if anyone knows anything about her.'

'Yes, boss.'

'Yes, boss.'

And out the door we go.

*

Just after four in the afternoon. Feel like I might work late tonight. Nothing to go home to. No fucking surprise there. Starting to feel like I need to visit a drinking establishment, but that's unlikely to end well. Then there's drinking at home, and by drinking at home, I don't mean having a bottle of wine as part of a Tesco £10 meal for two. So, maybe if I work late, the drinking is less likely to happen.

Drew a blank at the library. Old Maureen hadn't been in there, or at least, hadn't used her card, in over three years. It always seemed a stretch to think she'd be running some sort of online porn operation from a public library. I asked out of interest, and they said it wouldn't be possible. They have filters.

Now I have every internet café in south Lanarkshire and Glasgow to check out, which isn't so many. It's not like the centre of London here. If I have to go into the city it might take me into tomorrow, but there's one small place at the back end of Rutherglen Main Street to check out first.

Park the car outside Iceland, and take the short walk along. Almost dark, a few people around. It may be early November, but Christmas is in the air. Decorations in the shop windows, adverts for boxes of chocolates and turkeys and perfect roast potatoes that take five minutes in the microwave.

Beneath a tree across the road there's a guy standing on a box. A box that may, I suppose, be an actual soap box. I hear him first, the sound drifting across the road, intermingled with the passing cars. Don't particularly pay attention, but then, as I'm directly over the road from him, there's no traffic on Rutherglen Main Street, and everything is quiet. His voice drifts across, the words clear.

'After this I beheld, and lo another, like a leopard, which had upon the back of it four wings of a fowl; the beast had also four heads; and dominion was given to it....'

An articulated lorry passes by, travelling slowly. Tesco. *Every little helps*. I stare at it, my eyes focussed beyond the lorry on the space where the guy is. My heart starts pounding, and I think, Jesus, when this lorry passes he's going to be gone. That guy, who was standing there a second ago spouting some biblical shit, is going to be gone.

And then there goes the lorry, and the bloke across the road is still standing on his box, staring wildly into space, not looking at me at all, and now his words are lost as a wave of cars follow in the lorry's wake, the lights at the far end having changed. I watch him for a moment, as if expecting him to point in my direction, and then I turn and walk the short distance to the café.

The door pings as I enter, stop for a second, take a quick look around. There are a few tables down one side. Signs saying free Wi-Fi on the wall. There are a couple of teenagers sitting at one table. They're both on their phones, neither of them talking. The other side has six small booths with a computer in each. None of them are currently occupied. The kid behind the counter is reading a newspaper. The *Evening Times* more than likely. He glances up at the sound of the door, then looks back to his paper.

I approach the counter.

'You know that guy across the road, the Bible guy? Is he usually there?'

'Every day, man,' says the kid. I'm saying kid. He's like eighteen or something. 'He stands there and recites books from the Old Testament off the top of his head. Every fucking day, man. It's a bit fucked up.'

'I've never seen him before.'

'Can't have been looking.'

I flick open my ID and the guy gives me a glance to indicate his disquiet at me for luring him into conversation without letting him know I'm a police officer.

'DS Hutton,' I say.

'Yeah?'

He glances over at the table, but these teenagers aren't interested. Too cool to care that the Feds have just entered the building.

I place a picture of Maureen on the counter.

'You recognise this woman? She ever come in here?'

He looks at me for a while before looking at the photograph. He glances down, a smirk automatically coming to his lips. Well, at least now there'd be no point in saying he'd never seen her before. The opposite of poker face.

'Sure,' he says. 'Maureen. Comes here all the time. Haven't seen her in a few days, mind.'

'She uses the computers?'

'Sure. That's why she comes. Never has anyone with her or nothing.'

'You know what she does online?'

'What the fuck, man? Course I fucking don't.'

'You know her name, maybe she talks to you.'

'Aye, she does talk to me. You know why? 'Cause she's a lovely wee woman. Not a nosy prick, like some people.'

'Is there any way to go through your records so we can see what she looked at?'

'Fuck off, man.'

You just want to give people a big old bear hug sometimes, don't you? And while you're hugging them, bring your knee swiftly up into their testicles.

'Maureen's dead.'

'What the fuck, man?'

'Committed suicide last week. We're just trying to work out her last few days, trying to find some clue as to why she might have killed herself. We need to know the kinds of things she did online.'

I'll give him some bonus points for the fact that he actually looks disconcerted by the news.

'That's terrible,' he says.

'Yes, it is.'

'I don't have that information here,' he says.

'Can you get it?'

'Not me. You'll need to contact head office. I'm just, like, a guy here, you know. I don't own this joint. I know dick all about those things. Any problems, I call Livingstone, they send a guy out.'

'Livingstone?'

'Aye.'

'OK. Give me a contact, and I'll make some calls.'

He turns away, digs out a card, which is stained with coffee and God knows what else, then hands it over. I'm about to slip it into my pocket when he says, 'I need that.' So I write down the details and hand the card back to him.

'Thanks for your help,' I say.

'Why'd she do it?'

'Don't know yet.'

He doesn't reply, but as I turn away he mutters, 'Fucking polis,' at my back. I stop for a second, contemplate crushing his skull with a Khan-like death grip, then head on out the door.

Darkness has arrived with much greater intensity in the few minutes I was inside. I look across the road. Soap box guy is gone.

22

I got to go out into a miserable fucking November afternoon and speak to people. Morrow got to sit and look at online porn. Although, ultimately it came down to online granny porn, so I think I was better off.

He's not looking at it when I get back though. I slump down into my seat, check the time. Feeling hungry. That's good. I can leave it another few hours, then by the time I get home I'll be ravenous. I can stop and get a carry-out on the way, fish supper probably, have a couple of beers with dinner, then crawl into bed. Avoid hitting the pub and hopefully get to sleep before the demons start demanding something of me.

'You already find what you're looking for?' I ask.

'Oh, yes.'

He's not smiling anymore. I reckon a couple of hours looking at old women naked is going to wipe the smile from anyone's face. He types a couple of things into his computer, then swings the screen round to let me have a look. I'm immediately greeted by the sight of old Maureen completely naked, lying back on the sofa in her front room, her legs wide open. I could add more, but I can't bring myself to think about it. No one wants to visualise that.

'Holy fuck,' I say.

Morrow nods, but doesn't look at the screen.

'I've seen enough.'

'Sure beans,' he says.

He turns the screen back, clicking off the page as he does so.

'So, that's something you can't un-see,' I say.

'You get anywhere?'

'Yep. She was using the café on Rutherglen Main Street. The guy recognised her. Sounds like she went in there a lot. I need to make another couple of calls to try to get access to what she was doing. That account of hers, was there the opportunity to chat with her online, anything like that?'

'Oh, yes. All sorts.'

'How do you suppose she uploaded the pictures?'

He shrugs.

'Phone, USB stick, who knows? But she must've then gotten rid of whatever she took to the internet café.'

'It's weird, isn't it? Why didn't she just have a computer and internet in her own home if she was going to do this kind of thing?'

He nods.

'Yep, I thought about that. Asked around up there in her little block. Internet's shit, apparently. Always has been. Maybe she tried and it wasn't working. Maybe she didn't want a computer in her house in case the rays from it killed her. Old people have weird ideas.'

Ain't that the truth.

'You spoken to Taylor?'

He nods.

'Right, I'll just go in and update him.'

And off I go.

*

Fish supper dispatched, second bottle of Stella. 10.58 p.m. Pretty tired, not quite tired enough. Sitting in front of the television.

In the corner by the window is a large ficus benjamina, which, remarkably, has survived for over five years. I thought I'd kill the damn thing in days, but it's still going.

It'll outlive me. One day I'll be dead and it'll be sitting there for a while afterwards thinking, I haven't seen the Miserable Cunt much recently. I wish he'd come back, I'm dying for a pint.

There are three pictures on the walls. One is an original film poster from *Casablanca*. Worth something now, I dare say. Bought it in 1985 for £250. There's a painting of the harbour at Anstruther. It was a present. I stuck it on the wall to keep her happy, imagining that I'd take it down when she wasn't there. She's long gone and I never did get around to removing the picture. Then there's Grace Kelly. I never knew which movie it was from, never tried to find out. Someone said *Rear Window* once. Maybe they're right

There's something teenage about having a movie poster and a b&w movie star on your wall. Certainly, that's what Peggy used to say. I don't care. What does it matter? The women that come back here aren't doing it because they think I earned a 1.1 in classics from Oxford.

There's the air of cigarette smoke, but it's not as bad as some houses. I leave the windows open a lot, try not to smoke too much inside. Nevertheless, A Smoker Lives Here is more or less emblazoned on the walls.

BBC4 trundles round to the next show. The last one only finished a minute ago, and I've already forgotten about it. I don't even know what I was watching. It was just on, right there, in front of me. I have no idea what it was called.

'Now on Four,' says the faceless man on the television, over the BBC4 graphic, 'Dr Lesley Brothers travels to Israel to continue her examination of the Book of Daniel. With scenes of a graphic nature, that are liable to be upsetting to you in particular, Sergeant Hutton…'

The show starts.

What?

He never said that. He didn't. He couldn't have done.

Dr Brothers is saying something, standing in the middle of a Middle Eastern desert, but I can't hear what she's saying. The guy on the TV, he didn't just mention my name.

Is that a thing? Are they doing that now? They know who's watching and can tailor everything so that it's viewer-specific?

God, my head's swimming. Shut up! Shut up, Dr Lesley Brothers! Jesus!

I hit the remote, pressing buttons to turn it off. Keep hitting the wrong one. The volume turns up. What? What? Go away, for fuck's sake. Fucking television.

Just stop!

The remote control is a blur. I could get off my stupid arse and turn the set off, but do I even know where the button for that is? I never turn it off at the set.

Must be one of these buttons on here. Crap, come on. The channel changes. What? More noise? What?

There are images flashing by, images of a great beast, a beast with ten horns, crashing and breaking and destroying, images in black and white. The voice is talking, another voice. Not Dr Lesley Brothers. Someone else. Someone like her, lecturing us. Lecturing the viewer. Lecturing me. Telling me about Daniel.

Daniel. Why do I want to know about Daniel? Fucking Daniel!

Jesus, will you shut up? Shut the fuck up with your fucking voices!

I can't find the button on the remote. Go away. I can't leave the room, because it will still be here, louder and louder, eating at me. I need to turn it off. I jump out of my seat, so many voices in my head.

Stop it. Just fucking stop it! I don't know where the button is. The on/off button. I grab the television. The remote has fallen on the floor. I pull the TV forward. Not far enough. I shake it. Shake the TV. Grapple with it. Shut up, you useless piece of techno-shit! Fucking stop!

I push the TV off the unit. It falls onto the floor. The plug comes out of the wall. The picture dies. The sound stops.

Breaths are so heavy. Laboured. Fucking TV. You weren't speaking to me. Fuck you. Of course, you weren't. Fuck you. I stamp on the back of the TV. It's stopped now. I can leave. Where am I going to go? That's always the problem, stuck in this stupid little fucking piece of crap apartment. Me and Grace Kelly.

Fall onto my knees. Turn my back on the television.

Daniel. Fuck you.

Lean forward, head in hands. Breaths still short. Head. Head needs to explode. Squeeze it. Squeeze it harder. Maybe it'll stop.

23

Don't make it into work.

The alarm on my phone goes off at 6 a.m. as it always does. I haven't been in bed very long. Lay on the carpet a long time, fell asleep, woke up, felt cold, couldn't move. Shivered. Heating had turned off. Finally crawled into bed. The alarm goes off and it barely feels like I've been asleep. The alarm set to Nokia-supplied jazz music. The only thing that usually wakes me up. Set loud.

It plays and plays. Switches itself off after a couple of minutes. Comes back on, eight minutes after it turned itself off. I don't sleep through it. It's there, right next to my head, right next to my fucking head, right inside my head, but it doesn't make me move.

Finally turn it off, maybe the eighth time it's going through its cycle. Maybe the ninth. No one's counting.

Some time later the house phone rings. And rings. I think it wakes me up. Somewhere I recognise that it will be the station, looking for me. Sergeant Ramsay. I don't answer.

The mobile rings shortly afterwards. I let it. In some part of my brain I hear the conversation that's going on at the station. Ramsay reporting back to Taylor. Taylor not accepting that he can't get in touch with me, telling him to keep trying. Taylor irritated, the irritation covering up the worry. Has probably been waiting for me to fall off the cliff since I returned to work.

From somewhere I think of the toilet cleaner. The enlightened toilet cleaner, just trying to do a good job, trying to make peoples' lives that little bit better. I said I'd do something for him. I said I'd investigate ways to deal with the town graffiti artists. Investigate. Because that's what I do. Yet what have I done?

The home phone rings again. I don't have a phone in the bedroom. I'm not getting up. This time, however, I know I'm going to get the mobile. Taylor will be worried, and the least I can do is ease that for him. Albeit, I'm lying here at the bottom of the fucking cliff, so that thing he's worried about has happened.

The mobile rings as soon as the home phone rings off. I take the call without speaking.

'Sergeant Hutton?'

'Yes.'

'You all right?'

There's the question. I don't answer straight away, as I'm not sure what to say to that. Not in the mood for making shit up, not in the mood for pretending, but the thought of telling the truth ain't so fucking great either.

'No,' I say eventually. Look around for a clock, even though of course I know there isn't one to see. Take the phone away from my ear to look at the time. 10:13. Work starts officially at 08:30. Taylor gave me just over an hour and a half to be late before looking for me. 'Won't make it in, but I'm all right.' Bet I don't sound it. 'I'll take the day as leave, square it off with the boss later.'

'You'll be in tomorrow,' says Ramsay. Not a question, or an order, just a statement. Very straight, Ramsay. Knows who he's dealing with, but not judgemental.

'Yeah,' I say.

He clicks off. I lay the phone on the bedside table. The curtains are open, the morning outside grey and dull. The phone call has been little but a minor blip. It hasn't woken me up, hasn't penetrated the grey, hasn't allowed me to bounce back up from the bottom.

The toilet cleaner. That guy. I said I'd help him. I can't do it from here, can't do it today, but I can do it tomorrow, if I make it into work. He deserves it. Just a guy trying to help people. The least I can do.

This morning, that's all I've got to cling to. Not much,

and not enough. The grey swirls around, crawls over my head, crawls inside my brain. I curl up under the sheets. Still feeling wiped out. Maybe I can get back to sleep.

That's all I've got. Sleep.

*

Haul myself out for a walk just after two in the afternoon. Heading for the park at the top end of town, as that was where I so often found myself in the summer when I was getting over all that shit that happened in the spring. This time, however, I've no intention of going to the park. I time it so that I'll get to the church at the same time as Mrs Buttler. She said she was there at the same time every day. Practically invited me.

The person I really want to talk to, the person who's flitting in and out of my head, is Philo Stewart, but that's too complicated. I can't be having the feelings I'm having for her. It's not going to help anyone. Certainly not me. Mrs Buttler, sitting in silence in a silent church, is much safer territory.

Sure enough, the iron gates are closed but not padlocked. The door to the church is closed, but unlocked. I walk into the small entrance hall, along the short corridor, and into the nave.

Close the door behind me and take in the scene. Nothing has changed. Rows of empty pews in perfect silence. Empty, of course, bar Mrs Buttler. She doesn't turn to see who's there. I assume she knows it's me. Don't even consider for a second – having cast my instant judgement on him – that she will expect her husband to have come across. Not the type to step into the church. He likely would not even realise that's where his wife has gone.

I walk silently down the aisle and take my place in the pew across from where Mrs Buttler is sitting. We don't look at each other. I stare up at Jesus in blue behind the chancel.

Beautiful silence. So much more healing than it would have been sitting in silence in my front room, Grace and me. Nevertheless, I feel quite detached from the religion of it. It's not about God. It would be the same if this were a library, or an old stately home devoid of guests, or a magnificent old town hall, no one else inside.

That's what I tell myself. Jesus looks down upon me and begs to differ.

'I heard a guy on the street yesterday,' I say, finally breaking into the endless hush. Hadn't thought about saying it, the words just appear in my mouth. 'He's on Rutherglen Main Street every day apparently, quoting the Old Testament.'

I pause but she doesn't come in. Nothing to suggest that she knows the guy I'm talking about. Why should she, anyway? Rutherglen Main Street is two and a half miles from here.

'Said something about a leopard. A leopard with four wings on its back and four heads. I don't know, something like that.' I try to think of the exact words he used, but they've gone.

'Daniel,' she says. Her voice edges softly out into the silence.

Ah. The Book of Daniel. Of course. The book that's currently lying on a kitchen worktop in my apartment. That damned book.

'What does the four-headed leopard represent?'

'Well, there's the question. It's the same with all those old books. Scholars, priests, whoever, have placed interpretations on them, and who knows how accurately?'

I feel her looking at me, and finally I turn away from Jesus in Blue. She shrugs.

'Daniel had a vision of four beasts, which were supposed to represent four conquering rulers who would rise and fall.'

'The leopard was the first beast?'

'The third.'

'And the first two? A hyena and a giraffe?'

She laughs. 'A lion and a bear actually.'

'Of course.'

'Although the lion had the wings of an eagle.'

What if the Old Testament was actually written by the Monty Python equivalents of their day, and all that stuff was originally intended as surrealist comedy?

'And the bear had the wings of a dragonfly and the feet of a centipede?' I ask.

She laughs again. I haven't heard her laugh before now. Nice to hear. I don't suppose many of them ever laugh when they're talking about this awful church business.

'No, the bear didn't have wings. It just had ribs in its mouth. I mean, between its teeth, rather than as part of its mouth. I think that's how it is.'

Ribs?

'How many ribs?'

'Three. Why?'

Just like my gormless buddy in the internet café, I ain't got no poker face.

'Three ribs. What kind of ribs? I mean, the ribs of what animal?'

She looks away. Her eyes fall on the large Bible on the lectern. 'Don't think it says. You can look if you like.'

I don't move. Sit there staring at the lectern. Work has just intruded like a spear in the side of the head. That wasn't why I came here. I didn't want to think about work. Not yet.

Maybe I should just go to the park. Try not to think about a lion with wings and a bear with three ribs in its teeth, and Maureen with wings and young Tommy with ribs down his throat.

The third one, the leopard with four wings and four heads. Does that give us any clue as to who or when or why someone will next be killed? Should I be dashing into work with the information? Is it evidence? It's not evidence. A clue then? Something to shunt us off in the right direction?

Can't think straight. Can't think at all.

I've been looking at her the whole time, all this running through my head.

'You shouldn't go back to work,' she says. 'Whatever it is you're thinking, you look pretty messed up. It's like bringing your phone in here. You came here for something other than work.'

I don't speak. I can feel her compassion. At least, I think the compassion is hers. Perhaps it's the guy in blue up in the window.

'I presume there was something with ribs with regard to Tommy Kane,' she says.

'Sorry?'

There's no inquisitiveness in her voice. Resignation almost. As if she's saying, you shouldn't be thinking about work, but since you are, I'm just going to hurry you along, so that you can get past it for the day, and go back to the empty, maudlin thoughts you ought to be having.

'I saw Maureen hanging, same as everyone else around here. She had those wings on her back. They looked… it was bizarre. I didn't know what it meant. I'm sure no one did.'

'We thought they were meant to be angel's wings.'

'We all did. But if you're suddenly getting interested in Daniel 7, then presumably there was something about ribs with the boy. He had ribs in his mouth, or whatever.'

I stare across the aisle. Don't say anything else. The thought of work drills away, alongside its friend, inadequacy. I would have known this days earlier if I'd read the damned book; if I'd bothered speaking to a minister or Bible scholar; if I hadn't kept stabbing 'angel's wings' into fucking Google, like a deranged automaton, incapable of even the slightest lateral thought.

'Go home, Sergeant, or go for a walk.'

I look into the eyes of Mary Buttler. The large Bible on the lectern stares down at me sternly, pushing me away.

*

Wake up. Lie still for a moment trying to remember what day it is, what's coming in the morning. Work or weekend?

Work.

Reach out for my phone, check the time. 1.31 a.m. Have been in bed for four hours. Stare at the ceiling. Curtains open as always, the room dimly illuminated by the street lights.

Instantly aware of the usual problem. Awake in the middle of the night and straight away my brain starts whirring. Not necessarily about what needs to be done the next day. It can be anything, although it's invariably bad. Memories and thoughts ping in from all areas of the past – entirely random, never good – as though they're being catapulted from various points around the universe of my head.

Pushing that kid over when we were playing in the field. I was eight years old. Nine possibly. He fell into cow shit. He was off school for a couple of days. When he came back you could still see the bruises on his arm from where his mother had beat the crap out of him. Because I'd pushed him into cow shit. I didn't say sorry. Didn't know how. Just never spoke to him again.

That's what's in my head, that memory pinged in from the outer limits, from nowhere. Why did I just think of that?

I become aware of her before turning, think about it for a moment or two, as if the middle of the night is happening in slow motion, and then look over. She's standing at the window, looking down at the street. Holding something in her hand. I watch her for a while, wondering whether I should speak. I should probably get up first. Don't want to talk to her while lying in bed. Maybe if I just lie here long enough, she'll go away; or, at the very least, I'll go back to sleep and she'll be gone when I wake up.

I swing my feet out the bed and sit up.

'What's going on, kid?' I say.

She turns. She's holding a stuffed lion by the ear. It looks pretty old. She's wearing the same dress and cardigan as the previous two times that I've seen her. Is it two? Maybe it's more than that.

'Did you read the book yet?'

Shake of the head.

'I'm there, though. I know I need to.'

'Yesterday was a bad day.'

'Yes, it was.'

What? How does she know that?

'I'll read it in the morning. Going to get up early, go for a run. I'll read the book over breakfast, get into work early.'

She nods.

'That's good. You should.'

She turns back to the window, as though everything that had to be said has been.

'Anything happening out there?' I ask.

'Not tonight,' she says.

I wonder. All I need to do is look away, and when I look back she'll be gone. Is that how it works? I put my head in my hands for a moment, and although it's at first a slightly contrived action, it feels so natural. Sitting on the edge of a bed, leaning forward, head in my hands, feeling confused and wasted and miserable. Ah, you stupid arsehole.

Sit like that long enough that I quite forget that I initially put my head in my hands in the hope that the kid would vanish. So long, in fact, that I forget I'm not alone.

Except that, when I finally lift my head, it turns out I am alone.

Tiredness returns, for all the world like I've been rapped over the head with it. I slide back under the covers, lie down and fall asleep.

24

Woke up at just after 4 a.m. Went for a run. Stopped at the Esso garage on the way home and bought rolls and bacon and orange juice and milk and coffee. Came home, had a shower, drank two glasses of water, made breakfast, ate breakfast, read Daniel 7 while I ate, and now I'm walking in through the front door of the station at 6.27 a.m.

I'm not saying today's going to be a good day, it's just going to be a day, just any old day, but at least it's not going to be yesterday, and that's all that matters.

Sgt Collins is on the front desk. Will likely be going home at around 7.30. We nod at each other. I head to the stairs, walking quickly, but something makes me stop and turn. Collins isn't looking at me, it wasn't that, but something makes me realise that there are things I need to be told.

'Gerry,' I say, conversationally. He looks up. 'I didn't make it in yesterday. What'd I miss?'

'You see the news?'

Crap. It's never good when the news is mentioned. Ever. *You didn't see the news? There was, like, no crime, anywhere...!* Shake my head.

'Murder on Carmichael Drive.'

Just around the corner.

'Convenient.'

'Couldn't ask for better,' he says.

Don't often get murders around here. Although they seem to be becoming more frequent.

'Tell me everything.'

'Woman in her sixties. Part of this church business the DCI's been investigating. Got shot in the face. Some talk about whether it might have been an attempted fake suicide.'

He pauses. I let him think before bugging him with more questions.

'The husband, he walked in on it, didn't get a look at the killer. Nothing.'

'Might it have been the husband who then made up the interrupted suicide story?'

He shrugs. 'You'll need to speak to the boss.' Another moment's thought, then, 'Guess that's the basics. Puts a new light on the other two from last week, but you probably worked that out already. Being a detective.'

'Fuck off.'

We laugh, and I head up the stairs, the smile quickly dying.

*

'From here you can see the front path. Our guy sees the husband approaching, doesn't have much time. If he was going to try to make it look like suicide, and there's nothing here in fact to suggest that, he suddenly finds he has no time to arrange things. He grabs a cushion, hurriedly shoots the woman in the face, then legs it out the back door. The husband hears the shot, muffled but not that muffled, and by the time he's in the house, he gets to hear the back door close. And, of course, he doesn't run straight to the back door because he's too busy looking at what's left of his wife's face. Which is very little.'

'There goes the tender kiss goodbye,' I contribute to the conversation. As usual, not really helping.

We're in the front room. Body long gone, of course. Still plenty of blood sprayed around, and the marks of the gunshot in the sofa. The pillow is at the lab in town. Everywhere there are signs of crime scene investigation.

I look out at the front of the house to the middle-class detached homes across the street, in this middle-class area. Hands in pockets, I walk to the window. Beside me is one of those Lladro porcelain, I don't know, things. A couple of figures doing the tango. Well, I say tango, but what the fuck do I know about dancing? I watched *Strictly* one night because I was too drunk to press a button on the remote to change the channel, but that probably doesn't make me Lord of the Dance.

The two porcelain figures are on a doily, on a small, round-topped table, built specifically at great expense to hold porcelain figures of people doing shit. As this investigation continues, we turn more and more into Miss Marple. I'll be sitting in front of the TV one night, channel surfing aimlessly, then I'll stumble across ITV3, and there we'll be, me and Taylor, investigating the middle classes killing each other. *Taylor & Hutton,* the show'll be called. Or maybe just *Taylor*, and I'll be relegated to incidental sidekick.

'Foxtrot?' says Taylor, coming to stand at the window and glancing down at the happy couple, forever frozen in fully-clothed near-concupiscence.

'Fucked if I know. I thought it was a tango.'

'When d'you do that move in a tango?' he asks scornfully.

'During the boring bits? I don't know, do I?'

We stop looking at the stupid Lladro and stare out the window. Grey morning. A red car drives by, slowing down, looking at the latest tragic household in the community. It drives on, and once again there's silence from outside.

Autumn leaves sparse in the trees, thick on the ground. The threat of November rain. The kind of day that would be melancholy on any street, and not just when one of the residents has been murdered.

'How d'you know the husband didn't set it up?'

'Neighbour heard the gunshot when the guy was still outside. The killer was obviously rushed, didn't have time to try to muffle the shot as well as he would've liked.'

'Could've been working together, and it's all part of the setup to make us think the husband has nothing to do with it.'

He shrugs.

'Could've been, but I don't think so.'

'Anything to suggest he was going to try to fake a suicide, other than what went on with the previous two?'

'Looks like she was drugged, same stuff as the others. Then he's caught in the act, maybe as he's positioning her fingers on the gun or something, and he panics, knows that the wife is going to be able to identify him, so he pops the bullet in her chops. Takes the gun with him, as there was no point in letting it look like a suicide attempt.'

'What the fuck is he doing?'

'How d'you mean?'

'Drugging them all with the same stuff. Why on earth go to pains to make it look like three people committed suicide, but use this very obvious link?'

'Maybe he's an idiot.'

'But… it's not even like he'd have to be watching CS-fucking-I, is it? He must know that the police could have worked that shit out fifty years ago, never mind now.'

'That's where we're at, Sergeant,' he says. 'Lots of questions, no answers. And that's not to mention the damned turkey feather.'

I give him a look. I'd been wondering when the part about four heads and four wings was going to come into play.

'Just the one?'

'The one what?' he says. Distracted.

'Just the one turkey feather?'

'Yes, just the one turkey feather.'

'That biblical corollary we were looking for, the connection… Daniel 7, four beasts. First one has wings, which then come off, the second has three ribs in its mouth, the third has four wings of a fowl. The guy must have legged it with the wings, maybe intent on using them again.'

He's looking at me like it's me who's the mad person. I'm not the freak doing all the biblical shit.

'Right,' he says. 'Tell me about it when we get back to the station. Show me the damned book.'

'Will do.'

We stand, like two old women at a sea wall waiting for the first sight of the fishing fleet, staring out at the slow, grey morning.

'What d'you think we'd be called?' I say.

'What?'

'If we were a TV show.'

'Fuck's sake, Hutton,' he says, and turns away from the window.

25

Mrs Agnes Christie. The latest victim. The latest life to trawl through.

To which church did she belong? What kind of relationships did she have with the other parishioners? What part, if any, did she have to play in the great south of Glasgow Granny Porn ring?

Yes, all right, we're not really thinking about there being such a ring.

I think I might have slept with a woman called Agnes once, although I'm not entirely sure, and I used to have an Aunt Agnes, but nowadays every time I come across the name, I just hear Billy Connolly doing his two lions sketch.

'*Agnes*!'

It used to make me laugh. Don't laugh much any more, at least, not so that the laugh isn't verging on the psychotic.

Taylor had interviewed the husband, and the eldest two children. I get the third child, just arrived from the south of England. Jane Christie, unmarried, early thirties. A doctor working at the RUH in Bath.

I'd been dreading speaking to her, as I dread speaking to any bereaved relative, until I heard what she did for a living. I like doctors. They spend their days dealing with misery and death, pain, suffering and bereavement. By the time they're thirty they're already hardened against this shit. Hardened and practical. Less likely to burst into tears, which is a massive bonus.

Of course, there's also that thing we see more and more where the level of emotion displayed is directly proportional to the amount of reality TV the person watches. Someone who lives on a diet of *Jeremy Kyle* and *X-Factor* and *The Only Way Is Brigafuckingdoon* and all that shit, those people have come to see crying as the norm. Crying is what you do, it's the learned and correct emotional response. Letting people see how badly you're affected by X dying or by Y shagging your best mate's mum. However, the level of society that hasn't been assimilated into that world of cheap TV is far more likely to react to death/suffering/heartache in the old-fashioned, stiff-upper-lipped way of their forefathers.

Doctors, like police officers, don't watch *Jeremy Kyle* and *X-Factor*. Don't have the time. Not to mention that we spend our lives dealing with real life crap, so why would we want to watch more of it on TV?

'When was the last time you saw your mum?'

Sitting in the café across the road. The only room available at the station was one of those where we interrogate the prisoners. Didn't want to take her in there. Don't want the civilians to see the manacles. And, of course, there's too much blood on the walls. Yep, stick that up your arse, Shami Chakrabarti.

She's clinging on to her Americano with milk. You know, I'm not saying she's a doctor, so she like, doesn't give a shit that her mum's dead. The woman's working to keep it together. It's just, there's more chance of her being successful at that; there's more steel behind the eyes.

'A few months. Things have been pretty busy at work… but, you know, not that that mattered. We saw each other a couple of times a year. Was due up at Christmas…'

She looks off to the side. Being skilled in the art of getting women to talk – while sadly not so skilled in the more important art of getting women to shut up – I leave her to the silence, knowing that she'll fill the space.

'She loved it when I came up to visit and didn't make any other plans. A long weekend at home. She'd fuss over me, like I was a kid again. It was… you know, on the one hand it's a bit shit when your parents refuse to acknowledge that you're not thirteen anymore and can make an actual decision for yourself without destroying all of humanity, but every now and again...'

Her words drift away, hand to the face, then she reels it in and takes another drink of coffee.

'Did she ever talk to you about the church?'

She laughs. A nice laugh, and thankfully not one of those that precedes bursting hysterically into tears. Takes another drink of coffee, then shakes her head.

'The poor bastard.'

Can't help smiling. Somehow realise she's not talking about her mum.

'Who?'

'God. Mum'll be up there now, bending his ear about the church. And why did you let that happen? And what about this? And the next thing...'

I smile with her. The smile slowly goes from her face, but is not replaced by sadness. A physician's practicality, that's what I see.

'All the time. That was all she talked about.'

'She went to the Old Parish before the amalga—'

'Oh, no. She went to Halfway. Ever since it was mooted, I mean, way back, five, six years ago, when people first started talking about it being a possibility, she was all over it. She was wild, angry at the very thought, and then determined. She was so cross that there wasn't the same level of fight amongst the other elders.'

'And she was still fighting?'

'God, yes. She went to St Mungo's, but she hated it. She was still in court trying to overturn the sale of Halfway, even though... I don't know how far it's gone, but the new owners have already started the conversion.'

'Did she know Maureen Henderson?' I ask.

She looks vacant.

'Don't know the name. Was she an elder?'

'No, doesn't matter.' Shake my head, retract the carelessly tossed hand with which I'd dismissed the question. 'She was one of those who died last week.'

'Of course,' she says. 'Sorry, of course I knew the name.

Just wasn't thinking. She wasn't an elder, though?'

'No, and she was originally from the Old Kirk. She was just another one with plenty to say.'

'Mum never mentioned her.'

Seems weird, but backed up by the fact that we found no correspondence with Agnes Christie amongst Maureen's paperwork. These two women, now attending the same church and both utterly determined that their original church should not go under, probably never had anything to do with each other.

Shouldn't jump to conclusions, plenty yet to be uncovered.

'What was the problem with the other elders?'

'Not sure, really. You'd need to speak to Dad. He got a lot more of it than I did. Ultimately, for whatever reason, they weren't up for the fight. They seemed to rely on everything working out all right in the end...'

'Because that's what usually happens.'

'Exactly. Mum was all for, you know, she thought they should set up a war room.'

'Nice.'

A war room, eh? She would have had a natural ally in Paul Cartwright. If only they hadn't been on opposite sides of the fight.

'Great expression, but she had a point. A small committee that right from the off would identify the strengths and weaknesses of the four churches. Address our weakness, and exploit theirs, use our strengths and try to take theirs out of the game.'

'Good strategy.'

'It was, but she couldn't do it herself. She also said, right from the off, that we had the money in the bank, and we should use it before it got swallowed up. We ought to spend it before things went too far. Go over the buildings and halls with a toothcomb, find every single thing that could be used against us, and correct it before the process really got going.'

I like the way she says 'we' and 'us', although it can't be

often that she ever went to the church.

'Makes sense,' I say. Funny how many times we've heard this kind of talk in the past week.

'She couldn't get the support for it. God, she was so mad. So she talked to us about it. We got all the arguments, all the rage, all the bitterness when ultimately the vote went against us.'

And now she's dead, taking the bitterness with her.

'Had that lessened over time?'

'God, no. She was a broken record. I don't honestly think she ever imagined we'd get Halfway back permanently, but she had it in for the current building and all those wankers that run the show. God, sorry. Shouldn't use that language.'

'I'm a police officer,' I say.

She laughs. Dan fucking Brown would probably have called it a chuckle.

'You want another coffee,' I say. 'I think we've still got some talking to do.'

'Sure.'

*

That evening I have sex with the doctor. Ethically questionable, but that's just how it is. This is the kind of thing that happens.

Her dad is staying with the elder sister, husband and three kids. No more space, other than the sofa, so she booked into a hotel. The Premier Inn over by the site of the old Glasgow Zoo.

She spent a little time with them, dinner and what not, but couldn't stand to go through the entire maudlin evening. Excused herself. Stepped out of the family home, got into her hire car and thought, shit, the rest of the night alone sitting in my room at the Premier Inn when my mum just died? No!

She had my card. She called me. Didn't want to inflict herself on any old friends of the family in town, as it would have been an evening of melancholic remembrance, which she didn't need. Needed someone she could talk to without having to talk about her mother being murdered.

She called. I was still at the station. Morrow sitting across the desk. Just after eight. I was flicking through Daniel, wondering how long it was going to take me to pick up the phone to call Philo Stewart for expert interpretation of the book, with no reason why I should still have been at work, other than the fact that I hated the idea of going home alone.

The doctor asked me out for a drink. I met her five minutes later. We had two vodka tonics each, then it was back to the Premier Inn.

It was strange. I didn't actually want to have sex with her. I felt, almost, that I was just going along with it. Something to do. Something that was expected.

She was fit, mind. Much bigger breasts than you'd expect from someone of her slim build, though it took a while for me to get that far. She took charge, undressed me, threw me back on the bed.

Her mouth was straight over my cock. God, she was good. Painful at times, but that fucking great pain that you get. Hands all over, fingers squeezing my balls just that little bit too tightly. Tongue and lips massaging my erection, over and over, her long brown hair caressing my stomach and thighs. I wanted to see her naked, but if you're going to have to wait for that, it'd be tough to think of anything better to be doing.

Usually I'm too impatient to lie there for long, but she wasn't letting me up, so I gave into it. She said one thing. Looked up at one point as her lips were hovering above the end of my erection, a trail of saliva and pre-cum between us, and said, 'I love cock.'

Lost track of time. Didn't lie back with my eyes closed; watched her at work. She loved cock all right. I imagined she'd be happy to have more than one at a time. She kept drawing her mouth away, the juice on her lips, spitting down on my cock, and then swallowing me again.

Eventually, at a time of her choosing and completely unrelated to how I might have been feeling, she sat up, removed her jeans and underwear, knelt over me and lowered herself onto my desperate erection. She was soaking and I rammed easily inside her; we gasped together.

As she fucked me, she unbuttoned the top of her blouse and brought it up and over her shoulders, undid her bra and tossed it aside, and then leaned back, her arms to the sides, her face in rapture, putting her breasts on display for me.

I held her waist and drove my cock into her as hard as I could, all the time my eyes on the movement of her breasts as she fucked me, squeezing her pussy on my cock in time with the rhythm of my movements, and then finally I couldn't wait any longer, and I broke the rhythm so that I could lean up and take her breasts in my hands, caressing them and squeezing them, before taking them in my mouth and sucking forcefully on her erect nipples.

And so it went on. Like I said, this is the kind of thing that happens in life – we both had our reasons – but I was aware that I never committed myself to it in quite the way that I usually do.

Now it's 6 a.m. and the alarm has just gone off. The thought goes through my head that she's still here, in my bed, then I wake up a little more and realise that I'm in her bed.

There will be no nonsense when I go. No when-will-I-see-you-again. She stirred at the alarm, touched my arm briefly, probably just checking I was still here, and then turned her back. Thank God there was no arm draped across the chest, no head snuggled into the crook of my arm. She knows the score. We're all adults here.

Can't hear her breathe. It's as if she's not here. At any rate, I don't have to make any decisions around her.

The cars are picking up outside. I close my eyes and listen to the first birds of the morning.

26

We're back in Connor's room. He's standing at the window, hands in pockets, looking down on a bright November morning.

A good one today. Crisp, fresh autumn. Pale blue sky, a few clouds to the west. Kicked some leaves walking into work this morning. Didn't quite jump up and click my heels in the same movement, but there was something of the Gene Kelly about me.

The morning after the decent sex the night before, aided and abetted by the fact that when I left she said goodbye, kissed me on the cheek, and that was that. No expectation, no exchange of numbers. Perfect.

I shouldn't be complacent, because there's a bunny boiler around every corner – if nothing else, Hollywood has taught us that – but it felt right.

Thinking about it, I'm not sure that Hollywood has taught us *anything* other than that. Still, it's important enough a warning to us all to justify a gazillion dollars and one hundred years of movie making.

We're waiting for him. Been in here five minutes so far, maybe. Five minutes sitting in silence. I could sit here all day. It's like authorised skiving. Would have been nicer if he'd served coffee and doughnuts while we waited for him to pronounce, but you can't have everything.

Taylor is checking his watch. Taylor has work to do. He doesn't get sitting in contemplative silence the way I do. You know, the new me, the new sitting-in-contemplative-silence bloke that I've become.

'It's hard to even know where to begin,' says the voice from the window without turning round.

Taylor glances at his watch again, then at me. He's thinking that'd it'd be best to begin with investigating the deaths, not sitting around waiting to have a discussion about it. He's waited more than a week, and he's waited nearly two days since Agnes Christie was killed. Doing what he can, but with his superintendent unwilling to face the facts.

'The Church of Scotland community in this town...' continues Connor, then he shakes his head and the sentence slides away into nothingness. He turns and looks at Taylor. As usual, I've been requested to be in the room, but I may as well not be.

'Everyone, everyone of any importance in this town, obviously the Catholic community notwithstanding, attends the church on a Sunday morning, is a member of the session, is involved in some way. Everyone is on my back about this. You know how many phone calls I've had this morning? You know how hard this is for me?'

Ah, there's the rub. He gets quickly down to what's really important to him.

'Four churches are involved, with a combined congregation, before the merger, of nearly fifteen hundred.'

'Most of them never actually attended, sir,' says Taylor dryly.

Connor removes his hands from his pockets and makes a hopeless gesture.

'So that means we exclude them from the investigation?'

'Probably not, but when looking for suspects, it surely makes sense to concentrate on those who we know to have been upset about the merger, rather than those who didn't even notice the merger happened because they were casting their *X-Factor* vote.'

Connor emits some sort of weird snort and shakes his head again. Poor fucker. He arrived here so pompous, so self-assured, so confident that he would mould policing in this town to his own personal narrative. Then the Plague of

Crows happened and now every crime is a potential debacle, and the QPM he envisioned pinned to his jacket for his happy retirement days in fucking Braemar is drifting slowly off into the sunset.

That's just the way it goes. Life overtaken by events. Typical of the man, however, that he has to be a dick about it.

'Yes,' says Taylor, trying to be the grown-up in the room, something even I could manage in the face of Connor's hangdog catastrophizing, 'there are over a thousand suspects. But all we can do is speak to as many people as possible as quickly as possible, investigate any leads that present themselves, follow those paths that need to be followed. In short, do a good job as quickly as we can. It looks entirely likely that we're dealing with a triple murder. Accordingly we need to give the investigation the resources it deserves, and get on with it. If we need to speak to the kind of people who usually wouldn't consider themselves relevant to such an investigation, then those people are just going to have to... suck it up, sir.'

Bold.

Connor would have been chewing Taylor's testicles for that eight months ago, but now he knows he has ceded authority to the better police officer.

'What do we do, then?' he says.

'We give the investigation the appropriate level of manpower,' says Taylor. 'So far, the sergeant and I, along with DC Morrow, have been speaking to a few people, piecing things together. We need to throw manpower at it. We need more information. We need to start eliminating people from the investigation. We need to know who we should be pursuing.'

'Of course, of course,' he says. He waves a slight hand in the direction of the door. 'Get on with it. As many men as you need.' Women would probably be helpful too. You know you're in trouble when it's me picking someone up on his implicit sexism. 'If you're going to speak to... if there's anyone you need to interview who you think... let me know if you speak to anyone on the council. Or our service.'

'There's one more thing, sir,' says Taylor.

Connor strokes his chin.

'We got DNA from Mrs Christie's clothes that belongs to neither her nor Mr Christie. The killer was rushed, and possibly wasn't as careful this time.'

Connor asks his incredulous question with something of an eyebrow. Don't even fucking ask, his face says. Taylor asks anyway. Or, at least, he tries.

'If we could DNA test members of the—'

'Out of the question.'

'Sir, it's—'

'Out of the question. Go.'

And that's that. Taylor gets up, walks quickly from the room. Silently I follow, Sancho fucking Panza to the last. Close the door behind me.

Taylor stops, turns. The expletive is on his lips. He smiles and shakes his head instead.

'That guy used to be such a pompous dick...'

'Now he's just a dick.'

'Yep. Right, Sergeant, let's get to it. Give me half an hour to put some ideas together about how we're doing this, and then get everyone you can in Room B. We're looking for at least fifteen. Make sure DCI Dorritt's there, Stephanie, Sgt Harrison, Sgt McGovern, Jones. Get as many of them as you can.'

'Yes, boss.'

On my heels and off we go. At last we can start a proper murder investigation.

*

Taylor's quick and to the point. No bullshit, no artifice, no ego. A good officer doing good work. Everyone gets their tasks, and is sent on their way. Time to stop pussying around the investigation. We need to establish who else knew about Maureen and her thriving internet business.

We need to find out who hated whom and who fell out the most over the merger. We need to narrow down the list of potential suspects to something less than a thousand. One of these fuckers is guilty and it's time to start treating people as though it might be them.

At some point in the talk I come to realise that he's not including me in the list of instructions. I presume I'm staying with him, his loyal Chewbacca, to make the appropriate noises at all the right moments.

'Here's the rub,' he's saying, tasks divvied up, heading into the wrap-up. 'Victims one and three were vocal opponents of the merger, but we've yet to find anything about the kid in that context. You know the score. Was the kid against the merger, or is the opposition of the other two nothing to do with it? Everything on the table. Everything. Get out there, ask questions, bring the slightest suspicion to me, no matter how irrelevant it might seem.'

He nods. The collective realise he's finished, and off they go, heading out into the station. There's a much better feeling about this one than we've had with these things in the past. It feels like this person, whoever they are, is killing with some sort of purpose. Whatever it is, it feels easier to confront than the couple of psychopaths we've had around here the last couple of years.

Yes, all right, now that it comes to it I'd rather be in MissMarpleland than Psychoville.

'You'll have noticed the elephant in the room,' says Taylor, when all the others have gone.

'Eh…?'

'The Book of Daniel,' he says.

I'm not sure that's quite elephant-in-the-room status, although I can see that Taylor might think it relevant but didn't want to mention it because it's one aspect of this thing that's removed from the prosaic world of revenge and small-town politics.

'I'm hoping,' he says, 'that whoever is doing this Daniel thing, with the wings and the ribs and the God knows what else, is just doing it for a bit of extra flourish. Let's just not imagine that it's any weirder than that. I'd like you to find out about the book. All that Old Testament stuff is so damned fucked up, there are so many interpretations. What does it mean, all that stuff about wings and heads and ribs? Speak to someone. Have your own personal forty-five-minute BBC documentary on the subject. In fact, do the usual routine. Speak to a couple of people. Bible scholars. What we really need to find is some way to identify who's next because if we know one thing, it's that this ain't finished yet.'

Stand up. Suddenly think of the girl standing in my room in the middle of the night telling me to hurry up. Hurry up. I'd forgotten about her. That's strange. The girl who gave me the book in the first place, who was standing at the bedroom window looking out at the night. It wasn't my bedroom, though. Whose bedroom was it?

'What?' he says.

Shake my head. 'Nothing. I'm on it.' Check the watch. 'I'll try to be back by five.'

'You all right, Tom?' he throws at me as I'm on my way out.

Stop, take a moment, turn round.

'Sure,' I say.

'I doubt it, as you've not been all right since you came back to work. Two days ago you took a day off for... why?'

'I have my days,' I say. 'I just need to get through it. Day at a time. Today... today, I'm all right.'

'What about tomorrow?'

No answer for that. I never know about tomorrow. He rubs his hand across his chin. Clean-shaven, unlike his fellow officer.

'I'm good,' I say, and then turn and leave before he can respond.

I'm not good, of course, and he knows I'm not good. We're only a day or two away from me sitting in his office and him telling me that I'm being placed on sick leave, or at the very least, he's showing me to the door of the nearest psychiatrist.

It would probably be better if, when that happens, the psychiatrist were a man.

27

Fuck.

How many people in Glasgow are there that I could speak to about the Book of Daniel? Seriously, there have got to be, like, I don't know, a thousand. More than that. They do a theology course at Glasgow University. Find the guys who teach that, take it from there. Some of the students even. Ministers, priests, rabbis; Jesus, there will be guys down the fucking pub who can tell me the hidden context of the Book of Daniel.

As a concession to what I ought to be doing, I arrange to go and speak to a lecturer in Theology at the university. Any time this afternoon, he said. Sounds like he'll do me the Book of Daniel without all the shit attached. What we really need, of course, is the blend of scholarly and theological, because we don't know where the person who's using this is coming from. The practical side of me wants to talk to someone who doesn't think the Bible is anything to do with God, that it was all about politics and storytelling to perpetuate myths. However, who knows what our killer is thinking? So I have to get both views. From talking briefly to the guy on the phone, I decided that I'd get both sides from him. Sounded young, switched on.

First, however, I'm standing once again at the doorstep at the top end of Glenvale Road, the big house with the bedroom view (I'm presuming) down over the town and this half of Glasgow, waiting to speak to my current infatuation. The woman I can't stop thinking about. The woman with whom I hold imaginary conversations while walking to work, while eating breakfast, while standing in the shower. The woman who I tried not to think about while making love to someone else last night.

Taylor didn't say that I shouldn't speak to anyone from the four churches, but, of course, he didn't say it because *it went without saying*. It's obvious, and he trusts me to not do something that obviously shouldn't be done.

I ring the bell and I hate myself standing here. It's not about sex. It's not about how she looks in a V-neck sweater, it's not about imagining drawing the covers around us and pressing my erection against her. It's because I've fallen for her. I need to speak to someone who knows the Bible, and she runs a Bible study group, so it's like, huzzah! I actually have an excuse to speak to her, I'm not just turning up and saying, *oh, can I get your fucking flapjack recipe, I can't stop thinking about them?*

Shouldn't be here. Don't even know if she'll be in, or if the husband will be in. There's no immediate answer, so I ring the bell again and turn round. Nervousness beginning to ebb at the possibility that there's no one here. Look past the houses over the road at what I can see beyond. The old steelworks. The Campsie Fells in the far distance.

Used to think of them as the Misty Mountains, and would imagine going on a great trek across country to get there. If I'd ever done it, it would probably have been easier to catch a bus.

Think I hear footsteps and turn. Frosted glass in the door, but don't see any movement in the house. Aware that I'm holding my hands behind my back. Subconsciously trying to be casual? Fucking hell.

I go on waiting.

*

'It's a box of frogs, man.'

I laugh. I mean, he was being flippantly modern in his description of the Book of Daniel rather than trying to be funny, but I can't help laughing all the same. This guy is one of the new millennium crowd, about to answer all my questions as if he's trying to get a bunch of children excited about it. I suppose that's what he does for a living.

'Box of frogs,' I say, nodding.

'I mean, it's like they took this whole bunch of biblical stuff, I mean, like the distilled essence of the Bible, and tossed it into one book. It's bonkers. Split into halves. First one is stories about Daniel, told by, you know, like some unseen narrator we don't know. So, for example, you get the whole Daniel in the lion's den bag.'

'Sure.'

I read that this morning, had a bit of a face plant moment when I realised that that was the Daniel we were talking about. Up until that point I'd been thinking more of him as being the chap from the Elton John song.

'So, that's your chapters one through six.' No, he's not an American, he's just been watching too much TV. 'Then suddenly, out of nowhere, chapter seven switches to prophecy and is narrated *by* Daniel. And that's where you get the prophecy of the four beasts emerging from the sea.'

'So who was Daniel?'

He puts his hand on a mug of tea or coffee and takes a glug. Must be cold. You can see he's one of these weird guys who has his hot drink sitting on his desk for like three hours, only remembering to take a drink once every twenty minutes or so. He shrugs.

'There was no single Daniel. I mean, not in terms of writing the book. The whole thing wasn't even written in the same language. So, the first half you've got what are generally considered to be a collection of Aramaic folk tales that have just been, you know, assembled into one neat volume and ascribed to the same characters. Then you've got your regular biblical prophesies in the second half. Wars and monsters, the rise and fall of empires, God smiting the crap outta the bad guys, the Second Coming, et cetera, et cetera.'

You know, I'd read all that the previous morning, but it's so much easier to get it explained to you by someone speaking everyday, simple, American English.

'So, the variety of writers explains the smorgasbord?'

'Smorgasbord,' he says, nodding. 'Bang on.'

'OK, so the symbolism behind the four beasts?'

'Daniel 7?'

'Daniel 7.'

'They're meant to indicate the rise of four empires, the fourth crushing the first three. There's then all sorts of weird shit happens with the fourth and there are ten horns, and then a little horn comes up and flattens three of the other horns, and ultimately God, you know, et cetera, et cetera. That kind of thing.'

'And we know who the four empires were? Are?'

'Depends how much of a prophecy you want it to be? Each generation has their own interpretation. If we assume the guy who wrote it had someone particular in mind, generally they're considered to be Babylon, Persia, Media and the Seleucids.'

I nod, then say, 'You know, you started off talking about history there, but by the end it felt like you'd veered off into an episode of Star Trek.'

'Iraq, Iran, northern Iran, and then, you know, the Seleucids took over half of Alexander's territory, then expanded it, so they had some of Greece, the Levant, Turkey, Afghanistan, some of northwest India. Shedloads.'

'So, there's some modern day correlation?'

He makes a maybe-maybe not gesture.

'Sure, if you want there to be. Or else it can just be a bunch of messed-up weirdness from the second century BC.'

OK. Not really helping so far, so decide to go for one of those off-the-cuff judgement calls.

'We've got a case at the moment,' I say.

He smiles. 'Sure you have,' he says. 'Why else would you be here?'

'Fair point. We've had a couple of deaths... you watch the news?'

'Never,' he says.

'You *never* watch the news?'

Shake of the head. 'The trouble with watching the news is that you find out what's happening, and it's never good. Ever. I mean, do they ever start the bulletin with, *And here's a bunch of great stuff that happened today...*? No, it's not for me.'

'OK. So we've had a couple of murders out our way.'

'I heard about that.'

'I thought you just said you never watch the news.'

'Jeez, man, I talk to people. Holy crap.'

'OK, OK. So, the first victim, she had wings placed on her back. Two wings. The second victim had three ribs down his—'

'Ah, nice,' he says. 'I see where you're going. That explains the police's sudden interest in Daniel.'

'Quite.'

He nods, sits back in a slightly affected way. There's something of the young Robert De Niro about him when he does that. I wonder if he realises.

'There was a third, right?' he asks.

'Yep, but the killer was interrupted. However, we found a turkey feather in the vicinity...'

'Wings of a foul.'

'Yes. Presumably he legged it with them, because he didn't have time to do whatever he was intending.'

'Which means he might kill another third victim.'

'Don't know. Depends if he has a specific number of victims in mind, as well as specific people, or if he's trying to make some biblically related point or other.'

'What might that be?' he asks.

I give him the benefit of an eyebrow from across the desk and he smiles and nods.

'Ah, that's why you're here,' he says. I nod. 'Makes sense. Right.'

He stares at his desk. His face goes through a variety of minor contortions to indicate a variety of minor thought processes, then he smiles and kind of laughs and finally looks up.

'I'm not really getting anything other than what is kind

of obvious, you know, that it's representative of some sort of power struggle. '

All those minor facial contortions must have been him connecting remotely with the internet.

'These people are all related to the local church, is that how it's going?' he asks.

'Yes, which is where the Bible comes in.'

'People, you know, they like to bring everything down in scale, to bring it down to a very human level. These visions, they tend to speak on a grand political scale, empires and wars. This could be someone attempting to recreate that vision at the basic, you know, church level.'

I don't say so, but that's the obvious first thought to have. Nevertheless, you don't get anywhere by putting the interviewee's gas at a peep.

'Hmm, like the sound of that...'

'Because after all, what are these people doing in church every Sunday, but trying to recreate the ministry of Jesus in their own local setting? So why not try parochially to recreate some other biblical prophecy?'

Actually, although I've already had the thought, when he puts it like that it sounds pretty good.

'So, what do you think?' I ask. 'Does the killer see himself as the fourth beast, crushing the others, or do you think soon enough we're going to find another victim, and the guy's going to have ten horns on his head, or whatever?'

'I think your killer is going to run into trouble with the parallels. The fourth beast has ten horns, and then a little horn pops up and kills three of the other horns.'

'OK. So what do you think?'

He looks across the desk and then makes another one of his slight facial contortions, his head shaking slowly.

'No idea.'

'Any other interpretations of Daniel 7 that might be appropriate?'

The look doesn't leave his face.

'Officer, you can more or less put any interpretation on

Daniel 7 that you choose, and you'll find a passage from the text to back you up.'

28

Phone starts going as I'm leaving the University. Had thought of a walk down University Avenue, along Kelvin Way for a bit, maybe take a few minutes in Kelvingrove Park, cup of coffee, sit on a bench. A good place to get my head together. Not too many people about, a bright enough day, sitting beneath late autumn trees. Ignore the phone twice, a text and a call, but then it rings again almost immediately, and I can feel the few minutes sitting in the park being dragged away from me.

Taylor, telling me to meet him at the Old Kirk, although he's not forthcoming with information. I wonder if something's happened to Mrs Buttler, yet I can tell at least from his tone that he's annoyed rather than weighed down by another death.

I assume graffiti or some other strange act of religious vandalism. The fact that I couldn't even begin to guess what had actually happened points to just how out of my depth I am in this situation, and that I ought to be making more of a run at the learning curve.

*

Taylor's car is in the small car park outside the church, along with two police vehicles and a small crowd of spectators. Instantly intrigued. Too small a crowd, and too slight a show of authority, for it to be another murder. On the other hand, way too much for a bit of vandalism.

Vandalism. Crap. The guy at the toilets. Must do something about that.

So, somewhere between vandalism and murder. Doesn't

really narrow it down. Park the car, get out, approach the gate through the crowd. There's no need for the police to set up a barrier, as there's the six-foot wall and the heavy iron gates around the scene of whatever it is that's happened.

PC Wallace opens the gate to let me through. I step inside the grounds of the church. There are graves either side of the path. The path leads to the front door, and then away down to the right-hand side of the building. This is the enclosed side of the property, hemmed in by trees and a wall. To the left there is more open space, the bulk of the graveyard. The graves are old and worn.

Against the wall of the church, three people are standing with two police officers. Maureen Henderson's daughter, Margaret Johnstone, the church officer, Mary Buttler, with whom I've shared a few quiet moments inside the building, and a man in a dog collar I don't recognise.

Taylor is standing off to the side, about ten yards away from the church building, beside what looks like a newly dug grave. There's a guy in jeans and a Motorhead T-shirt talking to him with his arms folded. Must be freezing. Away to the side, lying on the grass, is a shovel.

I take in the scene for a few moments, trying to work out what's happened. A new grave, a gravedigger, a minister, the church officer, the deceased's daughter.

Maureen Henderson must be in the grave. Well, we had released the body after all, and this is a graveyard.

I approach Taylor. He sees me coming and dismisses Motorhead with a nod of the head, indicating for him to go and stand with the others.

I come alongside Taylor and we stand beside the grave, looking down at the neat mound of new earth.

'Maureen?' I ask.

'Aye.'

'What's the problem?'

He lifts his head and uses his chin to indicate the rest of the graveyard, then indicates the gang of four with a dismissive hand.

'Look at the graves, Tom. This place hasn't been used in decades. Been decommissioned.'

'So why'd they do it? Couldn't afford the crematorium?'

He smiles.

'Far more duplicitous than that. The last burial here was ninety-nine years ago. A couple of years after that, phhtt,' he says, dragging his fingers across his throat, 'they stopped using it. So, apparently graveyards cannot be sold within a hundred years of being in active use.'

'Ah…'

'So next year, this place, this ground could be sold. Sure, they could sell the building now, but it ain't that attractive when the garden's a graveyard. This time next year it can be sitting in an estate agent's window, glorious Victorian home in need of some work, 1.7 hectares of beautiful, well-fertilized garden, or however big this is.'

'I thought this building wasn't getting sold.'

He shrugs.

'That's not what they think. They reckon the committee down at the other church are just biding their time, and as soon as they can, this place is going to be sold as is or it'll become a deluxe development of two and three bedroomed apartments.'

'So…'

'So Mrs Johnstone got her mother's body from the undertaker's, they enlisted a former minister from this place, they got some young guy they knew, and they performed the ceremony.'

'Shit.'

'Aye.'

'Who's idea was all that?'

He points at the group again.

'The church officer for this building, Buttler. You met her, right?'

'Sure.'

'She seem the type that would come up with this kind of plan?'

I give it some thought. I'd come to think that sitting in

her company was the most relaxing thing I'd found in the last twenty years, but there was no doubt that she was passionate enough about the building to have suggested something like this. I almost smiled at her use of the word 'cunt' when talking about Cartwright. This, after all, wasn't the most heinous crime in the world.

'Yep,' I say, nodding. 'She was pretty pissed off about the whole merger, and she was worried about what would happen to this place. But the daughter, she went along with this? There must be other family coming in, intending to go to the funeral.'

'The daughter's switched on, Sergeant. Had good reasons. Firstly, and there's just nothing to be said against this, she felt guilty about not having seen her mother on her final weekend. People feel guilt, because that's what they do. She's also aware that most people hated her mum, so there was never going to be a big turnout at the funeral. One of her brothers wasn't even going to come, and she says she'll handle the second one. She thought her mum would love that her body has been used in this way.'

'Can't we just dig it up? Take it back to the undertakers?'

'Do you know the legality of that? You know, once a burial has been carried out by an ordained minister in a graveyard?'

I look away from the small gaggle of perpetrators and turn back to Taylor.

'No. And neither do you,' I say, nodding.

'Exactly. So, whatever we're doing, we're not picking up that shovel.'

*

Standing in Taylor's office later when Connor comes in, closing the door behind him. We'd already discussed his imminent arrival, although he's been longer than anticipated.

He looks from one to the other of us, but he's not really

166

interested in me. He's probably debating whether he should tell me to bugger off, but he goes for the alternative, where he just pretends I'm not there.

Several times he looks like he's about to start letting rip at Taylor, then he stops himself, thinks about it some more, tries to find other words. Finally he walks to the window and looks out at the car park. Taylor gives me a glance and then looks at Connor's back.

'Are we to assume that there are now lawyers involved?' asks Taylor.

Ah, of course. I never think strategically like that, but it makes sense. There are two things that get superintendents in a fankle. One is heat from above, and the other is lawyers. Oh, and the press. So three things.

'Just had a meeting with the lawyer representing Paul Cartwright, the property convenor at St Mungo's. He's been hired by Mr Cartwright to represent the church.'

As he speaks, his voice seems to drift off almost, taking on a peculiar quality. He hesitates again. Neither Taylor nor I speak. Leave him to it, he'll get there in the end.

'This is like… you know, apparently the church merger business was desperately ugly, but things had begun to heal. As they do. They just needed time. Now we've got these murders, which… it's impossible to say, but two of the victims at least were against the merger, so people are, rightly or wrongly, assuming that it's someone from St Mungo's who killed them. To shut them up. And now we've got this burial, these people using the victim's body to their own ends.'

He shakes his head. Wasted words, telling us things we already know, as though we'd walked in halfway through the movie.

'It's opening it all up again, tearing the congregation apart just as they were beginning to accept the situation.' Another shake of the head. 'And now I'm stuck in the middle of it.'

Ha!

'How are you getting on with the legality of this thing?'

he asks, finally turning to Taylor. 'The burial, I mean.'

'I've sent it up to legal. We can't just charge in there, dig up the grave and stick the body back in...'

'I need solutions, not problems,' snaps Connor. 'I don't think you people... you officers down in the trenches... understand what it's like in my position, how difficult it is. This is the tough end of policing, not your, whatever, your murders and your petty theft.'

Awooga! Awooga! Wanker alert!

No, really. Even if he'd been speaking to a couple of constables straight out of police school, his trenches remark would have been unbelievably condescending.

'Politics are the true crime,' he says, his voice displaying an affected weariness he must have learned from the movies.

'For the moment,' says Taylor, doing his best to get the conversation away from Connor's tortured id, 'the grave thing isn't really our business. We were called out by a complaint, but actually, someone was burying a legally declared dead body in a graveyard, with a gravedigger and a church officer, a family member and a minister. There's nothing we can do for the moment. What's more important is that we find out why three members of the congregation have been murdered.'

Connor lets Taylor finish his obviously absurd outburst of plain common sense, glances at me, and then starts walking to the door, shaking his head. He stands in the doorway and turns to give us another quick ejaculation of arrogant twattery.

'I need you to be part of the team, Dan. We all need to be on the same page. You're not dealing with a hold-up at the damned Pakis on the corner now. This is church and state. Doesn't get any bigger.'

He seems to remember I'm there and gives me a glance.

'Church and state,' he throws at the room, and leaves.

The door closes. Taylor and I stare at it for a second, then turn to each other.

'Can we be offended on behalf of the Pakistani

community and get the arsehole sacked?' I ask.

'Deep breath, move on, forget what he said.' Taylor glances at his watch. 'Right, get everyone together, briefing room, fifteen minutes.'

29

You don't run around in those rare investigations, when you genuinely have no idea who to suspect, necessarily hoping for the big breakthrough, the giant sign pointing at someone, screaming, *It was him! It was him!*

Progress comes in inches; if you're lucky, in feet. Never in miles. All you can hope for is that one thing leads to another, until the chain leads you to the end.

So, a solid meeting in the briefing room, where lots of strands are opened up. There are so many people potentially involved in this, that the whiteboards at the head of the room are cluttered. Overrun with names and connections. Part of the early process is to eliminate as many people as possible.

For example, Morrow has discovered that young Tommy was using a Gmail account in the name of *ywilson444*. The account was empty. If it had ever been used, everything was deleted. There were no contacts listed. Nothing. The last use of the account, however, had been the day he died.

So, might be nothing, but on the other hand, why would you have a fake e-mail address? We need to get the paperwork done and get full access to the records of the account. Of course, even if he was up to something, it needn't be the church. God, he was a teenager, he could have been doing any old shit. Contacting grannies, for example.

Yet, we know. We get that feeling. There's some weird shit going on around this church. The kid was murdered, and now something else weird has come up, It's going to be related.

Lots of people are ruled out, names come and go, many names that I don't recognise. We are down to five or six favoured candidates to have killed old Maureen, through a combination of mutual anger and resentment, unable or unwilling to provide themselves with an alibi, and personal interest in the merger.

Paul Cartwright's name comes up again and again. He's everyone's favourite to have killed Maureen. No one seems to have any idea why young Tommy might have copped it. No one outside the police seems to have had any idea that Tommy and Maureen had had inappropriate sex. (Look, I think it was inappropriate.)

The names on the hate list for Agnes Christie have been similarly narrowed down, reduced to well under ten. Cross-checked with the list for old Maureen, three names appear on both. Taylor will take them forward tomorrow. Naturally, Cartwright was mentioned.

More work divvied up for the morning, everyone told to go home and get a decent night's sleep.

Where am I? Been a busy day, haven't really had time to wonder where my head is. Those are the best days. I'll work for another hour or two, then head home, grabbing some crappy food on the way. I think Thai tonight. And a bottle of wine, maybe. It's not healthy, but it's healthier than the mental implosions that forever lurk just around the corner.

A bottle of wine, maybe... Aye, some *maybe* that is.

*

I leave the office at 9.32 p.m. Slightly concerned about Taylor. He can pretend to be ignoring Connor's bluster all he likes, but there's some serious shit going on here, and when that happens you need your boss to have your back. Taylor comes to work every day of his life at the moment knowing that he's on his own. He has a boss only too willing to pass the blame on down to the level below.

I try to get him to leave with me, but he sends me on

my way, telling me he'll only be doing another twenty minutes. I consider waiting, but he orders out. Ready for it, I finally hit the road.

Leave by the front door, look up at the night. Not many clouds around, some stars in the sky. Some stars? Like, several billion. I stay looking up for a few moments having a brief Total Perspective Vortex moment, but my heart's not in it.

Hey, want to have a real-life Total Perspective Vortex moment? Go online and find a running UK National Debt clock. Goes up by £5k a second. That, my friend, is a bit of a mind fuck.

I finally look down, for some reason smiling at the thought of the UK national debt, at the sound of approaching footsteps.

My heart skips a beat.

Jesus, it does as well.

Philo Stewart. She stops in front of me.

'Sergeant, good evening.'

'Hey. You were waiting for me?'

She nods.

'Sorry, didn't feel like phoning. Just been sitting in my car listening to music.'

'What were you listening to?' I ask, which seems like a really inane question, but I feel quite discombobulated by her arrival. That's what happens with sudden meetings with objects of your infatuation.

'Oh, Bob,' she says.

'Bob?'

'Dylan.'

'You're a Dylan fan?'

She nods.

'I know, try not to hold it against me.'

'I've seen him over a hundred and fifty times,' I say.

She seems taken aback by that for a moment.

'Wow,' she says. 'Me too.'

'No way.'

She nods. Jesus. She's a Dylan fan.

'You were at the SECC in June?'

'Of course,' she says. 'You seen him since?'

Shake my head.

'I went to the States last month. Saw him in Rhode Island, a couple of dates in Massachusetts. Toronto…'

'How'd he sound?'

We both laugh at the question. The laughter goes.

'Sorry,' she says. 'I shouldn't just spring on you like this. You called round the house earlier.'

'Yes. How d'you know?'

'I was in, sorry.' She makes a slight movement of the hand. 'You know, just had a lousy day. Couldn't talk. But I've felt bad about it ever since, so, you know, if you wanted to speak now. What was it you were after?'

'Eh…' I start encouragingly, then look over my shoulder and back. 'I'm going home, get a Thai takeaway, bottle of wine. You want to join me?'

'Sure,' she says. No hesitation.

We walk to her car. I don't ask where her husband is.

*

Bought the Thai food on the way home, now sitting at the small table in my sitting room. First time it's been used to its full capacity in forever.

This is inappropriate. I know it. Wrong in the first place to take my questions about the Book of Daniel to her rather than going straight to someone outwith the scope of the investigation, and all kinds of wrong to invite her back here after she'd turned up at the station.

But I'm getting the vibe, the inescapable vibe. She could have called, she could have gone to reception, but she waited for me to come off duty. So, effectively, that's what this is. It's off-duty time. And I shouldn't be doing it.

She's wearing a similar top to the one she had on a couple of days ago. Hair looks a little untidy but, as is often the way, it makes her even more alluring. We've hardly spoken, but we have to start some time.

'You came to see me,' she says. 'I'm not suddenly a suspect, am I?'

Shake my head. The mood seems strange, but it's borne, I presume, of mutual attraction, coupled with mutual acknowledgement that we oughtn't to be here together.

'Is that why you didn't answer the door?' I ask. 'You weren't worried, were you?'

'Just... doesn't matter, Sergeant. What was it you wanted to ask me?'

The Book of Daniel seems so irrelevant. The fact that someone somewhere is attempting to invoke it seems so mundane, so childish. If you have an out-and-out psychopath, whose actions are controlled by a complete lack of perspective and common sense, then somehow it's forgivable. But this has all the hallmarks of being carried out by a middle-aged guy in a suit, a church elder who's been watching too many Hollywood movies.

I don't immediately say anything. Trying to think of a way to pursue the reasons for her melancholy, without it looking, well, weird. Obsessive.

Obsessive is how I feel. Shouldn't have asked her back here. Should have been professional enough to tell her to come to the station in the morning.

'You've been in a war zone,' she says suddenly.

Oh, yes. I nod. She shakes her head.

'You know, sometimes...' she begins, 'sometimes you come back from these places, and the things you've seen... the things you've seen people do, the children you've seen, the burned bodies, kids with arms missing, kids who've lost their parents, parents who've lost their kids... It's all so... it's just such a mind fuck, you know? How can you live a normal life in a place like this when you've seen that, when you've lived through that, and you know the people you were trying to help are still there, still living through the same terrible shit?'

She laughs, throws a dismissive hand to the side. She's a strong woman. There are no tears coming. Hey, I know how to pick 'em.

'What can you do, Sergeant?' she says. 'What else can you do? You create a compartment in your brain, you put it in there, all the shit you saw and the people you helped and the people you couldn't help, and the things you think you should have done and didn't, you take it all and you put all that fucking shit in a compartment, then you close it and you never, ever open it. Not willingly, at any rate.'

'What happened?' I ask.

A rueful smile, another gesture of helplessness.

'What usually happens. Made the mistake of watching the news. There was a report from Syria. Was sitting at home, doing absolutely fine today, and then... fucko... hit me right in the face. Tony's away in Bishkek for a few days, and I'm sitting there on my own feeling bloody awful.'

She pauses, lifts her glass, takes a long drink. Third of a glass in one. Maybe half. I'm familiar with the need to do that.

'When you stopped by I was kneeling on the floor in tears. Bent double. It was, you know how it gets, like a physical pain. I... looked out when I heard your footsteps retreating. Almost called you back in. But... Anyway, I was feeling bad. Got myself together, thought I'd come by the station. Stuck on *Another Self Portrait*, and here I am. Right as rain!'

She laughs again. I always fall for the ones with a nice laugh. Not, on this occasion, that it's the primary attraction.

'It's nice that you stopped by,' she says.

'I...' I begin, but really, what the fuck am I going to say? *Well, sweetlips, I've been thinking about you all the time.*

'What about you?' she asks. 'You get that, or did you not see too much bad stuff? No,' she adds, shaking her head, 'I recognised it in you the other day. You saw plenty of bad stuff. You probably don't want to talk about it.'

Stare at my green chicken curry. Take a mouthful, dab

at my lips, a sip of wine. Going through the motions of eating dinner.

Well, she's right there. I don't want to talk about it. But if there's anything to kick out the careless and inappropriate thoughts of infatuation from my head, it's to be reminded of that fuck-awful night in a fuck-awful forest in the middle of Bosnia.

'It's not what I saw,' I find myself saying, 'it's what I did.'

Look up, shake my head. Shit, where did that come from?

She leans forward, elbow on the table, a hand running through her hair. Doesn't look at me. Eyes off somewhere, directed at the floor, but looking far off, looking into the past. I know the look.

'We all did things we shouldn't have,' she says.

People have said that to me before, but never like that. Never with such understanding. Where does her understanding come from? What did she do?

Shake my head, stare at the floor. Whatever it was, it's not going to be remotely close to what I did.

Jesus, here we go. Been in a shit-awful state, up and down and all over the damn place, and all that's been without thinking about the past. Haven't needed the past to feel shit, I've just been feeling shit anyway.

Close my eyes, and I'm back there. Looking at that woman. Feeling so desperately inadequate. Listening to the laughter.

'You ever tell anyone about it?' she asks.

I open my eyes. Fuck, I think I might start crying. Well, there's a bag of biscuits, isn't it? Pull yourself the fuck together, man! This is why you hate women. The tears. The emotions. You hate it.

I don't hate women.

God, head's pounding.

'No,' I say, bluntly.

'I can tell,' she says.

She's smiling. Smiling with me. For me. That's a

beautiful smile.

'You have to talk about it some time or else it destroys you.'

'I know.'

'Are you an alcoholic?'

Rueful smile from me, slight shake of the head.

'I... I don't think like that, but then... probably. I don't know.'

'Anything else?'

'You mean drugs and shit?'

She smiles. 'Drugs and shit.'

'Never.' Pause while I think of something else, and then it's there and on out my mouth. 'Sex, according to some.'

'Sex? You're addicted to sex?'

What am I saying?

'I don't know. Maybe, in the way I'm addicted to alcohol. I don't really think about it. Tell me about you. Alcoholic?'

'Possibly.'

'Drugs?'

'Cocaine. When we could get it abroad, and then back here for a while. Kicked it.'

'With God's help?'

'Self control.'

Well, here we are. Talking. Opening up. And suddenly I know what she's going to say, and I know I'm going to tell her. That thing that's hidden away inside.

'Tell me,' she says. 'Don't go into details. Let it pour out. The basics in thirty seconds.'

I put a hand to my mouth, another shake of the head.

'That won't cover it.'

'Give it a go,' she says. Her lips are beautiful. I watch the words come out. She looks at her watch. 'I'll time you, cut you off after thirty seconds. Just do it, soldier.' Another glance at the watch. 'Now.'

I start talking.

'I went out there as a photo-journalist. Bosnia. Wanted to be open-minded, not automatically vilify the Serbs like everyone was doing at home. Got in with a group of Serbian soldiers roaming the forest. They were feral.' Fuck. Taking too long. Too much detail. Just get on with it. Spit it out. SPIT IT OUT! 'They raped a group of women one night. Ordered me to join them. I refused. They said they'd kill one of them if I didn't fuck her. I couldn't get an erection. They killed her. Then they said they'd let the others live if I shot the old guy in the group. I should have shot myself. Or them. I shot the old guy.'

Neither of us checks the watch. I can hear them laughing at me. I can hear the laughter in the forest.

'Jesus, your poor man,' she says.

She leans across and takes my hand.

'I don't think so,' I say.

'The choice between doing something awful or dying is no choice to make. You can't hate yourself for it.'

I squeeze her hand. I almost say, *you weren't there*. What would be the point in saying that? Anyway, there are no words in my mouth. Her hand touches the side of my face.

'God, no wonder you're fucked up,' she says.

I laugh. We stare across the table. A moment. We both know. I might have imagined – if I'd given this any kind of aforethought – that she would have shown herself the door when finding out about me, but she's gone the opposite way. It's what I always say, isn't it? Women love tortured souls in the bodies of tortured men.

We lean towards each other across the table. Our lips meet. The kiss starts slowly, and then suddenly we're standing up, our bodies come together, and the sex starts in a wonderful, headlong, ecstatic, painful rush.

30

We're back at the small table in my sitting room, eating breakfast. She was still here when the alarm went off. I went for a shower, got out and she was in the kitchen. Eggs, mushrooms, toast and coffee, which is pretty much all there was to choose from. I'm not one of those guys who has eight-year-old bacon living in the fridge. Women like that too, if they ever get that close.

Had this brief moment of fear that she was going to kiss me without having cleaned her teeth. Yes, go on, judge me for being unromantic, but this ain't the movies. But, so far, she seems perfect. Gorgeous, understanding, great breasts, likes Bob Dylan. I've honestly never been so in tune with another person in my entire life. It's kind of fucking weird, really. So in tune, in fact, that the infatuation has just vanished, to be replaced by this... fuck, I don't even know how to describe it. I don't want to say comfort, because that might make us sound like Terry and fucking June.

Just feels like we've been sitting here eating breakfast together for the last fifteen years.

'This is weird,' she says. 'I mean...'

Smiling, she stops herself.

'Out with it.'

'It's, like, I don't know, Jane Austen or something. Instant romance.'

Can't help laughing. 'You're right,' I say. 'When you're reading those books you lose count of the amount of people who sleep together in the first few days. You're like, stop it, Jane, stop it with all the fucking...'

She laughs. The laugh turns to a smile and she indicates

Grace Kelly with a nod.

'What's with Grace?' she asks.

Food finished, two cups of half-drunk coffee on the table. 'Not that I'm judging. She was gorgeous.'

I have my back to Grace, but don't turn.

'Used to think… you know, she was perfect. Absolutely perfect. And then, I know, it's a bit sad, being this age and a picture of Grace Kelly on the wall. Had it up when I was a teenager, then it just kind of stuck with me as I moved my stuff from one crappy marriage to the next. Never put it up though. That would have been a bit unfair. That would've been like my wives having a butt-naked, erect picture of John Holmes hanging above the bed. Then I moved in here, on my own, and I had all my stuff, and there was the old picture of Gracie, and I thought, what the hell.'

She's smiling, the slight laughter still on her lips from the John Holmes gag.

'You're going to have to tell me everything,' she says. 'About what happened in Bosnia, I mean. You need to get it all out there.'

Nodding. Suddenly it doesn't seem frightening any more.

'I will. And you?'

'Well, you were right about one thing. I didn't do what you did, and nothing like it. But, of course I will. I think your need is greater than mine, but I'll give you a rough outline, and then I can take my full turn in the confessional after you.'

'When's this?' I ask, although, thank God, there's no unintended trace of neediness in the tone.

'Hmm,' she says. 'Got church business tonight. Bible study group in the halls. Then going to the airport at eight or nine in the morning to collect Tony. Possibly won't make it to church in the morning. So, not sure. He travels quite often, so we might just need to wait until the next time.'

Suddenly, waiting doesn't seem that hard a thing to do.

There's no rush. I've found someone to talk to, and the relief is tangible.

That voice, the voice that ought to be saying, *she's another man's wife!* is silent. The other voice that ought to be shouting at the police officer in me, telling me not to be so involved with someone within the scope of the investigation, is also silent. I've waited so long to find the person to whom I could talk, all other considerations are redundant.

Already I'm imagining that she wouldn't be here in the first place if her marriage wasn't on a shaky peg. I'm imagining the possibility that breakfasts could become a regular occurrence.

'Hopefully by then, this dreadful business at the church will be behind us,' she says.

I give a slight raise of the eyebrows in response, and look at my watch.

'Talking of which. Sorry, got to go. You all right to let yourself out? The door'll lock behind you.'

'Of course.'

Stand up and walk over to look out the window at the morning. She sits in her seat at the table and watches me. We don't speak. I turn, give her a brief kiss on the lips. We smile. I go to the door, grab my jacket and leave. I glance back at her as the door closes.

One last glimpse.

31

Back up at the graveyard by the Old Kirk. We've got a guy on watch so that no one can come and dig up the stiff.

One guy. Eight-hour shift. One of those things, isn't it? We have to do it at the moment; it's such a contentious issue. And Connor's in no doubt that we have to be seen to try to keep order, at least. We can't sit back while cadavers are used as pawns. Have to be neutral, although, of course, that's impossible, and we're now seen as protecting the interests of the little faction that buried Maureen's corpse in the first place.

However, it would be massive overkill to post more than one guy on it. I mean, how many spare police officers do you suppose we have for this kind of shit? I can tell you, if Connor hadn't been so concerned about his place in the church community, it would have been a big, fat none. Two, however, is still too many. So there's one poor sod there, standing in a graveyard for eight hours at a time. And what's he supposed to do if someone sneaks up on him through the darkness? How much chance will he have?

The first night, at least, passed uneventfully. I'm not going to be on duty, of course, just came to talk to Mary Buttler. She's in the church when I arrive. Stop off on my way down the path to speak to young Wallace, who'd been on the church gate the previous afternoon.

It's a cold day, bright, but high, grey clouds covering the morning sky.

'Stevie,' I say, walking past graves. Sgt Harrison told me his name, so now I sound like I'm in touch with the young constables around the place, when in fact I can barely tell one from the other.

'Sir.'

'Anything happening?'

'Nothing to report, sir.'

Check my watch. 'You've got another four hours?'

'About that, sir.'

'Do you get a break?'

He thinks about his answer, and what he's going to admit to, then says, 'Nip to the toilet, that's about it.'

Look around. There's a nice light to the morning.

'You want to go and grab a cup of coffee?'

'Sir?'

'I'll cover for you. Nip off for fifteen minutes. Toilet break. Get a drink.'

He's looking at me with slight suspicion. He's relatively new, but I doubt he's had a positive thought about me since he got here. Most of the others at the station probably think of me as 'that dick'.

'Are you sure?'

'Course. I'll be here when you get back.'

He nods.

'Thanks, sir.'

And off he goes. Watch him for a few moments, and then turn away. Look around at the gravestones in this nice light. Hands in pockets, and then decide it'd be all right, while on graveyard duty, to have a fag.

Light up, deep draw, turn and look as the sound of an approaching train starts to spill into the quiet morning.

The train accelerates on its way from Kirkhill station. I watch the tops of the carriages through the bare branches of trees as it disappears into the tunnel that runs beneath this end of the town. The sound is replaced by a low rumble that gradually disappears.

I turn at the sound of footsteps on the grass behind me. Mary Buttler, the keys to the church clinking softly in her hands.

'Good morning, Sergeant,' she says.

'Mrs Buttler.'

'They've got you on graveyard duty?' she asks, smiling. 'I thought it'd be considered the work of barely post-pubescent constables.'

'Just giving the kid a break.'

She nods, seems to take a closer look at my eyes. Moderately disconcerting, so I give her an eyebrow.

'I was going to ask if you were just up here again to sit in silence in the kirk, but that's not it, is it? There's something different about you today.'

'I don't think so.'

She nods. 'Oh, it's quite apparent, Sergeant. There's a weight been lifted.'

'Doesn't feel like I'm smiling,' I say, a little annoyance entering my voice, although admittedly it's only because she's seen right through me.

'You're not. It's deeper than that. It's nice to see.'

Nothing to say.

'So, what can I do for you?'

I look over at the small row of shops on the other side of the far road, the direction in which Wallace wandered off. No sign of him. There's no rush anyway. I may as well speak to Mrs Buttler here as anywhere.

'Wanted to talk some more about the burial. When did you think of it, who did you speak to, did you speak to anyone who hated the idea and thought you shouldn't do it? That kind of thing. If you hadn't thought of it, do you think someone else would've done?'

'That's a lot of questions,' she says, smiling. I join her.

God, she's right, isn't she? I'm not suddenly a grinning goofball, but there's no doubt the weight's been lifted. And it's not what I said, or what happened last night, it's the fact that I've got something to look forward to. Weird how the fact that Philo is married continues to impart not so much as a dent in my anticipation.

'Take me back to the start,' I say.

She went over this stuff with Taylor and one of the constables yesterday, but I thought I'd get her on her own, and with a bit of distance maybe she'd open up a little more. From the look on her face, she's well aware what I'm thinking.

'I was having tea with the Rev Forsyth a couple of days ago.'

'The former minister.'

'Yes.'

'He retired…?'

'He was minister here for around twenty years. Retired in '91. A very quiet man. Kept himself to himself, you know. I always thought there was an air of sadness about him. A bit like yourself.'

'Moving on…'

'When he retired he did some locum work around the place, but in the end he settled down here, and enough time had passed that everyone seemed happy when he came back and started coming to the church every week as a parishioner. He never got involved in the politics, though.'

'Not even after the merger was talked about?'

'He stayed well clear, although enough of us asked.'

'So what happened yesterday?'

She pauses, perhaps wondering if she's stumbling into talking too much. But then, perhaps that's just my natural suspicious police instinct. I don't think she has anything to hide.

'We were having tea on Wednesday.'

'Just the two of you?'

'Oh no, it was at our place. Wullie was there. Wullie and Compo are great pals. They could spend most of their lives talking about the bloody Rangers.'

'Compo?'

'The minister. Rev Forsyth. First name is Compton, and I'm rather afraid we all know him as Compo. I think he quite likes it.'

Compton's not a first name. It just isn't. Expect, despite what she says, most people actually call him Reverend Forsyth anyway; like Reverend Green, Reverend Moon and Reverend Spooner.

'Let's stick to Rev Forsyth for now.'

'Of course. He came to tea. They talked about football for God knows how long, then I managed to get the conversation on to the church at last. Wullie, of course, isn't interested, so he went off to wash the dishes and put the kettle on. There's a rumour going around, and it's just common sense really, we talked about it, that sooner or later they're going to have to sell our building. They don't need it, so why spend the money? Yes, they need the halls, but does it not make sense that they sell the church and the halls, and use the money to try to acquire something down there that they can use? The very idea sticks in my throat, but you can't argue that it's common sense.'

'So was it you or him who had the idea of burying someone?'

'Oh, good Lord, it was me.'

'You're sure? It wasn't that he put the idea in your head and made you think it was your idea?'

She looks me up and down, genuinely up and down, then shakes her head.

'I thought we had an understanding, Sergeant. Are you saying I'm just a woman whose easily pliable mind is ripe for manipulation by a man? Any man?'

Sigh, make a small hand gesture to indicate she should keep talking. It's a fair cop.

'No,' she continues, 'I had the idea a long time ago. A long time ago. Possibly the same day that talks of this ridiculous merger were first mentioned.'

'So you put this to Reverend Forsyth?'

'Yes.'

'What did he say?'

'Oh, he loved it. Thought it was a wonderful idea. He'd stayed out of the politics, but he couldn't bear to think of anything happening to this place. Imagine if it was turned into flats. Good grief.'

Over the church wall, I can see Wallace walking slowly back. Food in one hand, a cup of coffee in the other. I'm not done yet, and it's not been fifteen minutes. He sits on a bench as I watch, and I know I'll have another few minutes with Mrs Buttler before her flow is interrupted.

32

The guy lives in a small council house on the other side of the East Kilbride road. I decide to walk. Only takes about twenty minutes, and if I'm shouted for while I'm there, I can grab a taxi to get back if needs be. Along the top road, a couple of streets up from where Philo Stewart lives, past more of the same large old Victorian homes.

I've stopped thinking about her. Weird that. The infatuation bubble has been punctured, but not by despair or reality. Not that infatuation is ever punctured by despair. Infatuation is despair's sister in insanity. This, though, I don't remember ever feeling before. Infatuation has been replaced by serenity. Or some shit like that. I don't need to think about her all the time, because I know I'm going to be seeing her, and it's going to be fine.

I've found her, the one person I needed to find.

Weird, like I said.

Up by the new version of my old school, and then past the houses that replaced the place where I suffered through High School in the early '80s.

I stop as I come alongside the new blocks of flats and look back down the hill. A good view from here, over the top of the town, Glasgow sweeping away, the hills in the distance.

I notice a young girl playing in the trees down below, the other side of the path from the school. She's quite far away, but I know who it is. Running in amongst trees, running her hand across the long, dying grass. She doesn't look in this direction.

For the first time today I get the familiar feeling of unease, and suddenly I realise how genuinely awful I normally feel. On any given day, no matter what's happening, this is how I feel. Like there's something wrong.

I didn't see the girl last night. That feels unusual too. I hadn't been thinking about it, but now that I do, now that it's forced upon me, it does feel like she's there most nights. Prodding me. Trying to get me to do... something. I don't know what. Even that night, two nights ago, when I lay in bed with Mrs Christie's daughter, the doctor. Didn't I get up in the middle of the night and stand at the window? Wasn't the girl looking down at the road?

But not last night. Last night was fine. Last night I had Philo in my arms, and there was no strange visitor to drag me from my sleep. Or to enter my sleep.

Yet, now she's back. Why?

I turn away from the hill, and walk on up the road, the weight that usually drags me down suddenly having reappeared.

I find the ex-minister sweeping leaves in a small courtyard. He's in his mid-80s, I guess. Bit of a hump, exacerbated by being bent over a broom.

'Reverend Forsyth?' I say, standing on the other side of the gate.

He looks round a second and then he straightens up, his face breaking into a smile.

'Ah, you're one of the police officers from yesterday. Come to take me away, have you?'

'Just wanted to ask you a few questions.'

'Aye, well you'd better come in and have a cup of tea. If we stand out here the neighbours'll be all over us like a rash.'

He lays the broom against the wall, and I follow him inside.

*

'There you are, Chief Inspector,' he says, handing over a cup of tea, a bourbon biscuit placed on the saucer on the other side from the spoon. 'Sugar?'

'No thanks. And it'd be Detective Sergeant.'

'Ach, I'm sure you'll be Chief Inspector soon enough, son.'

That strangely doesn't seem as ridiculous today as it usually would, but let's not get carried away. If they were to make a league table of every detective sergeant in Scotland and their likelihood of promotion, I'd be dead last.

He settles down into the armchair on the other side of the rug. A regular sitting room, small, overcrowded with stuff. Ornaments and photographs everywhere, pictures on the walls and a couple of mirrors. It's an explosion of frippery, and it would drive me nuts to live here. Must be a nightmare to dust. And a quick glance at the side table next to me indicates that that's a problem he gets over by rarely dusting in the first place.

'So, if you're not here to arrest me, son, what can I do for you?'

'Just getting background,' I say. 'Every little piece of information helps.'

'Of course.'

'So, was wondering if you could talk me through the process of how you came to preside over a burial in a disused graveyard yesterday afternoon.'

He laughs lightly before slurping loudly at his tea.

And then he proceeds to talk at me, and talk, during the course of which he tells exactly the same story of how he and Mary Buttler arrived at the decision to plant Maureen's body in the ground, and how they approached her daughter and how they approached the undertakers.

Every now and again I try to ask a question, or to interrupt him, or to hurry him along, but he tells his story at a pedestrian pace, in complete control of the conversation. At some point it makes me think of driving round the Grand Prix track at Monte Carlo behind a slower driver who bosses the road and won't let you by.

The heating is up too high and I begin to feel tired. He

talks on, his voice low and steady, and I wonder how hard that must have been for the congregation on a Sunday morning. Worried that I'm going to doze off, or at least quite openly display my tiredness, I stand up and take a small pace or two – it's a small room – while he talks.

I stay awake. The Reverend Forsyth keeps talking. Eventually he pauses to slurp at his tea again and I take my opportunity. I ask one more question, and then I leave.

The air outside is fresh and cool, and I turn right out his front gate and start walking quickly back to the station.

*

Walk in, the place is the usual mid-afternoon bustle. Notice that Taylor's door is open. Morrow is in there with him. I stop for a second, take a look around, then go to my desk. Mountains of paperwork stare back at me. So much for computer systems.

From nowhere one of those little squeezy stress balls hits me on the forehead and bounces onto the floor. I look up sharply, but it's pretty obvious where it came from. Nice aim from Taylor, past Morrow, through the door and across the office, managing not to take out anyone else on the way.

Lucky for him that I'm in such a chipper mood.

Pick the ball up and toss it back into Taylor's hands as I approach the office. Stand in the doorway, eyebrows raised in expectation at what exciting new development could have had Taylor firing missiles across the room.

'Door,' says Taylor.

I guess he wants me to close the door, and isn't just randomly naming parts of the room. I close the door. Taylor nods at Morrow as he's obviously the one with the news.

'Our tech guys came up with the goods. The e-mail address was used to contact four other addresses. I have the names here, but again, they're all going to be cover names. What they managed to come up with, and man, I just love this shit—'

'Enough commentary,' says Taylor.

Morrow hesitates, then with a small shake of the head, continues.

'They've identified the locations from which these four e-mail addresses were operated. Three of them were used purely through home Wi-Fi systems. The one that wasn't, was used at the internet café we know Mrs Henderson to have frequented.'

'So, it was some sort of granny porn ring?'

He waves a finger.

'The three Wi-Fis are all at the homes of people related to the church. The first one, no surprise, is Agnes Christie. So, our three vics were all secretly e-mailing each other—'

'Did you just say vic?' says Taylor. 'As in short for victim?'

Morrow glances at him, then at me, as though I might give him some support.

'You have to stop watching American TV, Constable.'

'Yes, sir.'

'That's an order. Now, go on.'

Another hesitation. Taylor ain't in a great mood and Morrow is struggling.

'Constable,' I say, giving him a nudge.

'Yes. So, the next is from a home of a couple who, I think, are at the other church. St Stephen's. The guy is Mr Tony Stewart. You met him?'

Breath catches in my throat. One of those moments. An instant in time. It stops. Just for a second. The second extends, confusingly, and time and thoughts just become a jumble where nothing makes sense, and then with a great rush, like shooting to the surface of a deep loch, the cacophony of everything coming together, your breath is in your lungs and you're spewed back out into the present time.

'Yeah. No, not him, I met his wife. Spoken to her a couple of times, just saw the guy at church. Didn't speak to him.'

What was it that happened earlier? There was something that happened before I went to speak to the old vicar that took away the good feeling of the night before. I can't remember what it was. But I'd been fighting it. Fighting off the encroachment of anxiety. Of fear. And now there's to be no fighting it off. The fear comes barrelling in, an express train of instant torment.

'And then we've got, and this is the beauty, a Wi-Fi used at the address of Paul Cartwright.'

Still not thinking straight. That certainly doesn't make any sense.

'What?'

Morrow shrugs. I look at Taylor.

'Quite,' he says.

'Did you get access to what they'd been saying to each other? I mean, is it possible they were all into granny porn?'

What? My brain is like this tangled ball of yarn, strands of thought all wound together, impossible to tell one from the other.

'I'd say, definitely not granny porn,' says Morrow. 'There was very little substance in the e-mails. They were mostly discussing when and where to meet. It seems, however, that Cartwright – or someone at his address, or someone close by feeding off his Wi-Fi – was orchestrating it, meeting people one by one. There were some general instructions, but it's quite possible that the people in the group weren't aware of who everyone else was.'

'Why would the guy who was in charge of excluding the Old Kirk and Halfway, while making sure that St Mungo's won the merger building war, be in league with, well, at least a couple of his main opponents?' Trying to be coherent. 'Unless it wasn't him.'

'Possible,' says Taylor. 'We need to find out about his wife, any grown-up children that still live at home. And given that we've got the seventeen-year-old kid in this happy band, they don't have to be that grown up. What d'you know about this other couple? Which one of them is more likely to be part of this thing?'

Confusion edges its way back in. I really don't know. What do I know about Philo Stewart anyway, beyond the basics? She's told me little, and while I'm looking forward to finding out, all we've really settled on so far in the relationship, is that I'm the one going to be doing the talking.

And I know nothing of her husband.

'No idea,' I say. 'Need to speak to them again.'

'Right, you and I are going round there now. You know where they live?'

Nod. Almost blurt out that the husband is still in Bishkek. I mean, really. I want to sound like I know what I'm talking about, like I have information. That's what being a police officer's all about, isn't it? Information. However, I see sense, keep my information to myself.

'Let's go. Morrow,' says Taylor, 'make some enquiries about Mr Cartwright's family. Don't speak to him yet.'

*

I'm nervous going to Philo Stewart's house. Barely pay attention to the football on the radio. Thistle getting slaughtered 4-0. Doesn't seem to matter. Relieved when we approach and there are no lights on. Getting dark. She's not at home.

We stand on the doorstep ringing the bell, where I stood the previous afternoon. Another life ago. That other life which is threatening to come back, whatever happens. It could be that someone is killing all the people on that list, or that one of them is the killer. So far, however, I've been treating Philo Stewart as someone on the periphery of the investigation, someone with whom it was almost conscionable to have sex. (The married thing notwithstanding.) Now, however, she's been plunged bang, smack into the middle of it.

'Saturday afternoon,' says Taylor. 'Could be they have a

life.'

I'm looking down over the town, and on to the hills beyond. The lights are coming on as dusk encroaches. Don't reply.

Taylor knocks this time, but he knows there's no one there.

'Any idea where we can find them?'

Check my watch.

'She does Bible study group on a Saturday evening. Not sure where, but I expect we can find out from someone at the church.'

'Right, come on. We need to find these people as quickly as possible. If this list goes beyond coincidence, then either they're involved or their lives are in danger.'

He stops on the stairs and looks at the houses on either side of this one. 'We need to check out the surrounding area, see if there's anyone else from around here goes to the church. Might be piggybacking onto their router.'

He glances at me. I say nothing. He walks down the steps and gets into his car. For a moment I stand and watch the dusk. Night is coming, after such a short day.

33

And there it goes. Fought off the advance of darkness as long as possible – largely through wilful blindness – but now the darkness has won, and the feeling I had earlier is gone.

What would you call it? Contentment? Serenity? Happiness?

Serenity. That's the one. Everything seemed all right. Or seemed that it was going to be all right. It felt so all right that I didn't even see the warning signs. I didn't even stop to think, hang on a minute there, Buck Rogers, don't you be getting carried away with yourself. The minute you think everything's going to be fine, then fucko, Bucko, you're screwed.

Didn't think that. Everything seemed fine. The problems that were bound to arise seemed distant. Wasn't going to have to worry about them for some time yet.

Sex addiction? Alcoholism? Really? They both just vanished. For a few short hours, I was addicted to nothing. I knew I wasn't drinking tonight. No reason to. I knew the casual sex was gone. Just like that. I was waiting for Mrs Philo Stewart and the length of the wait wasn't an issue. Six days. Six weeks. Six months. Didn't matter.

There was a light, that was all. She was a light. That was all I needed. Someone who was going to understand me.

Fuck. Back to normal. Can't think thoughts like that without self-loathing cascading in like a putrid, fucking chemical waste spill.

Who the fuck was I kidding?

It's not that far a walk from the station down along

Main Street to the halls behind St Stephen's where they hold the Bible study group, but the rain is teeming down. Taylor is driving, Bob's on the CD player. Oh Mercy. *What Good Am I?* Ha! How appropriate is that? Jesus, they're all appropriate on that album. Every fucking song, every song wrapped in darkness, ripping through my fucking head.

Jesus. The drive's only two minutes. We won't even get as far as *Disease of Conceit*, although just the thought of it starts it off in my head, like a knife slamming through my brain, jabbing into my head, slashing and stabbing. *How dare you think everything was going to be all right, you fucking bell-end?*

There's still that little glimmer, the voice that says, *Hey, Sergeant, chill out, dude.* (Yeah, the little voice that doesn't exist is as American as Morrow.) *Relax, man. You know her. You know she's got nothing to do with this. In all likelihood this is either someone next door using her router, or it'll be her husband, and in that case the guy is either going to get murdered, or you guys'll get him for murder, and then she's all yours.*

Along Main Street, the rain hammering down. Going to get soaked walking from the car to the hall, even if we manage to park five yards away. A few cars dotted around when we arrive. We park about fifteen yards away. Taylor cuts the engine, doesn't immediately get out. Watches the rain.

'Guess we're about to get the answer to one of modern life's great mysteries,' he says.

Slowly pulled from the pit, I turn and look.

'What kind of person goes to Bible study group?'

He says it grimly, but it was supposed to get a reaction. I just stare at him. Can feel myself shutting down. I know how it works. I need to withdraw, retreat to the crappy equilibrium that counts for ordinary in my head, and then normal service can be resumed.

'Having a bad day?' he says.

Shouldn't let them notice.

'Sorry, just distracted,' I say, finally engaging. 'Come on, let's go and meet the freaks.'

I know she's not going to be here. I can feel her lack of presence.

I get out of the car, step into the deluge. Stop for a moment, feeling the full force of the downpour, and then follow Taylor as he runs to the doorway.

'Fuck,' he mutters as he stands in the small awning, opening the door. We both shake ourselves like dogs, and then walk inside. Immediate warmth. A small entrance hall.

Voices from behind a closed door straight ahead. Taylor gives himself another shake then steps forward, opens the door and we walk in, dripping water as we go.

There are seven people sitting in chairs in a small circle. We enter as one woman is saying, '…but you can't get the eggs…'

She stops talking. They all turn. Around the seven of them we get a range of looks from disappointment to curiosity to annoyance.

'We're looking for Mrs Stewart,' I say.

'Who are you?' says a middle-aged guy, getting to his feet. The words *the fuck* are missing from the middle of the sentence, but he nailed the tone.

I just think, *fuck you, dickhead*, but don't say anything. I've said my few words, and now Taylor can take over, as usual.

'DCI Taylor, DS Hutton,' says Taylor, stepping past me, ID in hand. 'This is the study group that Mrs Stewart runs?'

There are a couple of nods. The guy stands there for a moment or two, no doubt wondering whether he should call a lawyer, or maybe the bastard is a lawyer and is wondering how far to try to push us, so that he's got more to go on when he takes us to court for having the utter balls to barge soaking wet into the middle of their precious Bible study group.

Coppers Disrupt Bible Study In New Outrage! God

Eventually he lowers himself into his seat, but you can see he's doing it in a way that implies he's doing us a favour by giving us the floor.

'We're still waiting for her,' says one of the middle-aged women in the middle. The one in a blue cardigan.

'What time is she supposed to be here?'

Three of them check their watches.

'Forty-five minutes ago.'

Taylor looks around the room, contemptuously almost, as though it's the fault of these people that she's not here.

'Have any of you heard from her? Did you expect her not to be here?'

A few head shakes. No one says anything.

'Bollocks,' mutters Taylor, which will probably offend a few of this brigade, but none of them are speaking. They are all, it would appear, rightly intimidated by having the fuzz barge in on them.

'Is anything the matter?' asks one of the women.

'We can give you her phone number, although we've tried it and there's no answer,' says another.

'Tony, her husband, he usually comes too, but he's away this week. Travelling.'

'Where?' asks Taylor.

A few blank faces. Keep my mouth shut. Finally the only other bloke there says, 'Bishkek,' without looking at us.

Taylor looks around the small, reluctant collective.

'We do need to find Mrs Stewart. Does anyone have any other information that could help us?'

Blank Faces 'R' Us. Taylor gives them a few seconds, then nods a grudging acknowledgement, turns and leaves. I don't look at them, but feel their eyes on my back as I leave too. Close the door behind us, stand briefly in the small entrance hall looking out at the rain.

'Bishkek?' says Taylor eventually. 'Is that a real place?'

'Kyrgyzstan,' I say.

He looks at me in that way of his, the one that seems

surprised that I might actually know something other than how many times Bob's sung *Workingman's Blues* in concert.

'Huh,' he says. 'Come on. We better go back to their house, and if there's no one in...'

He clicks the car door open from the hall, takes a moment, and then opens the door on the deluge.

*

Standing on the doorstep, the house still in darkness. Lights on the houses all around. A regular November evening. Not raining up here, on the other side of town. Taylor's rung the doorbell twice, but we know there's no one there. Or if there is... well, trying not to think about that. Trying to keep my head empty. Not clear and focussed, there's so little chance of that. Just empty. If I could shut the thing down entirely, then I would.

That will be for later. And not much later. Already nearly eight. Go home. Get drunk. Fall asleep.

Taylor glances over his shoulder, looks up and down the street. No one around.

'Look, we'll go round the back,' he says. 'Don't want to get anyone around here peeing in their pants.'

And back doors are always easier to open.

Round the side of the house, no gate. There's a modern conservatory, but next to it is the old wooden door, old-fashioned window split into small frames beside it. It's overlooked by the house next door, but there are no lights on in any of the windows. We should be able to go about our business without anyone calling the police on us.

'Sergeant,' he says.

I don't even give him the usual eye-rolling routine. Pick up a small stone from the edge of the garden. If there's no key in the lock, then this is a waste of time, but people are careless. Better to try this first than put your shoulder out senselessly banging into solid wood.

I stand waiting for a moment, and then as a car goes

past the road at the front of the house, I quickly knock the glass and the small window breaks. Smooth out the edges as well as I can, hand through, fumble about at the lock at the back of the door, fingers on the key, and we're in.

Push open the door. It goes an inch and then jars against the chain that's been placed across it.

'Fuck.'

'That's what your shoulder's for,' says Taylor.

Half a minute later we're walking to the kitchen from the small vestibule at the rear of the house. Lights on. Look around the kitchen. An empty coffee mug beside the sink, the cafetière over by the kettle. Lots of gadgets, lots of utensils in modern, chic colours. Doesn't smell like anything's been cooked in here recently. Of course, she ate takeaway Thai last night.

Neither of us bothers shouting. Why are we here, after all? The husband is abroad, probably on a plane by now. The wife? She's not where she's supposed to be. She's not answering her phone, she's not answering her door. Either she's taken to bed because she's ill – although even then, presumably, she would have called someone from the Bible study group to let them know – or there's the other thing.

The other thing is what we're not talking about.

'Tell me about the fourth beast,' says Taylor.

He walks out into the hall, turns on the light.

'What?'

'We've had the wings and the ribs in the mouth, and the more wings, albeit that was a botch-job... What was the principal feature of the fourth beast?'

Stairs on our left, two doors on the right. He opens the first one, turns the light on. We look in. The dining room. Very elegantly furnished, minimalist, but not bare. A dining table with space for six. Modern art on the wall.

I think about the fourth beast. The very thought of it, of what we might find, has my stomach careering up into my mouth.

God, stop it. It's not that. It won't be that! She's not

dead, for God's sake. There are all sorts of reasons why someone doesn't answer their phone. There are all sorts of reasons why people fall off the grid for a few hours. They don't need to have been murdered for it to happen. They don't need to have been turned into the fourth beast...

I don't answer. Can't talk. He glances at me, shakes his head at my silence, and then opens the door to the front sitting room, turning on the light. The room where I spoke to Philo Stewart for the second time. The room where we laughed over flapjacks.

She's sitting on the same sofa in the same position as when I spoke to her in here previously. Resting back, her body upright. As we walk in we're slightly behind her, but there's no question of her being alive, no question that she's fallen asleep, no chance that we can assume everything's all right.

What's been done to her is obvious from the second we enter.

34

What was it I was thinking when I slept with Philo Stewart last night? That it was a little bit wrong, because I was getting involved with someone on the periphery of the investigation. The periphery, Sergeant? This is what you call the periphery? That is some tight-ass, incredibly focussed investigation, if that's the periphery.

1.15 a.m. Standing with Taylor and Balingol over the cadaver. She's naked. The ten small spikes banged into her head to mimic the ten horns of the fourth beast, have been removed. Her hair is a tangled mat of blood. There are no other noticeable wounds or injuries.

I feel sick. I want to run away, go back to my place and drink vodka from the bottle. I want to be bent over the toilet, puking up. I want to puke up everything. The vodka, what's left of the breakfast she made me eighteen hours ago, I want to puke up my feelings and the self-hatred and the guilt and the fear. I want to vomit and go on vomiting until every part of me is in the toilet and can be flushed away.

'Same dose of sleeping tablets used to sedate her and then, well, impossible to tell, but it could have been the first spike hammered into her head that killed her. Who knows? Pretty sure it wouldn't have been the tenth. Somewhere in between.'

'No attempt to fake suicide this time,' said Taylor.

'Obviously not.'

'Could be that the killer knew the game was up after they were interrupted the last time.'

'Not for me to say,' says Balingol.

Taylor turns to me.

'You're the Daniel expert. Any thoughts?'

I don't look at him. Still staring at the pale, cold face on the slab.

'Maybe you're right,' I manage to say, every word a struggle. 'It could be his original intention was to fake suicide and place some sort of headgear on her, something to indicate ten horns. Then when he was rumbled before, he just thought... this,' and I indicate the matted hair and the dried-in blood.

'Anything else?'

'She'd had sex in the last twenty-four hours,' says Balingol. 'Seems that everyone I see on this damned slab has had sex in the last twenty-four hours. There's all this bloody sex going on... if I ever end up on this damned slab, the pathologist is going to think I'm a virgin, it's been so long.'

Taylor gives him a glance – no one wants to think about Balingol's sex life – and then turns to me.

'Interesting. The husband's away, and she gets to play. Any ideas?'

I don't need to worry about my face giving anything away. I'd already known. Balingol never fails to find out when someone's been having sex. There was no shock when that was mentioned, no, 'holy fuck, man, I've been exposed.'

He's already said that time of death was around midday, an hour either side. That means I had sex with someone the night before they died, and breakfast with them about five hours before they were killed.

I need to tell Taylor. I should have told him already. There's not a good time to do it. There's not going to be a moment when it will be all right, no moment when Taylor will say, 'Gee, thanks, Sergeant, that's valuable information that we can feed into the investigation going forward.'

I just need to get it out there, but I know what's going to happen. My jacket's been on shaky enough a peg for some time now, one shitstorm of hopelessness after another, on and on, with me completely incapable of getting off the rollercoaster.

Rollercoaster? Seriously? Rollercoasters also go up. Where's the up been with me for the last three years? The last twenty years?

I need to tell him. Not in front of Balingol, but as soon as we walk out the room.

Shake my head.

'We just talked about the church,' I say.

'What was her angle?'

'That it was like Syria.'

Balingol barks out a laugh.

'She wasn't far fucking wrong, was she?' says Taylor.

Fuck. As soon as we get out the door.

'Any clues to the age of the guy?'

'Not yet. I'll let you know in the morning.'

Taylor nods, taps Balingol on the shoulder.

'Thanks, Bill.

Balingol grunts. Taylor turns away and I follow.

This is it. Career down the toilet. You know, sure, I didn't have anything to do with it. I didn't kill her. I wasn't to fucking know, was I? But I couldn't just fucking wait, could I? And coming on top of everything else that I've been piling up for the last year.

Jesus.

The door opens. Connor. Looking like I feel. Oh, the poor bastard. Must have so many of his friends upset at him.

'Dan,' he says.

'Just heading back to the station,' says Taylor.

'Stay and talk me through it,' says Connor.

'Of course.'

We turn back. My spirits have slumped so far into the pit, that the presence of Superintendent Connor makes no difference to them. They couldn't go any lower anyway.

'Go home, Tom,' says Taylor.

'No, it's OK. I'll speak to you after.'

Taylor looks at his watch.

'We're going to be a while,' says Connor. 'Go home, Sergeant. It's an order. You look terrible.'

35

Me and Grace Kelly. One of us dead, one of us might as well be.

What's it going to be? Tomorrow morning, I get in there and I tell Taylor that I fucked the murder victim. That I was in love with the murder victim. Do I tell him that?

I thought I might come home and tip the vodka down my throat, straight from the bottle. Glug vodka until I threw up and passed out. Instead I got home, feeling unbelievably tired, but agitated with it, so that I knew there was no point in falling into bed. Opened the vodka, got a glass, got some ice, got the tonic, got a bag of crisps. Poured a large one. Drank it while I was still standing in the kitchen. Poured another, went through to the sitting room, slumped into my usual seat in front of the TV. Didn't turn the TV on.

An hour later. Still sitting here. The ice has long since melted, the vodka and the tonic have flowed in and then back out the glass. The crisps are long gone. That was dinner. Crisps and vodka. Bob playing on the CD player. *Oh Mercy* on a loop. All those slow songs dredged in warm, sticky mud. Sucking me in, drawing me down to their level.

The small red light is flashing on the phone. There's a message, but I don't want to hear it. I don't want to listen to the sound of anyone's voice. No voices, no conversation. Just the sound of Bob crawling through my veins.

So, what now, Slim? Ready for bed yet?

I don't think so. I don't want to go to bed. If I lie there, I'll be lying where she was. The bed might still smell of her. And she's dead.

Drain the glass. Bitterness washes through me.

Is that what we want, the tragic poets of the world like me?

Did you just call yourself a tragic poet?

Hopeless, doomed love. So much better than that other thing, where you get to move in with the person you fall for, and everything goes smoothly, so that eventually, with nothing in the way, it grows stale and old and tired.

I can see her smiling at me from that table. Just over there. The table just behind me. Maybe if I look round, she'll be there now. Perhaps I can imagine her there forever. Sitting at that table as I looked over my shoulder on the way out the door. What was the last thing she said?

Of course.

That was it. Her final words to me. Of course. Hardly eternally romantic. Doesn't matter. The thought of her, the sound of her voice, her body beneath mine, the smile across the breakfast table, it's all there and the wave of grief floods over me, breaking down the walls and I bend double, face crumpled, and Bob's singing *Most Of The Time*, and oh fuck, he wasn't singing about someone who was dead, but he might as well have been, and I can see her and feel her and touch her and her body is next to mine, and that agonising, tortuous pain that comes with grief, the one that makes you think you can't possibly bear to be alive for even another fucking second, the one that fills your head and rips out your heart and tears you to bits and spits in your face and crushes you, it fucking crushes you, consumes you, pummels you so badly that you can barely breathe, that pain is squeezing me, crushing me into a tiny, helpless black ball, one that is nothing but pain, and I can't think of the next morning, or the next minute, and I fall forward off the chair onto my knees, lift the bottle and now I'm tipping the fucking thing into my mouth, pouring it so that it's glugging out, as much dripping down my face as is getting in my mouth, come on you fucking piece-of-fucking-shit drink, take it away, take away the fucking pain.

Please.

Please, take it away. That's all I want. I had someone to take away the pain and now she's gone.

You can do the job. Come on vodka, you fucking piece of shit, come on!

I know. I know, it's not the vodka that's the piece of shit.

Finished. Throw it at the TV screen. It misses, hits the wall. Breaks.

Fall forward, tears flowing, great retches.

Bent double, knees at my face, lying on my side.

Take me away.

*

'You need to get up.'

Cold. Have been shivering for some time, but haven't been able to move. Too tired. Feel terrible. Arms around my knees. How long have I been like this? It's still dark. Did I set an alarm? Of course not. I need to set an alarm. I should have set an alarm. I feel sick. That's why I'm not moving. I feel sick. When I move, I'm going to throw up.

'You need to get up.'

What?

Who said that?

The girl's voice. The young girl. Who is she? Why does she keep showing up? She wasn't there the night I spent with Philo Stewart.

Philo Stewart.

'You need to get up. Get up now. Please.'

Sharply drawn breath.

I sit up quickly. Look around the room. There's no one here. Street lights still on, no sign of the dawn.

Fuck, here comes the sick.

Bathroom.

36

The night before was one of those that could have led to me having a day off, but I couldn't afford that. Knew it as soon as I was awake. Knew it as I was leaning over the toilet, throwing up everything that had ever been in my stomach.

Didn't even check my watch, just knew that I had to get up and get on with the day. Drank two large glasses of water. Walked through to the kitchen, made myself some toast. Ate the toast. Back to the bathroom, threw up the toast and the water.

Showered, for half an hour. Began to feel better. The vomiting was over. Shaved, got dressed. Shirt and tie. Made myself some coffee and ate a bowl of granola. More water. Cleaned my teeth, gargled with mouthwash for a minute and a half. Hoped the stench of 1 a.m. vodka was gone.

Now walking into work. 8.15 a.m. Sunday morning, the streets are quiet. The utter desolation of the night before has gone. The sorrow has been washed away by the morning. The walls are back up. I don't know what's going to happen, but I need to tell Taylor. Get it out there. I suspect it's going to be a very short day on the job. He just can't leave me on the case when I slept with one of the victims. That's the kind of thing that the papers say causes outrage.

Outrage As Randy Copper Fucks Victim! they'd cry, without actually being able to specify who exactly is outraged by it.

Along Main Street, with its pound shops and charity shops and boarded-up windows. I always think of

Springsteen as I walk along here. Not Bob. Just the Boss, with his songs of urban decay. Same thing this morning.

Nod at some old guy I helped out once, and who I often see on Main Street. He nods back. He doesn't wince at my appearance, thank God, so there's that. After a night like last night, the following day could be so fucking awful. Head in the right place for this, head in the right place.

Taylor worked late, so hope I get in before him. I want to be waiting for him, get him alone in his office. He won't get mad. He doesn't get mad about this. He'll think about it. He'll tell me to go home. But I'm not going home. I don't know where I'm going, but not home. Not today.

Home is the last place I saw her. Home is where the sheets will still smell of her, where a red light flashes relentlessly at me on the phone, with some message from Peggy or my mum with news of a dead relative or God knows what. I don't want to think about home. I don't want to think about anything.

Maybe I'll just go away somewhere completely different. That might be what I need. Up north. See some snow. Taste some different air.

Up the hill, into the office. Collins is on duty. I nod, he nods back. Again, nothing exceptional. I've pulled it together. There are practically commentators in my head, as though they're describing my comeback to the football pitch from a bad injury, or drug rehab.

Into the office. Morrow not in yet. Well, that's good. The Detective Constable has been looking better than me for the better part of two years now. I need to take these minor triumphs when they come.

Change of shift, the office slightly busier than normal as people come just before people go. Stand at my desk, to which nothing new has been added, and look at Taylor's office. No one there yet.

Right, need to do something useful before he gets in.

The Book of Daniel. Get back there. There's got to be some clue in it, but no one else is looking. I don't *think* anyone else is looking.

Hear footsteps first, and then suddenly, as I begin to turn my head, the cup of warm coffee explodes in the side of my face, the words, 'You fucking idiot, Hutton, get into my fucking office!'

Coffee across my desk, down my jacket, over my shirt and tie. The office stops. Taylor walks past me, looking straight ahead. Catch a glimpse of his face, filled with anger. He kicks his door open, barks out, 'Fuck!' kicks his desk, and stops by the window.

I'm still standing by my desk. Coffee drips from my face. The office is quiet. Pin drop. How many people are in here at the moment? Fifteen? Twenty?

They all stare at me. I look up. Catch the eye of Mrs Lownes. Her look is not at all judgemental. Sympathetic perhaps.

'Hutton!'

I wipe a hand across my face and go through to Taylor's office. Close the door. Stand just inside.

Taylor doesn't turn. Outside the door I can hear the office start to come back to life. They'll remember this. The last day that wanker Hutton came to work.

'What the fuck were you doing, Sergeant?'

I don't answer. He doesn't turn. I don't think I've ever seen Taylor this pissed off. This enraged. This is my level of rage, although I get angry at all that crap that's in my head, and at old people in the supermarket and at old people driving too slowly.

'You were seen, outside the fucking station, two nights ago, talking to Mrs Stewart. You were seen getting into her fucking car.'

He can barely restrain himself. He's trying. I can feel his rage. I know it. The anger where you want to grab something and kick fuck out of it. Hit it and hit it and keep on hitting it. And I'm the it.

'Sergeant!'

'Yes.'

'You slept with her?'

'Yes.'

'Fucking hell.'

He turns. His face is pale. Blanched with anger and betrayal.

'Is there anyone, I mean, fucking anyone on this entire fucking planet, that you haven't slept with?'

Nothing to say. She was going to be the last one. She was. Maybe she will be anyway, despite being dead with ten spikes in her head. That probably won't mean anything to him. Would probably sound pretty weak. Although I'd mean it.

'What the fuck were you thinking, Sergeant? And I don't want any of your glib, defensive crap. What were you thinking? You'd spoken to her as part of an on-going investigation. What?'

Exhale a slow breath. The only thing to do is tell the truth. That's all there is. It's not a defence, but it's all there is.

'She was the one,' I say.

Oh crap, did I have to put it like that?

'What?'

His voice is incredulous, and so it should be. I try not to be glib, I try to be forthright, and I end up sounding like the worst Hollywood fucking movie of all time, uttering a stupid fucking line that makes me sound like Ben Stiller, Adam Sandler and someone else completely shite all rolled into one.

'I could talk to her. She understood.'

'She understood what? That you were a fucked-up piece of useless, washed-out crap?'

Well, that pretty much nails it.

'You all know that's who I am,' I said. 'She understood why. I could talk to her. That's all.'

He takes a moment. Can see him step back from the precipice, the precipice where if he falls over it, he comes at me swinging.

That was better. Might still have been a bit Hollywood, but it cuts to it. He knows that's my problem. He knows that beneath all the shit, the fights and the alcohol and the women, he knows that what I've needed is someone to talk to.

His anger begins to dissipate, but it's not making this any easier.

'You didn't kill her,' he says. It's not a question. He knows. She died around midday, I'd been in work from before eight, although I had gone off on my own. Where had I been when she died?

'No, I didn't.'

'Why did you sleep with her, Sergeant?'

That, I don't have an answer to. And if I do answer it, it's liable to create a breach in the walls. Not these four walls in this room, as Taylor gets going again. My own walls. The walls that I've constructed to help me get up today, to allow me to not go straight back to the vodka bottle. The walls that separate me from her.

I don't want the walls to be breached. I can't let that happen. I don't want to go back to last night.

'Before you leave, is there anything that I need to know?'

Before I leave.

I shake my head. 'I'd told you everything prior to seeing her that evening. We didn't discuss the church. It was personal.'

'There's no hint of her being in a group with these other four?'

'No.'

'She talk about Cartwright when you spoke to her previously? You know, we're going to have to get that guy in. Is there anything we can use?'

Give it a second, but I'd been thinking about it on the way in here. One of the reasons I walked. So I could think. But she never mentioned him.

'Nothing. She was at St Stephen's, and they thought themselves quite detached.'

'She wasn't that detached if she was in collusion with the others.'

'I got no hint of that.'

Hands in his pockets, nothing else to ask. It would have been better if I'd had something else to give him, although, of course, the more involved I'd made her seem, the worse it would have looked for me.

He finally leaves his position at the window and goes to sit down behind his desk.

'What are you going to do today?' he asks.

'I don't know. Hadn't thought beyond seeing you this morning. Presumed you'd show me the door.'

'You knew I'd find out?'

'I was going to tell you. Was going to tell you last night, then Connor turned up.'

'You look terrible,' he says.

Nothing to say to that.

'If I send you home, are you just going to go to the pub for breakfast?'

'It's Sunday. There's a pub I can go to for breakfast?'

He smiles ruefully, puts his elbow on the desk, rubs his forehead.

'I'm sorry, sir. Didn't mean to give you the extra headache. I should get out of your hair. It doesn't matter whether you're suspending me, or whether I'm taking the day, or the rest of the week, or month, off sick. I should just go, and let you get on with the investigation. You can get someone to let me know what the situation is.'

'You had breakfast yet?'

'Some.'

'Go to the canteen. Eat breakfast. You all right to drive?'

'I feel all right to drive. Not entirely sure that I'd pass a breath test.'

'Give it an hour, eat something…'

'Not sure that'll make a huge difference.'

'We've been needing someone to go up north, speak to the Reverend Baxter.'

'He's in Golspie.'

'Yes, he's in Golspie.'

How long will it take to drive to Golspie? I don't

actually ask the question, but obviously it's written on my face.

'About four hours. It's early enough. Take a while, eat something, try to get your head into as right a place as possible, then leave. Drive up there. Speak to the guy. Come home this afternoon. Come and see me when you get back.'

'Are you sure?'

'I'm getting you the fuck away from Dodge, Sergeant, but I can't promise you that Dodge won't be waiting for you when you get back.'

*

Sgt Harrison joins me at breakfast a few minutes after I've sat down. I've got bacon, sausage, two eggs, toast and coffee. She's got a poached egg and some toast.

She nods as she takes her seat across from me.

'I was wondering who he'd send,' I say.

'Who else was it going to be?'

'There are thirty people up there.'

'He knows you won't even countenance talking to men about anything personal, and I'm just about the only woman in the entire place you haven't slept with.'

She smiles as she says it, and what can I do but smile with her?

'You're not here to get me to spill my personal crap out over the table, are you? That would ruin breakfast for everyone.'

'No, probably not. I think it's more of a, you know, it's like putting paracetamol down in front of someone with a headache. Up to them whether they take it or not.'

I nod, slight smile on my face.

'Am I to have the paracetamol option all day on the drive to Golspie?'

You know, that wouldn't be too bad, I suddenly think. I'd been surprised by Taylor sending me off on a day out. I can see his management thought process, of course. If he did the natural thing and punted me off into the long grass, then I might never recover. Worried that I'm going to fall off the cliff. Instead he gives me something to do that none of us have had the time to, but which has needed doing. The thought of all that time on my own, Bob on the CD player, or not, was all right. Having a purpose, I was less likely to fall back into brain-splitting melancholy. But having Eileen Harrison along for the journey? That'd be all right too.

"Fraid not, kid,' she says. 'He probably thought if we spent all that time together you'd turn me.'

She laughs at her own line. God, I love lesbian police officers.

'You want to talk about her?' she says suddenly.

'Really, I don't. Can't.'

'You're actually hurting?' she says.

'I could be if I let it. If we keep talking about it.'

'Maybe that's what you need.'

'Jesus, Eileen, what are you trying to do? I thought you'd been sent here to help, not push me into the fires of Mordor.'

She laughs again.

'All right, all right.'

A moment, share a glance over the table, both look down at our food, take a bite. I remember the night when she was in exactly the same position that I'm in now. She'd had sex with a police constable, who'd then been killed. Worse, for Sergeant Harrison, it dragged on much further. There were people actively trying to establish with whom the deceased had slept. She got a couple of weeks in police purgatory for that, an investigation, escaped with a reprimand.

But that's not what I'm thinking about. I'm thinking of the moment when she told me about it, when I was the one to whom she confessed. And what use was I to her then?

'I probably don't deserve your time,' I say.

'Don't be daft,' she says. Knows what I was thinking. 'We were all pretty screwed up back then.'

'Now it's just me.'

'Don't kid yourself.'

We eat breakfast. We talk a little. The thought of Philo Stewart is a volcano spewing lava, but I've got my back turned, and am refusing to look at it.

37

OK. It's just me, Bob and the open road.

Driving up the A9 is as close as we get in our country to replicating the feel of an American movie, driving across Montana or Idaho or Wyoming, endless straight roads, with nothing in the distance for mile after mile after mile. And it's not really that close. But once you're up past Stirling and Dunblane, the countryside is more open, and the longer you drive, the more different it becomes, and you know that wherever you end up, it's going to feel considerably different to where you started off.

Stop off once at the House of Bruar. Cup of tea and a piece of cake. Don't stay too long. Wander through the men's clothing department on the way back to the car park. This is the kind of shop where rich people buy their clothes. Shooting jackets. Fishing waistcoats. Mustard trousers.

When I retire to the Highlands I'll stop off here on my way up to refresh my wardrobe.

Fucking right I will.

Run screaming from the place before I turn into one of *them*. It may be the place where rich people shop, but most of the poor sods mooching through and looking jealously at £150 casual shirts are the kind of middle-class wankers in whose midst we currently find ourselves, up to our eyes in murder. The civil servants and the Tesco managers and the personal assistants, desperate to be part of the big leagues and wondering if all it takes is to fork out more than you can afford on a pair of giant, fuck-off waders you'll never use.

Up past Aviemore, snow on the hills, down the hill

towards Inverness, then over the Kessock Bridge, passing Inverness Caley's ground on the way, where I once watched Thistle in one of those mind-numbing 0-0 draws that make you want to never watch another game of football in your entire life. Across the Cromarty Firth, and on up past Tain and Dornoch. Arrive in Golspie at 1.17 p.m., go straight to the old fellow's house. If he went to church, or was preaching, he'll hopefully be back by now.

Get out of the car, and stop for a moment. Look out on the sea, land in the distance. A lot of grey cloud around, not much blue sky. There's a wonderful quality to the light, and the smell of the air. I stand there for a few minutes, just looking at the water. Feeling it all. I only move when I get the sudden thought that I wish she was here with me.

I hadn't even got as far as imagining the weekends away we'd have been able to take together. Had spent the drive up the road with the old favourites, *Bringing It All Back Home* and *Highway 61*, trying not to think about it. About her.

Up the short garden path. Ring the bell. The immediate pad of footsteps and the door opens. A woman in her late 60s, an apron on.

'Hello.'

'I'm looking for the Reverend Baxter. DS Hutton, Police Scotland.'

'He said you were coming. He always takes Joey for a walk around this time. Keeps them both young, he says. You can come in and wait, or you'll find him along the Dairy Park.'

'Dairy Park?'

'Aye, if you go along to the end of the town, then instead of turning up the road to Brora, go straight along, park at the end of Duke Street, then walk across the bridge.'

'OK, thanks.'

'No problem. If you don't find him, just come back and you can wait.'

Into the car, along to the end of the street, following the

directions. Park the car, and cross the bridge. A wide stream running on down to the sea, with a ford for cars to cross, albeit there's nowhere to go other than to park at either of the houses on the other side.

Onto the field, that beautiful feeling in the air, no hint of rain and just a bit too cold in my jacket and tie. Hands in pockets. Say hello to a couple of women walking by, dogs in and out the grass. See a single guy with a dog in the distance, heading back in my direction.

As we get closer, I can see he looks about the right age. Green wellingtons, big warm jacket. His clothes much better suited to the weather than those of the soft southern police officer who's here to greet him. Joey, if this is them, is a golden Labrador, old and not terribly excited about having to walk as far as he's being made.

'Reverend Baxter?' I say, as we come upon each other.

'Aye, you must be the policeman. Call me Jim.'

'Jim... Jim Baxter?'

'My name's Morris, but everyone started calling me Jim back in the day. It stuck.'

He pauses, takes a look around.

'You want to go back to the house or sit on a bench and look at the view?'

I get enough sitting in houses, so I indicate the bench.

'Joey!' he calls out after the dog, and the mutt comes ambling back towards us from ten yards along the path.

We sit down on the wooden bench and look at the sea and the rocks and narrow stretch of beach, the sand covered in seaweed and old buoys and those coloured, random bits of rope that you always get. Orange and light blue.

'Where's that?' I say, indicated the low land on the horizon, far across the water.

He gives me a curious glance. The dog approaches, looks vaguely interested in the fact that his owner is talking to someone, and then wanders off again to rummage around the beach, no doubt in search of some faeces or other to rub himself in.

'It's Scotland, son, where'd you think it was? Norway?'

'Which bit?' I ask, not rising to the bait.

'The Moray coast. Ardersier, Nairn, along there.'

I picture the map of Scotland.

'You come along here every day?'

'Rain or shine,' he says. 'Seems to be mostly rain at the moment.'

Everything seems like a potential lifestyle choice, and I'm forever slotting myself into other people's lives. Could I do this or that? Could I live this far north, with this seascape and this magical light, and walk along this coastal path every day with a dog around my feet?

I forget for a moment that I'm here to interview him, and let myself fall into the view.

'Are you going to ask me something, son?' he says soon enough. 'It's a beautiful day 'n' all, but a man my age sits on one of these benches too long, we're looking at month-long haemorrhoids.'

Funny.

'What age are you?'

'Sixty-seven,' he says. 'You'll be there soon enough. It may not sound old by today's standard, but just you wait. Every day is an exercise in pain management and limitation. Now, what can I do for you? You're up here to talk about those damned churches, I suppose.'

'Yep. You've seen the news? You surprised about what's been happening?'

'Only surprise is that it didn't come sooner.'

'I hear that a lot.'

Philo said it.

Think of Philo. Immediately kick the thought away. I know the technique of getting something out your mind, having used it so often in the past.

'Which has got to make you think,' he says.

'Why is it happening now?'

'Exactly. The merger, well, I don't know who you've spoken to, but I expect you've heard it plenty enough. It was an ugly business. Usually is. These things are happening all over Scotland. But I spoke to a couple of people from the Presbytery, and they'd never seen anything like it. There was so much lobbying taking place, a real political slugfest. People were getting threatened. It was—'

'Who was getting threatened? Who was making the threats?'

'Listen, son, the whole atmosphere was toxic. These people are supposed to be Christians. I'm not going to go giving you names, he said that and she said the next thing, I'm not handing some guy on a plate to you so that you're going to go charging down there saying, we have it on good authority that three years ago, et cetera et cetera. All that stuff is in the past. There may have been people continuing to bang on about it, because that's what people do, but it was settled. Done and dusted. The fat lady had sung. Why would someone who'd won the argument kill someone who was still trying to have the argument? You win the Cup Final 1-0, you don't have to kill the guy who keeps banging on about the offside goal. You get to move on, and you've got the cup.'

'Surely the aggrieved party is capable of sustaining the grievance at a level that's going to cause enough irritation to—'

'Maybe you're right, son,' he cuts in, 'but you should have been there when it started. Some part of me wanted to stay there to try to help guide these people through, but I'm afraid there was another part of me that was quite sickened by it, and couldn't get away fast enough.'

He shakes his head, stares grimly at the ground. 'How do any of us understand the mind of a murderer? Yet it seems strange. For it to be happening now, you know? Strange.'

'So, you think there's something else? That talk of the merger is a smokescreen?'

He doesn't glance round, doesn't immediately reply. I like this guy. Sometimes you speak to people and you know you're going to be left trying to wring out the merest fragment of information, and that everything they do say is going to have been run through the arsehole filter. This guy though, he has a way about him. This is a guy whose comments are automatically given weight.

'I'm not on the ground, son, not any more. What I'm saying is common sense, that's all. It might have nothing whatsoever to do with the merger, or perhaps it's related to it, but the connection is more tenuous than you're currently thinking about.'

'There's a girl,' I say. Don't know where the words come from. Hadn't been expecting to say them. Didn't even realise I'd been thinking about them. Suddenly the thought is in my head, and the words are out there. *There's a girl*.

He smiles. I don't look at him, but I can feel it.

'Aye, son, there usually is. What's she like?'

'No, not like that,' I say. Now I'm thinking more carefully about what I'm going to say, but I'm still saying it. 'A young girl, twelve maybe, not sure. Seems as though she's twelve, rather than it's me looking at her and thinking that's what age she is.'

He doesn't say anything. I notice the slight movement of the fingers, a minimalist way of encouraging me to keep talking.

'She… she's in my dreams. I'm not sure what she's doing there, but it started at the same time as this church business.'

'What does she do?'

'I'm not sure. She's just there.' Pause for a second. What *does* she do? 'She directed me to the Book of Daniel, and then it turns out that the killer was using the story of the four beasts from Daniel 7 as, God, I don't know, a reference point for the murders. Something like that.'

'I didn't know about the Daniel 7 link,' he says. 'Hmm, that's interesting. The Book of Daniel is…'

'A box of frogs?'

He laughs. 'I've never heard that before, but yes, if you like. And this girl had you looking there before you

———
224

realised that was the path the killer was following?'

'Yes.'

'Hmm... You know who she is?'

'Never seen her before.'

'You think she might be dead?'

'What?'

Turn and look at him sharply.

'The dead speak to us in all sorts of different ways, Sergeant.'

'I'm not communicating with a ghost,' I say.

'No,' he says, 'obviously you're not communicating with her.'

Discombobulated? Yep, that's the word. I've been discombobulated by him. I look across the water. There is a closer bank of land, and then the more distant one, which he said was the south bank of the Moray coast. They probably don't call it the south bank. There's a fishing vessel out on the water, that's all you can see. I realise I'm watching something black and round bobbing in the water, wondering if it's a seal sticking its nose in the air.

'That's the Portmahomack lighthouse over there,' he says. 'You ever been along that road?'

Shake my head.

'Beautiful.'

We fall once more into silence. Fall is the word. I tumble into it, and I could sit here for hours looking at the view. Sea and low-lying land, that's all. No mountains, nothing dramatic. But I could look at it all day. The landscape equivalent of sitting in the Old Kirk back home.

This is what my recovery could look like, if I wanted to try to make it. Sitting in silence looking at views. Yet, haven't I done a lot of that in the last year or two? Plenty of time off work, and when I'm not in work, I'm fine. I sit and look at views. It's going back to work, and once more subjecting myself to the daily grind, or the occasional terror, that's what brings it all back.

There you have it. What I need is not to go to work. Go and live by the sea, and look at the waves.

Fuck. Maybe when I'm sixty.

'Obviously you need to find this girl,' he says. 'Whoever she is. Dead or alive.'

I neither turn nor reply. Soon enough I'm going to have to drive back down the A9, and the stop for the cup of tea and the large piece of cake and the walk through the posh man's clothing department is never quite as enjoyable on the road home. For the moment I'm just going to sit in silence and look at the view.

And he's right. I need to find the girl.

38

Get back to the office at three minutes after seven. Felt melancholic on the drive down the road, as if I was leaving home rather than returning to it. Listened to Bob's *Time Out Of Mind-Love And Theft-Modern Times* trilogy all the way. Well, people call it a trilogy, never saw it that way myself. Don't reckon Bob does either, but who knows what he's thinking.

If I listened to the news I might have been ready for the media scrum outside the station. Glad that I decided not to leave the car at home, then walk in to work. That's what I would have done if I'd been aiming to go to the pub afterwards, but my head's in good enough a place this evening that I don't need it.

So, I don't have to walk through the cameras and the journalists at the front of the station; round the back, they've locked the gates on the car park. The constable on duty lets me in, and I can park and get out of the car without some dick of a journalist sticking his microphone in my face, asking who the fuck I am and what the fuck I'm doing at the station, so that they can then stand breathlessly on camera, above rolling text screaming BREAKING FUCKING NEWS, YOU BASTARD in ear-piercing letters, saying, *'I've just spoken to some cunt! I've absolutely no idea who he was, or whether he's connected to this dramatic breaking story! He told me to fuck off! Incredible scenes! Back to you in the studio, Kate!'*

Into the station, up to the front desk. Ramsay's in position, his usual rock-like self.

'Shit's hit the fan?' I say, barely slowing down.

'An arrest in the four churches horror,' he says.

That almost has me breaking my stride. Not at the fact there's been an arrest, because it was one fairly obvious explanation for that stramash outside; it's at his use of the phrase *four churches horror*. That, there, is an expression straight from the tabloids.

I slow down a little, but don't stop. I'll get the information from the horse's mouth.

Up the stairs two at a time, into the office. Expect to see the usual headless chicken waltz, with people running back and forth in general ferment, but there is an air of calm. Maybe they've actually got him, they've actually made the breakthrough and the arrest in my absence, and tied it all up inside nine hours.

No, I don't think so.

Taylor's in his office, door open. I knock and enter. He looks up, acknowledges my return and nods for me to close the door, then gestures for me to sit down.

'One of you fellows win the lottery?' I ask.

'As a matter of fact, no,' he says.

Doesn't look pissed off, which is unusual in situations such as these.

'You didn't find Bible John, did you?'

He laughs.

'We did get his modern day replacement. Or, we arrested someone. It remains to be seen whether we have the right person, and I seriously doubt that we do.'

'And the winner is…?'

'Paul Cartwright.'

'Oh, nice. Did you get a confession?

Shakes his head.

'Evidence?'

He makes a maybe/maybe not sign with his hand.

'You read it was him in a fortune cookie?'

'That, obviously, was our starting point. Then we established it was definitely Cartwright at the centre of this little group of five. He admitted that, at any rate.'

'Did he say why?'

'He did. Seems he wasn't happy with his successes so

far. He wanted more. He wanted, in fact, to get hold of St Stephen's. Or, more to the point, the congregation. Says it was his intention to sell the building, and invest the money back into the parish, i.e. St Mungo's.'

'He had a plan?'

'He was working with someone from inside each of the four congregations, including your Mrs Stewart at St Stephen's. Says that none of the other four knew exactly what his plan was, or anyone else's part in it. He admits it was all very Machiavellian, but that that in itself isn't a crime. Which is a fair point.'

'And so…?'

'He just happens to have no alibi for any of the four murders, which seems a bit odd for someone like him, with a family, and a lot of church and business contacts. DC Gostkowski was taking a look at his involvement in the church, and one thing she turned up was that he made a reading in church on average once every three months, and every single time he read, he read from the Book of Daniel.'

That's interesting, and yet one of those glaringly obvious clues that ultimately never point to anything.

'That's a very public thing, though, isn't it?' I say. 'And then, if someone else was looking to set the guy up, you have this obvious weird connection with Daniel to use.'

'Exactamundo.'

'So…?'

He lets his gaze drift out the door and off in the direction of Connor's office.

'The superintendent brought you a valuable new piece of evidence that absolutely nailed Cartwright's arse to the mast?' I ask.

'Not quite.'

'In need of a quick result and some good PR after a week of shit, the superintendent jumped hastily to a conclusion and ordered you to arrest someone first, build a case later?'

'Ah, Sergeant Hutton,' says Taylor, in some sort of

generic, mock continental European accent, 'I see that you are a student of the superintendent's methods.'

I laugh, shake my head.

'You're fucking kidding, right?'

'Sadly, no.'

'What about the DNA sample you got from Mrs Christie?'

'Didn't match.'

'Of course not. You think you'll be able to build a case?'

'We can build a case of some sort, no question, but whether it's good enough to get a conviction... and whether it's the right case...' He tosses a dismissive hand to the side.

'What else have you got?'

'You mean, things like fingerprints, DNA, witnesses, motives and murder weapons?'

'Any one of them would be good.'

'All of them, Sergeant, would be fantastic. However, none of them, which is what we have, puts us a goal or two down at this stage.'

'Cartwright must have some high-price legal representation.'

Taylor takes a moment over this, nodding slowly. 'Yes, he does. Almost seems to be enjoying his time in police custody. Must see a big lawsuit in it at some stage. Wrongful arrest and all that.'

'So,' I say, because Connor being a total bell-end is not exactly unusual, but Taylor taking it with a smile on his face is kind of weird, 'what's with you? You're practically Gene Kelly in here. The place is chilled, and you've near as dammit got a smile on your face. Weirdest thing I've ever seen.'

Taylor again indicates Connor's office.

'It's all on him, Sergeant. Just following orders. He told me to make the arrest. I outlined, at as much length as he would allow, why I thought that was at best premature, and at worst, unbelievably stupid. He ordered me again to make the arrest. I asked if he could give me that in writing.

He obliged.'

'You're covered?'

'Yes, Sergeant, I am. I even noted my objections in writing, and he replied to that. So, I'm doubled covered. I hate this sort of political shit that you get when your boss is someone like him, but you just have to get on with it and do what needs to be done. If, against all our expectations, it turns out Cartwright is guilty, then the superintendent gets to go and lick his own balls in front of the media. Never been much of a one for ball-licking myself.'

'Is it possible Cartwright's guilty?'

A dismissive wave of the hand. 'Who knows? I mean, at this stage it's more or less impossible to rule anyone out, and the field is still wide open for new entries. This guy, however, at least had motive for two of the four killings, because both Maureen and Agnes were a pain in his arse, and he's a known covert collaborator with them. So, there's as much chance it's him as anyone. In fact, quite possibly a little more.'

'Did you do an interview before you nicked the bastard?'

'Well, obviously I did Lorraine and Jeremy Kyle...'

'Funny.'

'We brought him in. We interviewed him. He called his little ragtag collection of amateur conspiracists, his War Room II.'

'Yeah, he said he convened a war room in order to win the contest in the first place. Hey, and that's something else. According to Agnes Christie's daughter, her mum always said their church should have had a war room.'

Hand across his chin, your classic detective's pose.

'Suppose it's not that unusual a phrase. A decent thought, but in tying them together we have Cartwright's admission in any case. Anyway, the superintendent watched the interview. Or, at least, enough of it to be convinced. When Mr Cartwright was not immediately able to provide an alibi for any of the four murders, the super seemed to find this compelling.'

'Ah, so we have at least coincidence on our side.'

He nods, smiles ruefully. 'Now we're at the case-building stage, and we're full-on with that.'

'Oh, Cartwright did tell me that he'd had nothing to do with Maureen, had never replied to her letters, no contact ever.'

'Always good to catch them in a lie,' says Taylor. 'And it does explain why she stopped writing to him.'

Nod in agreement, decide to ask the question that I probably ought not to.

'You speak to Tony Stewart?'

Shadow across his face, lowers his head slightly. It's all right to feel slightly upbeat about making a false arrest, especially when it's your boss who's making a dick of himself, but it's a tough copper who's chipper about anyone finding out their wife has had her head spiked.

'Aye. Poor bastard. Hadn't been able to get in touch with her for about twenty-four hours before he got on the plane, so he was shitting himself anyway. We got someone to meet him off the plane at Heathrow. He went to pieces down there. Met him at this end as well, and he was still in pieces.'

Nothing to say. I was right, I shouldn't have asked the question in the first place. Don't want to think about some guy whose wife I slept with being in pieces. Don't want to think about the fact that he wouldn't have been able to get in touch with her for some of that twenty-four hours because she was in bed with me.

I'm not in pieces. I'm not. But that's a bucketload of denial keeping me together.

'I take it you're responsible for some of that time he couldn't get hold of her?'

A moment, then I nod. He exhales a long breath. Checks his watch.

'We'll talk again in the morning. It's not out of the question that you'll be temporarily suspended pending further investigation, but at the best, I'll need to remove you from this investigation.'

'Of course.'

Been a while since I managed to see a big investigation all the way through to the end.

'How'd you get on up north?'

'I could have stayed,' I say. I could too. I could move up there and clean toilets.

Hey, if I'm kicked off this case, then I can at least go back to the toilet guy. Maybe helping him will give me some level of job satisfaction akin to what he manages to achieve.

'I bet. You talk to the minister?'

'Aye. A decent old sort, out walking his dog, worried about his piles sitting on a wooden bench. Didn't have a lot to say, except surprise that it was happening now and not previously. In fact...' Pause to think about the old fellow, and the nuance of his words. Nuance? I don't think so. I think he was quite straightforward. 'No, he was pretty clear. Said it was extremely nasty before, and that he wouldn't have been surprised if there had been murder back then. That it's happening now surprised him. So he wondered if the merger ultimately might be a red herring. Not, obviously, an intentional red herring, but something that's distracting us from the case.'

'Possible,' he says. Another check of the watch, then he waves his hand towards the door.

'You should go home. Write up your interview with the minister in the morning, ping it over. I'll tell Ramsay just to get you back onto the usual thing. We'll talk when I get the time.'

Nothing else to say. The situation does not allow that I let the conversation turn to anything else. He's being unusually polite about it, but the bottom line is I'm getting my due.

Kicked off the case, with the not entirely outside possibility of being kicked out of the police.

*

Nevertheless, I don't leave work just yet. The thought of going home is too awful. Just too awful. She'll still be there, sitting at the small dining table, smiling at me as I walk in the door.

It didn't go so well when I went home last night, after all.

Find the girl, that's what Reverend Baxter said. So I go down to records, make myself known to the woman on duty – who just so happens to be Cheryl, with whom I had the brief fling until our passion crashed and burned on the unsavoury matter of anal sex – we exchange barely a word, and I find a computer to sit at.

I could do the first part of it, checking back over missing persons from the last few years, at my desk, but Taylor doesn't want me there, which is fine. I just need to hope that I don't walk into him on the way out. He'll likely be working much later, so I'll give it half an hour or an hour and then head off.

Sit for a moment staring at a blank screen. Haven't been thinking of the reality of this until now. Searching for missing or dead children is awful. There's a lot of shit in this job, but Jesus, this is right there at the top. Out in front. The shittiest thing any of us ever has to do. So, here I am, voluntarily giving myself the task of searching through one tragic story after another.

And what is it I'm hoping to find? Who, or what, is this strange little girl who keeps speaking to me?

My thoughts are too prosaic for that. Can't think about it. I just know that what Baxter said makes sense. I need to find the girl, and this is as good a place to start looking as any.

39

An hour, all I could stand. Such an overwhelming feeling of sadness. So many lives lost or ruined.

Out the station, do my best to shove everything that I've just read into the necessary compartment. No sign of my girl, whoever she is. If she went missing in the last few years, it wasn't from around here. Or, indeed, anywhere in Strathclyde.

I don't go home. I get in the car, start to head in that direction, but then I see Philo sitting at the table, and I smell her scent on the sheets on the bed, and I can't go there. I just can't. Yes, I need to face this grief at some point. Everybody has to face grief. But I need to be in a better place before it happens.

Where do I end up? In the car park at Morrison's down by the river. Somewhere to sit and think. It'd be good to have someone to talk to. Perhaps I shouldn't have left the station so quickly, because that's the only place I'm going to find anyone. But then who would it be? My new pal, Eileen? Someone I've known and more or less ignored for the last six or seven years.

I contemplate, seriously, going to see Peggy. Turning up on my ex-wife's door, needing to talk. She'd love that. Might actually let me in, as I don't think she has anyone else on the go at the moment. But what then? What would I say? *Hey, Peg, you know how for all those years I was keeping some dark secret that I just never got close enough to you to tell you? Well, I found someone I could confide in, someone I'd only known a few days, but who I quickly realised I loved more than I ever loved you. But now she's dead. You got a couple of hours to chat?*

I think of Margaret Christie, my doctor from three nights ago. Just three nights. What do you think? My last ever casual shag? That's what it feels like at the moment. She was staying at the Premier Inn at the Black Bear. Wonder if she's still up here. I could probably talk to her. But then, if I called her, she's going to think I'm looking for something more than conversation, and I won't be.

I end up driving to the Black Bear anyway. Sitting in the bar. Watching Sky Sports. Eating a gammon steak and pineapple, drinking two glasses of wine. She's not in the bar. Why should she be?

I should go home, but I can't. It's as though there's a wall up. I walk next door to the Premier Inn and book myself a room. Pay for a toothbrush and toothpaste.

Go to the room, turn on the news. Brain in neutral. I'm here now. I can stop thinking about going home.

The news leads with our story beneath the wonderful graphic: *Bible Paul?* Watch the media scrum in front of the station. A press conference in which Connor, unusually, takes the lead. Obviously wanting to be the face of the arrest. Nice for him, his brief moment in the sun. Possibly doesn't understand that no one ever remembers the police officer on these occasions. They watch the news item, the basic facts of the case might stick with the viewer, but all they will have seen is the uniform. No one remembers the face of the officer.

Fuck, I don't know him. Perhaps he fully understands that, but it's not about public perception for him. It's about positioning himself so that he looks good in front of his superiors, attempting to regain some of the reputation that he will think he lost during the Plague of Crows debacle. He must be confident, because he's going to look like a total cock if he's wrong.

And I think we all know he's wrong.

After the news I find a documentary on Egyptian treasures on BBC4, which I manage to watch in its entirety without falling asleep, as some young academic chap strides around ancient monuments in his pale blue shirt, talking excitedly to the camera.

Where do they get these people? What is the genesis of these random three-part series that crop up continuously on BBC4? Do people sit around in an office and come up with titles for new shows, such as *What The Ancient Greeks Taught Us* or *Who The Fuck Were The Phoenicians?* or *How Many Visigoths Did It Take To Change a Light Bulb?* after which they put the idea out to tender? Or do academics like this guy sit in the bath and think up a show such as *The Mongols Invented Golf And Other Astonishing Facts Of The Ancient World* and then take it to the BBC?

If it's the latter, I could do that. It'd give me something to do when I leave the police. Make a documentary for BBC4.

My imagination wanders, Mitty-esque, as I watch the show. I struggle to think what it is that I'd have the expertise to discuss other than Dylan, Thistle and my own fucked-up life. Decide on a TV series entitled *Echoes Of Dylan, From Firhill to Mesopotamia*, and then the show is over and I take myself off to bed.

I lie there, trying not to think about Philo Stewart, painfully thinking about her in my attempts not to.

I think about her husband, the guy in a suit, in tears. The guy I had cuckolded the night before. He hadn't heard from her for twenty-four hours before he returned. Some of it he was on the plane, some of it she was in bed with me, making love, sleeping. We ate dinner the night before, breakfast the following morning. But it doesn't all add up to twenty-four hours.

Why didn't she text him when she got home from my house? And now, thinking about it, I realise of course, that I have no idea when she left my house. Why have I only just thought of that? Because you were trying not to think about it at all.

She would have had no reason to linger, so I don't suppose that she did. Why did she not call, or at least text her husband when she got back home? It would have been mid-afternoon with him. He must have been texting, calling. Maybe beginning to pull his hair out.

The sorrow floods in with the thought that she couldn't bring herself to do it, because she knew. She knew she'd found someone else, and that the someone else was going to bring an end to her marriage.

How much conceit is there in that thought? It doesn't matter. It's there, it's in my head, it won't leave.

The thought that I could have had someone. Someone to really talk to, someone who understood, someone with whom the sex was unbelievable, someone with whom I could share. Someone to whom, at last, I could actually give something of myself.

The inevitable tears on my pillow. Fuck. I don't move. I don't get up to get something with which to drown out the pain. Eventually the tiredness takes over and I fall asleep.

*

'I'm pure like that, by the way, she can go and take a fuck tae hersel', so she can.'

10.23 a.m. Head has been swirling since just after six. Woke up with the image of Philo sitting in that chair, in my head. Her face streaked with blood, her head pierced with spikes. Eyes open.

Yes, great romance has to be doomed. If it's not, you end up sitting together watching TV. For the romance to last, there has to be separation and pain. No greater separation than one of you being dead.

If this was Shakespeare – you know, one of those Shakespearean police procedurals you get in school – I'd find out who killed her and then drink poison. At the moment I'm shaping up to do neither, although I'm trying to distract myself from doomed love by thinking about the former, and can never rule out the latter.

What I should be distracting myself with is the small domestic matter with which I'm currently dealing. A neighbourhood dispute in the new houses beyond the park.

You're not usually going to get a detective sergeant packed off to one of these – not even a washed-up bum of a detective sergeant – but this one has been escalating.

Started off with the age-old *she's parking her car in front of my house* complaint. We get fifty of them a day. They don't usually get as far as the shit through the letterbox, anonymous death threats and a whole host of other tit-for-tat, petty-tending-to-serious shit that I get bored thinking about.

'Are you not embarrassed that I'm here?' I say. She wasn't expecting that. Big woman. I mean, round big, as opposed to tall big. Rough. I don't mind saying it. She's rough. Probably used to getting her own way around here. That appears to have changed when her physical and intellectual equal moved in next door.

'Wha'?'

She looks as if she's about to lamp me. I can handle her. Or, at least, I'd be able to run faster than her, and PC Wallace, who's standing by the door, can deal with her.

'We're pretty stretched at the moment,' I say. 'There's a quadruple murder investigation in town. We currently have four missing persons on our books, as well as the usual dreadful crimes of child abuse and child pornography and child neglect. You're keeping me from helping those children, all because you can't speak to your neighbour. You can't compromise. You can't be bothered making the effort to come to some accommodation. Instead, you need an adult in uniform to sort it out for you.'

'Are you finished?' she says, not picking up on the fact that I'm not in uniform.

We all have to be so nice to people these days. Jesus, it sucks. Why can't you just tell people how it is, without having some do-gooding dickhead of a police lawyer up your arse?

Obviously, this morning, I'm not in the mood to care.

'As police we can't really do anything, and I mean, something in the region of nicking one of you and thus separating you—'

'You're no' fuckin' nickin' me!'

'—until one of you commits a serious crime. So, either one of you is going to have to kill or seriously kick fuck out of the other one, or burn the other's house down, or whatever. Then the one doing the kicking'll get nicked, and the other one's in hospital. If that's what you want... However, if you want to be pragmatic, then you're just going to have to tuck your balls back in and compromise. You're going to have to ignore the occasional car parking, she's going to have to try to park there less frequently, and you're both going to have to ignore the shitstorm of trivial revenge you've been cooking up for the last two months.'

'Are you for real?'

'Yes,' I say, getting to my feet. 'I'm going to go next door and say the same thing to Mrs Walker, at the end of which I'm telling her that you've invited her in for a cup of tea. So get the kettle on...'

'She's no' fuckin' comin' in here!'

'Up to you.'

I pause for a moment before walking out. She stares at me like I'm some new species of arsehole. Time for a last few words of candour.

'Mrs McLean, I'll be honest. You people, you know,' and I cast a hand around to indicate her type who live in this small housing estate, and it's just as well I don't sound like I went to Eton or Fettes, because then there would be absolutely no doubt that I mean what it sounds like, although at the moment she might just have enough confusion to let me out the door without swinging for me, 'you can't just forfeit personal responsibility and community responsibility, so that every time a problem comes along you ask someone else to solve it for you.'

'Can I no'? You think I give a fuck what some polis says?'

'You think, just because of my badge, I give a fuck about you and your neighbour squabbling like kids? Sort it out between yourselves, or come back to me when one of you's in hospital. I'm going next door.'

Look at Wallace, nod in the direction of the door.

She throws a 'fuck off!' at our backs as we walk out.

Down the short path, through the gate. Stand on the pavement, looking across at the trees of the park. Hands in pockets. Don't really feel like going next door and delivering the same pointless message, but pretty much have to now.

'What'd you think?' I ask.

'Sir?'

'What'd you think? Of me telling her she had to take responsibility for her own actions?'

'Thought it was well-judged,' says Wallace.

'Did you really?'

'Yes, sir. If it was obvious one-way harassment then it would have been inappropriate, but since it's apparent that both sides are as bad as each other...'

'Hmm.'

I'll take that. A bit of brown-nosing from a constable. As if that's going to get him anywhere.

I look at the next house, the frames of the door and the windows peeling blue paint, a tricycle lying forlornly on its side by the front path.

'Word of warning, sir,' says Wallace, as I open the gate.

'Go on.'

'Mrs Walker makes Mrs McLean look like Donkey from *Shrek*.'

40

I let Wallace drive back to the station on his own, while I walk through the park.

I wonder how long I can keep that up. Moving from complaint to complaint, telling people they need to sort out their own problems. Chances are that by the time I get back to the station either Mrs Walker or Mrs McLean will be dead, and whichever one is still alive will be able to say that I more or less encouraged her.

Cold, damp day, bit of a chill wind. Not a good one for walking. Cut down to the path at the lower end of the football pitches rather than taking the longer high road, the path round the top end of the gully. I know where I'm going. Back to the church. Not part of the investigation any more, so what exactly is it that I'm doing?

I need the peace, that's all. Like sitting looking at the waves in Golspie.

I need to work it out. It doesn't matter that I've been kicked off the investigation, doesn't matter whether I get booted out the police. I need to focus for a day, or a week, or however long it takes, and work out what's going on here.

There is surprise that it's happening now and not two or three years ago. Perhaps it's as a result of lingering resentment over the merger, but if that's the case, then I need to leave it to Taylor. He's thinking about that, and trying to collect evidence in the case against Cartwright.

I need to cast aside thoughts of the old enmities and decide what else there could be. A group of five. The architect, the doctor's mum, the pupil, the granny porn star, the ex-war zone Bible study teacher. What could possibly bind them, and could it be that Cartwright is due to be the next victim rather than the one who killed the first four?

I emerge up the hill from the park back onto the road and walk round to the church. The gate is open, and once again there is one of our lot on duty beside the new grave of Maureen Henderson. Constable Webb.

I walk over, glancing casually at headstones as I pass.

'Marcie,' I say. 'Quiet morning.'

'Dead quiet, sir,' she says.

I stop beside her and look around.

'Anyone coming or going?'

'There's a woman in the church. She had the keys.'

'OK, thanks.'

I stand there for another moment or two, and then move away. The graveyard is not too large, sloping away at the back down to a fence, the railway line beyond. I walk further in amongst the graves. A low, grey light, and somewhere a crow cries mournfully against the cold morning.

I look at the names on the headstones, worn and battered by time and the weather, many of them difficult to read. Simple messages in memory of the departed. Nothing elaborate or mawkish or maudlin, just Victorian austerity of language.

Hey, Sergeant, what the fuck do you know about the Victorians and their language?

Yes, good point, whoever that is in my brain. The language is simple, unassuming, sometimes biblical. That's all.

Get a shiver as I pass a grave near the far end of the cemetery. I shake it off, stand for a moment. Look down at the headstone.

In loving memory
Charles McMann
Born 14th January 1821
Died 27th October 1897
And they that be wise shall shine
as the brightness of the firmament

Fuck. I recognise that quote, which means it can be from only one place. I'm not so well read up on the Bible that I can tell one quote from another. The fact that this rings a bell can only be because I read it a few days ago. The Book of Daniel. Fuck, fuckity-fuck.

Keeps cropping up, and this one gave me a shiver before I'd even looked at it.

I stand over the gravestone reading the lines a few more times. Memorizing it, as I know where I'm going next.

I finally lift my head and look around the graveyard. Constable Webb is still in position. I don't see the girl, hadn't expected to, yet I get the feeling that she was watching. The gate is slightly open, the way I left it, yet looking at it from across the other side of the graveyard, it feels almost as though there's something missing. Something that was there a moment ago is gone, and has left a part of itself behind. An invisible part.

I walk back up the slope towards Webb. 'Did anyone come in?' I ask, as I come alongside.

'The graveyard?' she says.

'Yes.'

'No. No, I don't think so. There was someone, a young girl maybe. I saw her standing at the gate, just outside, but she never came in.'

I don't need to ask what she was wearing.

'OK, thanks.'

I turn. Stand and look around. I've learned that there's no point in sprinting out after her. She talks to me when she needs to.

She talks to me?

Why is there always so much to think about? Simplify. Simplify. Simplify.

'Sir?'

I turn back, having started to walk away.

'The girl,' says Webb. 'There was something weird. I mean… I can't… can't put my finger on it.'

'I know.'

What else am I going to say? *Hey, don't worry*

Constable, the kid's fine. She turns up every now and again in my apartment and gives me a kick up the arse.

I want to say more, but there's nothing else. I attempt to give Constable Webb some sort of reassuring smile, but I probably just look like Gordon Brown during that absurd five minutes of the 2010 election campaign when someone suggested he tried grinning, then I turn and walk towards the church. Glance at the gate as I come to the church doors, but the feeling is gone.

*

Back in my position. Fifth pew from the front, right hand aisle, sitting at the end of the centre pew. Looking up at Jesus in blue. Perfect stillness.

I need to leave, that's all. The police. This town.

I feel a bit of a mess today, yet strangely it's not the mess I'm usually in. A different mess, but not the same intrinsic, black, cancerous mess that usually exists in the pit of my stomach. Philo cured me of that. Snap of the fingers, pretty much, that was all it took. She crept inside my head and sorted me out.

Today's mess is because the woman I'd fallen for is dead. That's all. Jesus, that's the kind of mess that thousands of people, millions of people, are dealing with every day around the world. Right now, this second, there are millions of people grieving. And I'm one of them.

At least it's normal.

I'm alone. The door to the church was open. Constable Webb said that Mrs Buttler had come in here, but I haven't seen her. In the vestry perhaps. I haven't gone looking for her.

Jesus isn't saying much up there in his window. Doesn't speak to me. Thank God.

Ha!

Dylan said that he started writing all those religious albums after experiencing a vision of Jesus in a hotel bedroom in Tucson, Arizona.

Yeah, I know.

I was glad when Jesus turned back up in Bob's hotel room in Glasgow one night and told him to go back to writing about women making him miserable.

The wooden door at the end of the aisle opens and Mrs Buttler emerges. She smiles when she sees me, then comes and sits in her usual spot on the other side of the aisle.

'Here to interrogate me about the burial?' she asks. Light in her voice. I suspect what we have here is a woman who's quite happy that Paul Cartwright has been arrested for murder. If happy's the word.

'Off the case,' I say.

'Didn't expect that,' she says.

'Reassigned,' is all I say. No requirement for details.

'Just here for the peace, then?'

'Yes.'

'You'll need to start coming on Sunday mornings,' she says, smiling again.

'I'd have to listen to people talking about God,' I say, and then stop myself getting more flippantly profane. 'Anyway, there aren't any services here at the moment, are there?'

'We'll see about that.'

'What does that mean?'

'Well, I'm just saying, that's all. With that man in jail for those murders, the lot down the road are going to be on the back foot. Now would be as good a time as any to strike.'

'You think he did it?'

She seems surprised by the question, which is fair enough, given that I'm part of the organisation that arrested him in the first place.

'You surely didn't just arrest him because he's an odious creature, did you?'

'I didn't arrest him at all. I was off the case before the arrest was made.'

'Did you speak to him?'

'Yes.'

'What did you think?'

Look away from her and back to the front before I answer. I'm not one for sophistry and obfuscation. Might as well get it out there.

'After hearing so much about him, I was expecting not to like him, but you know, there was something there. Pompous, yes. But he was clinical and focussed. He had a plan, and he executed it perfectly.'

I glance back at her. She's not looking too impressed. I don't think I even get a look of grudging acknowledgement.

'The man was dreadful, and if that's what being a Christian means, then I want no part of it. I'm glad he's gone.'

'There's the difference, I suppose. I'm not looking at it from the point of Christianity or the Church.'

'Well, under the circumstances, Sergeant, forgive me if I do.'

Look down at the floor. The nagging doubts are breaking through the barricades of wilful blindness. Words come out, even though I ought to be keeping them to myself.

'It doesn't make sense, though, does it? He has this immaculate plan which he carries out to perfection...'

'I wouldn't use the word immaculate.'

'He'd been bang on in everything he'd done, didn't care whether or not he made enemies. You can see that he was the kind of man who accepted antagonism and bitterness as part of the way he carried out his business. So, why now? Now that he had what he wanted, he'd won, everything was settling down, why now avenge himself in such a public way? Why, when you've done all the hard work, open yourself up to ruin?'

I turn and look at her. She doesn't seem impressed.

'Well, whether it was you personally or not, Sergeant, it was your lot who arrested him, so maybe you want to go and speak to that policeman who was on the television last night.'

Perhaps not him.

'No one will thank you if you get Cartwright released, however,' she adds.

I should shut up about the case. Every name is on the table, after all, and why wouldn't Mrs Buttler be on the list? The e-mail thing reeks of a scam or a set-up.

'There's a headstone out there,' I say, moving the conversation off the contentious subject of Cartwright. 'The lettering seems clearer than most of the others. *And they that be wise shall shine as the brightness of the firmament.* I mean, it's not been done particularly recently, just looks…'

She's nodding.

'I know the one,' she says. 'It's always been like that. I mean, the thirty years or so that I've noticed it. I presume one of his family had it added at some point. Maybe after the war? I don't know if anyone ever looked into it.'

'The quote is…?'

'Daniel 12:3.'

'Daniel. There's a lot of Daniel.'

'It's one of the popular books,' she says, smiling. 'Sometimes even when people don't realise it. Stories of oppression and apocalyptic visions.'

'A box of frogs,' I say. 'I know, I've read it.'

'Frogs?' She shakes her head, smiling.

'That's what they say,' I reply, returning the smile.

I sit for a little while longer. I think I just about rescued my relationship with Mrs Buttler. She might still welcome me back the next time.

Out the church and stand for a few moments in the late morning tranquility of the graveyard. Look over at Webb, who is there with her hands behind her back, a long few hours ahead of her. Take a few moments, check the time, and then decide to extend the offer of a fifteen-minute break that I previously gave to Wallace.

She accepts, and I stand at the graveside of Maureen Henderson while Wallace grabs a coffee.

41

In the coffee shop across the road from the station. Lunch. Went back in, filed my report on the angry neighbours; wrote it in fifteen minutes, spent close on forty-five before I finally managed to upload it. Made a couple of calls in relation to a small betting shop stramash from a couple of nights ago, will have to follow up one of them with a visit later this afternoon. Sat and stared at my desk for five minutes trying to think what we'd do about the toilet vandalism situation. Contemplated dipping further into the melancholic world of lost children. Finally decided to come across the road to grab a sandwich.

Mind is blank as Taylor pulls the other seat out at my table. My mind was blank because Philo Stewart keeps intruding, and I'm not ready for that yet. I'm not ready to embrace the tragedy of doomed romance.

'Tom,' he says.

I nod. 'You looking for me in particular, or did you just come out for a break and think it'd be rude not to sit down?'

He gives this a little thought and then shrugs. 'Neither,' he says. 'How's your morning been?'

'The usual kind of thing. A bit of UN peacekeeper, a bit of paperwork, a lot of getting fucked off at the dumb-ass, piece-of-shit filing system.'

He smiles briefly.

'You all right? At a guess, I'd say you're wearing the same clothes as yesterday, which is rarely a good sign.'

'I'm fine. Just couldn't bring myself to go home.'

'Why?'

He waves away the question almost as soon as it is out

of his mouth, a slight look of guilt on his face at the intrusion into my grief. Perhaps an acknowledgement from him that that's what I'm suffering. Grief. Unlike the usual suffering.

'Went to the Premier Inn over at the zoo. Watched some TV. Got up this morning, came into work. I should go home tonight. Just need to get on with it.'

'I heard you were at the church.'

News travels… well, you know the rest.

'I was just along the road. Still getting my head together. Went in for a moment's peace.'

'Did you get it?'

'Yes.'

'Have you found God, or are you just going to start listening to *Slow Train Coming* and *Saved*?'

'Funny. Neither.'

'Thank God for that. You speak to anyone while you were there?'

'Mrs Buttler, the church warden.'

'You discuss the case?'

'A little. You pissed off about that?'

He shakes his head. Takes a sip of coffee. Black filter. Hot as fuck, it looks like. He takes the regulation glance over his shoulder to see who else is around. There's no one that we particularly need to avoid.

I take a bite of my cheese and tomato ciabatta with Italian basil, whatever the fuck Italian basil is compared to any other kind of basil.

'What did she think about Cartwright?'

'She's delighted. She hates him. Immediately, and you know, this is what bothers me about it, immediately you can see she's thinking, *maybe this'll be the catalyst for us to get our church back.* So why would Cartwright do it now? Why crack now? He had everything where he wanted it. He'd nailed the fucker with an inch-perfect, geometrically precise plan. Every eventuality thought of and schemed for. Nailed it. Absolutely fucking nailed it. So, why now? Why do this thing where he's not only taking a chance by murdering people, but he's doing it in this ostentatious manner, this balls-out, look at me you fuckers, look what I'm doing with all my fucked-up, crazy Book of Daniel shit. Makes no sense whatsoever.'

Taylor doesn't answer. Looks at the table, winces as he burns his lips.

'You get any more out of Cartwright?' I ask.

'Not a huge amount. Sticking to his story which, if it's true, slightly contradicts your perfectly reasonable assertion that he would've been stupid to risk anything else, because he'd already won. This guy had let the glory of success get to him. Still chasing St Stephen's. He even had actual architectural plans for how he'd redesign St Stephen's church to allow him to get planning permission, with a view to selling it off. This guy was ahead of the game. Which doesn't mean, of course, that he killed anyone, because there's a difference between scheming and, as you say, balls-out murder.'

'But what about the rest of the gang? At least two of those people hated him. And the kid? He was there because he liked granny porn?'

'He called them a committee of all the talents.'

'He didn't.'

'He did.'

'Wanker.'

'Quite. You know, you said it yourself, Sergeant. There's something about the guy. Sure, he comes across as, you know…'

'A total douchebag.'

'Aye, that. But he knows what he's doing. He's in control. He had this fired-up woman from Halfway, just desperate to make a difference to something, and duping her with the possibility of getting her church back. He had an influential woman on the inside at St Stephen's. He had the crazy woman from the Kirk, who was just dying for someone to bring her into a circle, to make her part of a team. To be somebody in this business, rather than the outsider, screaming at the moon. And the kid… quite legitimately, he was going for all ages. There are more young people at St Stephen's than in the parish now, so the kid was there to get the youth vote. So, overall they had this plan to undermine and brief against the Reverend Jones, while spreading pro-merger propaganda amongst the congregation, and he had these people briefing and lobbying for him right across the congregations of the town. The guy was good. So, yes, it really doesn't make sense that he would then kill these people.'

'And Philo Stewart was in on this?'

He nods. Finally ventures another sip of coffee.

I bite into the ciabatta and think about what she'd said. She hadn't been very forthcoming on that, but really, we'd hardly known each other.

'Why didn't she say something? You know, I... I slept with the woman. If three of five people in a little group of hers had been murdered, wouldn't it have occurred to her that she might be next?'

'They didn't know who the other members were. He wonders if they thought they knew, guessed perhaps, but they wouldn't have known for definite.'

'Fucking internet,' I mutter. 'It was so much easier when people just met in dark corners to plot and scheme.'

'Well, I don't know that it was, but it is a bag of spanners. It could go off in a thousand directions.'

'So, is it possible that Maureen and Agnes didn't even realise it was Cartwright who was running the operation, given that they hated him?'

'As a matter of fact,' he says, now more confidently swigging down coffee, 'that's right. He had a front man, who the others all thought was heading up the operation.'

'Jesus?'

He laughs.

'Sadly, no. The vicar who presided over the illicit burial of Mrs Henderson.'

'Really? I spoke to that guy yesterday.'

'Tell me about it. I'm about to head off there now.'

'We didn't get into any kind of discussion about the

church and the merger and all that. Just talked about the burial. How it had come about, et cetera. He pitched the exact same story as Mrs Buttler.'

'Did you buy it?'

'Seemed legit.'

He glances at his watch, takes another swig.

'What's the plan for Cartwright?' I ask, through a mouthful of cheese and tomato.

'Hasn't changed. Still getting ourselves together. We can certainly make a case, just not sure it'll hold up. You want to come?'

'To interview the vicar?'

'Sure,' he says.

'You're not very good at kicking me off the case.'

'You have a different air about you,' he says. 'Just for this interview, see if you pick up anything different from this guy now you know there's something to look for. After that I'm speaking to Mr Stewart. Chances are I won't let you sit in on that one.'

I'm no stranger to guilt, although not usually in connection with the husbands whose wives I've slept with. Guilt, nevertheless, chooses its moment to arrive.

Taylor takes another slurp of coffee, leaves half of it and gets to his feet, perhaps sensing that I may be about to take one of my regular trips to Melancholy Street.

'Come on,' he says, 'let's move. You can finish that in the car.'

42

Waiting in the sitting room for the old guy to make a cup of tea, in amongst the total debauchery of the collected ornaments of his life. Thousands of little figures in crystal and china, and teacups and plastic flowers and wooden flowers and photographs in frames, and photographs out of frames, and frames without photographs, and wooden animals and porcelain dolls and bronze Adonises.

Adonises? Adoni?

Wonder if he's gay. Hmm. I'm not, you know, going to say that out loud. Just thinking it now as I look around the collection of stuff. Several naked male bottoms, that's all that put the thought in there.

Perhaps he's not gay, and he's got like fifty grandchildren and every Christmas they all think, what the fuck are we going to get Grandpa? Then they think, oh, I know, he likes all that boring ornamental shit, like Greek dudes with their tackle out or, I don't know, a fucking Smirnoff crystal figure of a fucking dolphin.

It's not Smirnoff, is it?

Jesus, sometimes I wish I could just switch off my head.

'This is like old person Hell,' says Taylor.

'I know.'

'Gay or recently widowed?' he asks.

I laugh as the door opens and the old fella comes in. I'm talking like he's a hundred and ten, but the guy is in his late seventies probably and still reasonably fit. There's something about him that doesn't tie in with the total bunfight of ornamentation. He's carrying two cups of tea in saucers. No biscuits.

Don't like tea without a biscuit. Taylor would probably lamp me if I asked for one of the bourbons he brought me previously.

'Chief Inspector,' he says, taking a seat. Taylor is still standing. 'What can I help you with?'

'You know Mr Paul Cartwright?' asks the boss, cutting to the chase.

'Yes.'

'In what capacity?'

'Through the church, of course. I must admit I wasn't terribly familiar with him before the merger, but we got to know each other over the last few years. And, of course—'

'And what do you think of him?' asks Taylor, cutting him off. I'd warned Taylor of the man's tendency to ramble.

He pauses, takes a loud sip of tea, gives me a glance and then smiles as the tea cup comes away from his mouth.

'He can be trying,' says the Reverend Forsyth.

'When was the last time you spoke to him?'

He lays his cup down on a side table, somehow managing to find space among all the crap.

'Last week,' he says. Taylor indicates for him to keep talking with a perfectly timed eyebrow. 'A small matter we've been discussing.'

'You want to tell us about it?'

And now you can see the thought processes running. They're all the same, whether they've got something to hide or not. Doesn't matter, the same thing goes through everyone's head when they're talking to the police: how much do the Fuzz already know?

'Oh, it was nothing,' he says, then he smiles and indicates the room with a casually thrown hand. 'Look at all this. Can't say no to a beautiful ornament when I see one.'

'I'm going to have to ask you to accompany us down to the station,' says Taylor.

The Reverend Forsyth seems surprised at first, and then

resignation takes hold of him as he realises he made a misjudgement.

One might also question his judgement of an ornament 'n' all.

*

Back at my desk. Looking through statistics on public toilet vandalism. Yes, I am. Has to be done. Not down interviewing with Taylor. He thought it best that my continued involvement on the case be kept at the unofficial level, and not paraded about the station.

It's nice that Connor hasn't come back to him on it, yet. He's obviously just completely forgotten about me. My superintendent makes me feel so warm. Of course, I got to shag the previous one, so on some sort of law of averages, I was bound to come up against someone who doesn't realise that I exist. Definitely for the best.

Just thinking that it might be time to head out and do a tour of the public toilets of the area – there's a job – without as yet getting back in touch with my erudite toilet cleaning officer, when Morrow's phone rings. I watch it for a few moments, not that a ringing phone looks so different from a silent one, the little red light aside, then lean over and lift the receiver.

'Morrow's phone.'

'Hutton,' says Ramsay. 'Morrow around?'

'Haven't seen him in twenty minutes.'

'Got someone for him at the front desk. Can you come down and show him to a room?'

'Sure beans,' I find myself saying, out of nowhere. Jesus. Must be the phone. It automatically translates you into the person whose call you've answered. The things they can do nowadays.

Ramsay hangs up without speaking, which is as appropriate a response to *sure beans* as you can get. Last look at toilet vandalism statistics, without any of it going in, and then out the office and down the stairs.

Into reception, and there he is. Fuck. Hadn't even thought about it.

Tony Stewart, standing a few feet away from the desk, swathed in misery, melancholy and self-loathing. Jesus, it's like looking in a fucking mirror.

He doesn't see me coming, he's so distracted. I'm up in front of him before he lifts his head.

'Mr Stewart,' I say. 'Thanks for coming in.'

The words feel like dirt in my mouth.

He looks pathetic. Acknowledges me standing there in front of him, but says nothing.

*

Jesus, I don't want to have anything to do with this guy, but it feels unbelievably cruel to leave him on his own. Stick him in a room and say, go on, my cuckolded friend, suffocate to death in your own misery, why don't you? We will provide the unutterable gloom of the setting, if you can bring along your own melancholy and suicidal depression.

I stick him in an interview room, one of the non-intimidating ones with a first floor window onto daylight, or what passes for daylight in November in the west of Scotland, nip out to get two cups of tea and instruct Constable Grant to briefly interrupt Taylor to let him know that his next in line is here. If the Reverend Forsyth is taking longer than expected, hopefully Taylor can park him for a bit and then come and deal with Stewart.

I walk back in, two cups of tea, place one on the table in front of him, sit down opposite.

Now, I'm nobody's conversational go-to guy at the best of times. No one ever thought, *fuck me but I need to be doing some small talk, where be Hutton*? No, conversation and I are uneasy bedfellows, and this situation is the Mount Doom of small-talk scenarios. Obviously there is serious interviewing to be done of the guy, establishing what he knew about his wife's involvement with

Cartwright, but the interviewing isn't for me to do.

I'm here to stop him throwing himself out the window. You might think the bastard's not going to throw himself out the window, but sitting here, he sure as fuck looks as though that's what he wants to do.

'I'm afraid we need to wait for DCI Taylor. He's the lead officer on the case.'

He doesn't look at me, but there's a small movement of his head to indicate that he at least heard.

Feeling a tightness in my chest, which has been coming on since I saw him in reception. I want to apologise. That's nuts, isn't it? Why the fuck do I want to apologise? I never want to apologise to the husband. Ever. To me it's always about the women. If they didn't want to do it, then they wouldn't do it. I never force any of them to do anything. Why is it, and we see it often enough, that husbands get pissed off at the guy who sleeps with their wife, rather than the wife? As if the wife was not at all complicit.

I suppose if they feel the need to physically hurt someone, they're less likely to hit the woman. Not that you don't also get the beaten wife, so let's not get carried away.

I know what was different this time, of course.

Just like that, with that snap of the fingers – or the snap of the fucking heartstring! – I was in love with her. She felt the same. We were going to be together. Shit, there was a lot I didn't know about her, like what she was doing in this bizarre little group with Cartwright, but at some point in the near future, she was going to look at this man who's currently sitting across the table from me wearing his sorrow like a fucking death mask and say that she was leaving him, and that when he got back from Bishkek or Ashgabat or fucking Samarkand or wherever the fuck it was he was going next, she wasn't going to be there.

And I feel guilty.

'When was the last time you saw your wife?' I ask.

Can't help it. Have to say something.

He stirs, looks across the table. Eye to eye. That thing I thought earlier, Jesus Christ, I was right. Looking in the fucking mirror. That's what I'm doing. How many times have I crawled into the bathroom, thrown some water in my face, raised my head and seen those eyes looking back at me? How many fucking times?

That hand around my chest is squeezing ever more tightly.

'Last Sunday,' he says. His voice is ragged and small. 'At church. I travelled to Bishkek just after.'

I nod. He recognises the acknowledgement in my eyes.

'You knew I was in Bishkek,' he says.

'Philo told me,' I say.

What are you doing? Taylor knew the guy had been in Bishkek, and he'd never met the wife. The police met the guy off the plane, fucking Bishkek National Airlines Flight 101. I didn't need to go there.

His shoulders straighten a little. His eyes are slightly curious.

'When did you speak to my wife?'

Oh fuck. Here we go. I walked right into that, didn't I?

Speak to her, my sad sack friend? I fucked her! Ho ho ho!

'I saw her at church on the Sunday, then I spoke to her a couple of days later at the house. Just getting some background on the situation at St Stephen's and how the relationship with the churches had developed over time.'

'We were new to the church. We didn't really get involved,' he says. 'Why did you speak to her?'

Hesitate. I'm the police officer in the police interview room and I'm the one who's being put on the spot.

'Background,' is all I manage. Which isn't entirely inaccurate.

He looks hurt. I want to know why he looks hurt, but I can't ask. As it happens, I don't need to.

'She was Philomena.'

I don't say anything. A loud expletive of *fuck* explodes in my head.

'She was Philomena. She was always Philomena. She told everyone that was her name. She was proud of it. The only time...' Voice breaking, likelihood of tears, 78%. Crap. '...the only time she ever called herself Philo was when she met me. That was how she introduced herself...'

Voice breaks, he closes his eyes, fights to keep it together. Swallows, struggles his way through a few facial contortions.

'Why did you call her Philo?'

And you know, that should have the guilt and the fear and the self-loathing coming winging its way in on a grey fucking horse named Death, but it doesn't. Instead I sit there looking across the table at this poor fucking bastard, and all I can think is this. She knew. Right there at the church, walking up to me to introduce herself. She knew.

All right, maybe she did it all the time, and the sad sack knew nothing about it. But that wasn't it. She and I were perfect for each other, right from the off, right from that first damned minute.

I'll take your misery, my wretched friend, and raise you a thousand.

The door opens.

43

Walk out the station. Cold wind outside. Head thumping, hurt flowing like blood.

Hurt flowing like blood? Jesus, what a dick.

Look at my watch. 16:01. I stand there, looking down the road. It's an actual fact that wherever you are in the west of Scotland, you are never more than a hundred yards away from the nearest pub. Look at my watch again. I need a drink. I need lots of drinks. I need to drown myself. I need one of those garbage evenings soaked in alcohol that ends with me flat on my face in my sitting room in front of some bastard on BBC4. The thought of trawling through town looking for women doesn't even enter my head.

What are the odds of me making it into work tomorrow? Taylor's already going to be pissed off that he just walked in on me talking to Stewart; turning up hungover, or not turning up at all, is going to be one of those final straws they talk about.

How many chances is the guy going to give me? He keeps giving me them, and I keep drinking them down with a double shot of vodka, ice and lemon optional.

What was I doing? I need something to do. Need to pick up one of those strands that was lying around.

Baxter. I think of Reverend Baxter, the two of us sitting on that bench, looking out on that amazing sea, the water the most incredible colour.

Find the girl. That's what he said. Find the girl. Does she have anything to do with this? Really? Some strange recurring nightmare?

Did I feel, when I was making my previous check on

on-going missing persons investigations and those from the recent past, that I was doing something useful? You know yourself, don't you? When you're doing anything in life, anything at all. You know whether what you're doing is of any value.

I don't know what I thought. I can barely think about anything. She's there, right in front of me. Philo Stewart. I'm looking over my shoulder at her as she sits at my small table. One last look.

Fuck.

Look up. Standing outside the pub. Hadn't even thought about it as I'd walked here. Like I'm drunk already, no control over my movements.

The girl. That's what Baxter said, and as soon as he'd said it, I knew he was right. That girl isn't springing in and out of my head for nothing.

I need to check open murder cases and archived missing persons. Neither makes sense, of course. She's not just in my dreams. How can she be? She gave me a book. I saw her at the graveyard. Constable Webb saw her too. How can she have been murdered? And if it's an archived missing persons report, she's not going to be this little girl. I already checked back fifteen years.

Yet I know that I need to go and do some more checking. Don't even look at the pub. Turn, walk back to the station. Don't go to the office. Round the back, into the car. The stuff I'll be checking is old enough that it likely won't be on computer. I need to look at files.

Maybe I'm being ridiculous. There's some sort of explicit acknowledgement in even looking at this stuff that the girl must be dead, in which case she's in my imagination or she's a ghost or some other inexplicable shit that I don't want to think about. So, I'm not going to think about it.

Off in to Glasgow to look at the old records.

*

It's apparent that I'm not currently fit for the job because this stuff is depressing the shit out of me. On the one hand, of course it's depressing. Endless reports of dead and missing children, ruined families, wasted lives. But that's policing every day, and the only way to do it, the thing that we all do, is not let it get to you. And this, this right here, is getting to me.

The dead two-year-old, the five-year-old who wandered off in the shopping centre, the young teenager who left one night and never came home. Story after story of heartache; sometimes it's laid out for all to see, and sometimes you can only read between the lines at the utter misery which led to the events.

Sitting at a desk in a storeroom in the basement, like every research scene in every movie you ever saw. Lighting isn't great, no windows.

There are three others down here with me. Three women. Two of them archiving, or doing whatever it is they're doing, working in this place. Another officer, searching through old documents.

Had a brief word or two with the archivists when I came in, established whereabouts I needed to be looking, and got on with it. Flicked through quickly at the beginning, taking no time at all with the boys, stopping to look at the photographs of the girls.

As I move through the boxes, and the dates pass further back into history, I start to come across the odd report with no pictures attached. What can I do then? Have a quick read through the report, establish if there might be some age connection with the girl I'm searching for, perhaps some geographical connection, and then move on.

Bob plays in my head. I put the tune there when I can. *You Ain't Going Nowhere*. What's it about? No idea. But it's a jaunty little tune, and I try to think about it sometimes. I try. Fight off the demons, such as those fuckers are. And the demons are on the move today.

Finish with the seventies, move back to the sixties. *You Ain't Going Nowhere* struggles on. Tapping a finger.

Humming. Unaware if either of the archivists will be looking at me. Think the other officer might have left.

A report from 4th August 1967 leaps out at me. No photograph. Daisy Compton. That's all. Daisy Compton. Missing, aged eleven. Last seen going to play in a park in Tollcross. She'd disappeared eleven months earlier. The first report I see is the one that basically admits defeat. I look back through the previous reports, nothing else of significance to be gleaned.

However, it's none of this information that jumps off the page. It's the name of the child's father. Reverend Archibald Compton. The Reverend Compton. Has me thinking of our old chap, currently in custody. Sure, Compton's his first name, but it leaps out all the same. Of course it does. You get attuned to looking for the slightest thing.

Closer check of the document, and there's nothing else. Make a couple of notes, then look up. One archivist left. Check the time. After six. Will be long since dark outside.

'Are you needing to leave?'

She looks up, smiles.

'You've got another thirty minutes or so.'

'I need a computer.'

'Of course,' she says, and she nods in the direction of three monitors sitting against the far wall.

Leave the files behind, but still lying out on the table, and walk over to the computer.

44

Rain is falling, one of those set rains, heavy, consistent, little wind, rain not going anywhere. Early evening, driving out to Newton Mearns. Windscreen wipers on full, the night-time traffic a blur of water and lights. Slowed to a stop in Cathcart, now heading up through Clarkston.

On my way to see Mrs Juliet Faraday, the ex-wife of the reverend Archibald Compton, the man who changed his name to Compton Forsyth, and was moved to another church in Glasgow after their daughter went missing and his marriage broke up. No photographs on the internet, so I've really no idea what it is I'm going to say to this woman when she asks why I'm there – nor, indeed, how I would explain it to Taylor or Connor should either of them ever ask – but I've switched off that overactive part of my brain, and am not trying to plan anything out. What happens, happens.

Begin to get a strange feeling of nervousness as I get closer to my destination. As I make lights, and don't get held up, I begin to wish that the traffic was heavier. I don't want to get to this woman's house, although I'm not sure why that is. I'm not worried about it. What's the worst she can say? *Bugger off, Sergeant, I don't want to talk to you.* We get that fifteen times a day.

I used to get nerves on the job, but it's been a long time. In the old days the nerves were always related to big man activity. Apprehension at facing a regular Glasgow hard case. They don't bother me anymore. Nothing does.

Except now, as I pull up in front of this semi-detached house on a quiet residential street, I feel incredibly uncomfortable. I called ahead and she knows I'm coming, although she has no idea why. Perhaps she thinks I've found her daughter. Perhaps I *have* found her daughter. In my nightmares, at least. I doubt she'd see that as a positive.

Sit in the car for a couple of minutes. Don't want to get out. Turn Bob off, sit in silence. Well, silence is relative. The rain is stoating off the roof.

Fuck it.

Out the car, up the garden path, ring the bell, stand close to the door beneath the short awning and wait.

*

'You're sure I can't get you a cup of tea?'

'I'm all right, thanks.'

'Very well.'

She takes a seat on the sofa beside her husband. He's looking at me that way people usually do. She seems nervous. I'm standing with my hands in my pockets, having refused the offer of a seat as well as the tea. There's the hum of a fake-log fan heater; in another room the television is on. News. Somewhere something shit is happening.

Inevitably I take too long to say anything, which allows the bloke to say, 'What's all this about, officer?'

Good question.

'I'm sorry to trouble you, Mrs Faraday,' I say, ignoring the bloke, 'but we have your ex-husband in for questioning at the moment, and I just wanted to ask a few background questions.'

'You've arrested him?' says the bloke sharply.

'No,' I answer, although what do I know? They could have done all sorts in the last few hours, albeit my phone has been silent. I'd been expecting, at least, Taylor to call to rap my testicles for sitting in the same room as Tony Stewart.

Jesus, don't think about that.

'How long were you married?'

Mr Faraday has that regulation pissed-off-at-the-coppers look on his chops, but what do I care? The dude's like eighty or something. I'm sure I could take him.

'Fourteen years,' she says, looking up after a few seconds' adjusting to the fact that she's going to have to talk about something she doesn't even like thinking about.

'That was in the fifties, sixties?'

'Yes.'

'Can you give me a brief outline of your marriage, why it didn't last?'

'Really?' snaps the wounded prick, standing up for his wife. 'Do you—'

'It's all right,' she says, squeezing his hand.

Yeah, dickhead, listen to your wife. I give her the space. The guy mumbles and looks vaguely like he's been defenestrated.

'There's really not a lot to say,' she says. 'We were married in 1953. Nothing especially interesting about it, much like any couple in those post-war years. Archie was a trainee minister for a while, took some time to get a full-time job, but finally got a placement in Tollcross in the early sixties. There was nothing exceptional…'

She lets her voice go, because there might not have been anything exceptional at first, but there was something exceptional coming. Again I give her the space, while the husband holds on to her hand.

'Then one day our daughter disappeared.' She hesitates to shake her head, but there will be no tears. This woman is in her early 80s, and has had a whole other life since then. She must have found the ability to talk about it at some point. 'She was outside playing. You didn't think anything of it back in those days. But one day she never came home. There was some suggestion that she might have run away, but she was only eleven, and such a happy little girl. So happy…'

At least I've managed to take my hands out of my pockets. Don't push her though. Everything I need to learn is coming.

'Archie blamed himself, the poor man. He felt terrible.

And I'm afraid, for a while at least, I passed my anxiety…
my grief… on to him, and was happy to blame him too.
We never recovered. He started drinking. We both did.
Eventually he wanted to leave, get out of Tollcross. At the
time I didn't. I wanted to spend every minute there, every
minute looking out at the street as if she might come
running round the corner.'

She smiles. Dangerous territory. You can see it; now
she's about to start crying, and when that happens old
fucktard chops will get terribly defensive on her behalf and
no doubt attempt to escort me from the premises.

'Why did he change his name?'

Keep 'em talking on matters of practicality.

She gives a slight shake of the head, a slight smile.

'Why do women cut their hair after a break-up? No one
knows. He got the church in Cambuslang, and I wouldn't
go with him. He just wanted to start over. Had always
hated Archibald. Took the opportunity to lose the name.
Stopped drinking, as far as I know, got himself together.
Got the new life that he wanted.'

She squeezes the bloke's hand again, gives him a bit of
a reassuring glance and says, 'So did I.'

Well, I know the rest. Compton Forsyth didn't go
straight to the Old Kirk. He got the Halfway gig for a few
years, and then got promoted to the bigger church. Stayed
there until he retired from full-time work, a few years
before he actually had to.

So, I could probably ask several more questions in
relation to the missing kid, but I don't want them thinking
that's solely why I'm here.

Do I suspect the old minister of having done something
to his daughter? Just because he was guarded, bordering
on evasive, with Taylor earlier? We weren't really
accusing him of anything.

'Have you got a photograph of Daisy?' I ask.

'Good grief!' the guy barks.

Good grief? How fucking old are you, grandad?

Well, probably about eighty-five, actually.

'There wasn't one in the file,' I say, directing all my conversation to the woman, even though there wasn't one on the file isn't exactly an explanation for the question.

She gets slowly to her feet. Hip replacement.

'Of course, just give me a moment.'

She walks from the room. The old guy looks daggers at me. No doubt he was a fucking soldier or something and thinks he can still take me. I give him a glance, and then look back at the door.

Those nerves, which had mostly gone while talking to Mrs Faraday, suddenly come raging back.

What do I possibly expect from this photograph? There's no third alternative. Either the girl is not the one who's been running through my head, in which case, why am I here? Or, she is. In which case, Jesus fucking Christ, a young girl who's been missing since 1966 gave me a Bible.

Nerves.

Mrs Faraday walks slowly back into the room, a small picture in her hand. Now she's crying. Mr Faraday gets to his feet to defend his wife's honour.

She stops in front of me, takes a moment, and then hands me the photograph.

45

And they that be wise shall shine
as the brightness of the firmament

Driving back through the rain and the traffic. Fewer cars, so everyone going faster, the air filled with spray. Wipers flying back and forth, back and forth, umbrellas scurrying by on the pavements, blurry lights flashing all around, everything smeared with rain.

I'm crying. Why am I crying? For Philo Stewart? For the ghost of a little girl who vanished nearly fifty years ago? Or is it just me? I'm crying for myself, because I'm so utterly fucked up, because I really haven't a fucking clue what's going on.

How could I? How could that happen? How could I be seeing that little girl? The daughter of Mrs Faraday and Reverend Compton Forsyth?

She's not just missing. If she had gone off somewhere to live some other life with some other family, then I wouldn't be seeing her. I'm seeing her because she's dead. I'm seeing her because forty-seven years ago someone killed her, and she wants me to find her body.

And the scariest fucking thing of all is that I know where the body is buried. I know. I knew as soon as I saw it, but I didn't like that thought, did I? So I pushed it away. On one level it was obvious, yet on another so utterly preposterous, so stupidly, insanely far-fetched, that it was easy to push away. Easy to hide in some remote part of my head.

Stop at Wickes on the way home, buy the first shovel that comes to hand. Don't compare the price, don't compare the quality of the shovel.

'Y'all right, darlin'?' asks the woman at the checkout.

Answer with the merest of nods. Look at the shovel the whole time. She's probably wondering if she should sell me the shovel, because a shovel's the kind of thing you could do some damage with. Maybe I look like I'm intending to do some damage. Maybe, she's thinking, she should call the manager. Or the police. She does neither. She hands me my change and the receipt. I leave with the shovel.

Why me, Daisy Compton? You could have come to anyone. It didn't even have to be someone involved in an investigation. It could have been anyone at any time in the last forty-seven years.

Maybe she has. Maybe I'm her second, third, ninth, fifteenth, fiftieth attempt.

How many accidents do I nearly have? No idea. Barely notice the drive, don't even think about going back to the station. Along Glenvale Road, past Philo Stewart's house. Can't stop myself looking. No lights on. Nobody home. Where will the cuckold, the widow, be spending the night?

Up the road to the Old Kirk, into the small car park between the hall and the church. Grab the shovel, step out into the rain. Streaming down. I'm still wet from walking to and from Wickes. That kind of rain. Only takes a few seconds. At least you can't tell my tears for the water.

Head is exploding. Jesus! Make it go away. Just stop, come on Hutton, make it stop. Put it in one of those fucking compartments you're so up your arse about, you're so convinced that you have littered all over the fucking place in your stupid, fucking head.

Through the gate, a lone figure in a massive waterproof stands by the grave. As soon as he sees me he starts to walk towards me. In the rain and the dark he won't recognize me, just as I don't yet recognise him. All he'll be seeing is a guy with a shovel walking towards the grave he's protecting.

'Stop!' he shouts.

It's Wallace. I stop. It's not like he's about to pull a gun on me, but there's no need to wind the kid up.

Lift my hand, shout, 'It's Hutton.'

God, the rain is so damned loud. The rain is loud. He slows, recognises me.

'Sergeant,' he says.

I acknowledge him with barely more than a nod that he probably doesn't even see, then walk past him. Shovel in hand.

'Sergeant?' he says, falling in behind. 'Sergeant?' he repeats, a little louder.

I stop, more or less next to the grave of Maureen Henderson, and turn.

'Constable Wallace?'

'You're digging up the grave?' he asks. Sounds worried. Of course he's fucking worried. The last thing you want when you've been given one crappy duty to do for eight hours is a ranking police officer turning up and doing precisely what you've to stop anyone doing.

We stand a yard apart, me with my shovel, Wallace with his worry, but also his determination, separated by pishing, soaking, cascading rain.

'Not this grave,' I say. 'You're all right. Another one, just down here.'

'Sir?'

'You stand there and guard your grave, Stevie, this has nothing to do with you.'

'Have you been drinking, sir?' he throws at my back, just as I've turned away.

Hesitate. Keep my temper in check. It is, there's no denying, a fair bloody question.

'No, Constable, I haven't. You do your job, let me do mine.'

Start to move away.

'Maybe I should call it in, sir,' he says.

I answer that with a dismissive wave. He can do what he wants, but I'm starting to dig up this grave right now.

I stand looking down at the headstone, the slightly

272

clearer words beneath the name and dedication to the deceased.

And they that be wise shall shine as the brightness of the firmament.

Why did he do that? Why would you bury someone in an already marked grave, and highlight the headstone with a new engraving?

But I know. I know already. Those words, they have nothing to do with the man who dug up this grave and placed another body in it. Those words just appeared, the same as that girl has appeared in my head so often.

Shovel into the grass and into ground, the earth soft with the cacophonous rain. Not trying to do a neat job, or an anything job. Just need to get it done. Cut a square of grass, lift out the first wedge. Aware that Wallace is standing over me.

'I'm going to call it in, sir,' he says.

I pause, my back to him. Good lad.

'Give me twenty minutes, Stevie,' I say, turning, 'then you can call it in. OK?'

He stares down at me. The rain falls straight, without a breath of wind.

Wallace leaves. I start digging. Head's not screwed on straight. I dig, don't think. A few minutes later, I'm aware that he's back. I've barely begun. I don't want him to tell me that Taylor's already on his way. He surprises me by appearing with a shovel, and starting to dig from the other end.

I pause for a moment, watch his first couple of scoops.

'Thanks,' I say.

'You were never going to do it in twenty minutes, sir,' he says.

*

We dig. No idea about the time. And he was right. The constable knows a lot more about digging a hole than I do, it appears. Whatever the time is, it's a lot longer than

273

twenty minutes, even with two of us. At some point we hit the lid of the coffin. Only space for me in the pit, Wallace at the side, moving earth out of the way.

I've no intention of attempting to make this a clean operation. I don't need elaborate space around the coffin. I'm not looking to raise the thing and carefully remove the lid. I just need to clear the earth from part of the lid, to smash the top with the shovel, to break in, to find what I know I'm going to find.

What if I'm wrong?

The thought barely crosses my mind. Occasionally flits in and out.

Am I still crying? Jesus, I don't know anymore. Maybe I have been the whole time. Consumed. Consumed by the need to open the coffin, and find the body of the girl. She's going to be here, I know she is.

Standing at the thin end of the coffin, the shovel now scraping along the lid at the top, picking up the sodden dirt, tossing it in clumps up to the surface. Soaking rain, pitch darkness. How am I even going to see anything? Thinking of problems as they arise.

'You got a torch?' I shout.

Why am I shouting? Above the pounding of the rain, the pounding in my head.

I pitch up some more earth. He doesn't answer. I look up, and then he shines a narrow beam of light down onto the top of the coffin.

Hear a car pull up outside the church. Someone in a rush. Not the only ones.

The light shining down on the dirty, sodden coffin lid, I lift the shovel and thump it down as hard as I can in the confined space.

Footsteps. Aware of more torchlight bouncing around above my head.

Another hit with the shovel, a crack of old, damp wood.

'Constable!'

The light shining on the coffin lifts. Drive the shovel in again. Louder noise. Do it again, quickly.

'Constable?'

Taylor, barking. Not alone. Constable Wallace says nothing. Suddenly there are two torches being shone down onto my coffin, another in my face.

Bring the shovel back down onto the lid.

'Hutton? Hutton! What the fuck are you doing?'

Angry words. Angry words and rain and light all pouring down. With the light, I can see the coffin lid is cracking.

Taylor's not stopping me. Doesn't know what to do. I don't look up to see who's with him. Feet to the side of the coffin, jam the shovel into the crack in the wood and start to prise it open. The wood is cracked and old and damp, getting damper by the pouring, bloody, torrential second.

'Jesus, Hutton,' shouts Taylor.

The light goes into my face again for a second, and then back down onto the coffin lid.

Rain. Rain. So much fucking rain. Fucking Scotland.

The wood doesn't give as much as I think it's going to. Bring the shovel back down onto the lid. Again. Again.

'Hutton!'

Try to prise it open again, but it's not breaking apart yet. Toss the shovel up onto the ground, then wedge my feet against the sides of the pit and lean forward. Grab the wood, start pulling it. Immediately hands cut and splintered, pain jags into them. Ignore it, rip wood.

A large piece lifts up from the middle, bend it perpendicular, then push it back with my feet. A ten, twelve-inch gap opens up. Three torches shine into it. With the rain and the confused light it's not all immediately apparent, but I know what I'm looking at, and soon enough, those other three see it.

'Hutton?' says Taylor.

The urgency has gone from his voice. Now he's questioning.

In the dark and the rain and the convergence of torches there's a mat of long hair, bones, skulls, one lying on top of the other, a faded dress, a faded cardigan.

I know the dress. I know the cardigan.

Oh, I'm crying now. Not just the rain. On my knees, on a broken coffin lid. In the dark.

'Hutton!'

46

Sitting in Taylor's car. The rain has stopped. Fuck. Wouldn't you know? Doesn't matter.

Cup of coffee. Voices outside. Windows steamed up. Soaking, cold, hands circled around the coffee, hoping the warmth travels up my arms. Shaking slightly, tissues wrapped around cut fingers, but slowly pulling myself together.

More of our lot have arrived. Mrs Buttler has been alerted. Lights are being set up prior to a proper excavation of the grave taking place. Only been a few minutes. Fifteen maybe. Twenty. Look at the clock. Realise I've lost track of time. 20:37.

Car door opens and Taylor gets in. Doesn't have coffee. Puts the key in the ignition, but doesn't start the car.

'You need to go home,' he says.

'The girl,' I say, before he asks the question. 'The girl who gave me the book. I told you about the girl. That's her in the grave.'

He looks sharply at me.

'What? When did she die?'

OK, that was a bad start. Straighten myself out. This is no place for ghosts and absurdity and whatever the fuck this is. I don't know who gave me that Book of Daniel, but it wasn't her. She's dead, and has been for over forty years.

'There's been a girl haunting me. In my head. Can't explain it, but, you know, if anything, it's probably because I've been so fucked up. I don't know, I've been open to this kind of thing. Whatever that is.'

More coffee. Keep talking. Don't let him ask questions.

'Baxter, the old guy, the old minister, he said, find the

girl. You need to find the girl. I checked back. Old records, missing persons, murders. Discovered that the vicar, Forsyth, he'd been married in the fifties, sixties, had a kid. The kid vanished. Never seen again. His marriage fell apart, he came to live here. I found the wife, she showed me a picture of the missing kid. It was the girl in my nightmares. I'd seen this grave, I just knew that's where she'd be.'

'What's her name?' he asks.

That's good. A request for basic information, taking for granted everything else. I can't handle disbelief.

'Daisy Compton. It's her. I recognize the dress.'

'You think... I don't know, what do you think?' he says.

'He killed her. Who knows why? Maybe it was an accident, maybe he was abusing her and she was going to talk. Who knows? He buried her in a graveyard, and then got a position in this town to watch over her. And he was going to make damn sure no one ever sold this land and dug up the grave.'

'Fuckity,' he says.

Fuckity?

More coffee. Finally turn and look at him. Getting back to normal. He's helped me by not expressing incredulity at how I came to be scraping away at a coffin lid in the pouring rain and the dark.

'You still have him in custody?'

He shakes his head. 'Let him out...' checks the clock '... more than four hours ago.'

'We need to go and see him.'

'You need to get home.'

'We need to go.'

He starts the engine.

*

Pulling up outside the old fella's house. Looks like a small light on in the hallway, nothing else showing. Wonder if he's taken the opportunity to leg it, yet why would he?

'What was going on with him and Cartwright?' I ask, breaking the silence of the previous few minutes.

'He was part of Cartwright's plan,' says Taylor. 'That's all. Asked them both separately about it. They obviously had no opportunity to confer. They said the same thing. A grand conspiracy. Think they just enjoyed, God, I don't know, the intrigue. Made them feel like they were in a Dan Brown novel.'

Stops the car and we get out. The air is damp and cold, but no rain.

'So it could have been this guy who killed the other four, just as much as it could have been Cartwright?'

He nods.

'Did you let Cartwright go?'

'Yep. Just didn't have enough to charge him, so we had to. Connor was spitting.'

Up the garden path. Ring the bell, wait in silence.

Turn away, look across the road. Curtains closed, can practically hear the televisions of the street blaring out their mindless crap.

Taylor tries the handle and the door opens. He gives me a glance and walks in. We pause in the hallway. Little sign of life other than the small lamp, but looking down we can see the timer plug behind it, meaning it will have come on automatically.

'Forsyth!' he calls out.

Looks up the stairs, then he mutters, 'Fuck,' and pushes open the door into the front room.

Reverend Forsyth is dead, a single spike hammered into his eye socket.

The room feels cold, and for the first time in a while I'm aware of my soaking, dripping clothes.

47

Three hours later. Almost midnight. Standing over Forsyth's dead body. Taylor and I have just arrived and Balingol has been doing his thing.

The spike has been removed from the eye. A dark, bloody, empty socket looks back at us. Have barely seen Taylor since we found the body. I stayed with the stiff and headed up the on-the-ground investigation. He legged it over to Cartwright's joint to speak to him, possibly to re-arrest him.

Naturally enough, this time the man had alibis coming out of his ears. He'd just been released from police custody. It was pretty inevitable that his wife and more than one other member of his family would be there to meet him, then take him home for a cup of tea and a biscuit.

Then Taylor had the job of informing Mrs Faraday that we might have found her daughter. We don't know for sure, yet. It wasn't like the body we found was obviously identifiable from the picture the woman had shown me earlier, or from the girl that had walked through my nightmares for the past couple of weeks. We should be able to complete formal identification tomorrow.

Forsyth. A single spike in the eye. The words Daniel are just sitting there in my head. How does that happen? I only read them once or twice.

'Same sedative as previously administered?' asks Taylor.

'Indeed,' says Balingol.

'Anything other than the obvious?'

'Doesn't seem to be. Single spike to the eye socket, and

as you can see here...' and he indicates the spike, which is lying on a small table next to the cadaver, 'it's long, fairly blunt and quite thick. Hammered in, I imagine. Might have caused the victim a peculiar sensation or two before he expired.'

Expired. Nice. Like a parking permit.

Feels cold in here. My clothes have not really dried out. Beginning to get shivery. Need to go home, get out of these. Dreaming of a warm shower.

'Time of death?'

'I think, quite possibly within an hour of him being released.'

Taylor lets out a long sigh. It's unavoidable. If he hadn't released him, he wouldn't be dead. Although, of course, the only reason to have kept him would have been because of some belief that he was the killer, which he very clearly was not. Unless, of course, he was part of a team, and someone else is tying up loose ends.

'There's a pattern to these, is there?' asks Balingol.

Taylor looks at me.

'"I considered the horns, and, behold, there came up among them another little horn, before whom there were three of the first horns plucked up by the roots: and, behold, in this horn were eyes like the eyes of man, and a mouth speaking great things."'

They look at me. The words are just there, in my head. I don't know how.

'This was the little horn, you think?' says Balingol, having come to terms with the fact that someone unexpected was spouting badass biblical shit.

I nod. Taylor, however, is still regarding me as a curiosity. He turns back to Balingol.

'You had a chance to look at the girl?' he asks.

I look round. Hadn't noticed it when I came in, but there she is, the small figure on the other side of the room, shrouded in white.

Shrouded in white, and impossibly sad. Jesus.

I wonder if I'll see her tonight.

Shiver again, rub my arms, once more try to throw melancholy out of sight.

'You look cold, Tom,' says Taylor. 'You should get home.'

'Will in a minute.'

'Blow to the head,' says Balingol. 'That's what I took from a cursory glance. If you don't mind, I think I might go home and do a more thorough investigation in the morning. Maybe I'll get Dr Baird to look at it.'

'Of course,' says Taylor.

He turns away, rubs his eyes, looks at the door. Is he expecting Connor to walk in here any minute, demanding answers and action?

'Fuck,' he mutters. Voice low. Balingol gives him a glance, a raised eyebrow, then pulls a sheet over the top of the Reverend Forsyth's body.

'See you in the morning, Bill,' he says.

Balingol replies without speaking. Taylor starts to walk to the door and I fall in behind.

'You get home, Sergeant.'

'You too.'

'Just going to tie up a few things at my desk. You need to get a shower, get into bed, or you'll be coming down with the flu, some shit like that. We don't want you off sick when you get suspended, now, do we?'

A bitter laugh from me. Nothing from him. We walk out the building in silence.

*

I guess this was how it had to be when I finally came home, when I finally came to sleep in my own bed for the first time since she'd been there. Knackered and drained, no thoughts of alcohol or depression or of the woman I'd decided was the love of my life. No thoughts. Just needing to tumble into the shower, fall into bed.

Walk into the flat, close the door behind me. Jacket on a peg in the hall, walk into the sitting room. Don't turn on the lights. As ever the room is illuminated by the lights from outside. The thought creeps back into my head. Will the girl be here?

She'd wanted me to find her body, right? That was all. She'd wanted to be found, so that her mother could bury her. The thought of her drifts away.

I walk into the middle of the room and stand in silence. Looking out the window. Suddenly my brain, which has been switched off, begins to wake up. But I wish it wouldn't. It has nowhere to go tonight, other than sorrow, the great weight of sadness. All this death, love found and immediately lost, that haunting little girl. And where are we for it all?

One more dead body, one less suspect.

The reflection of the red light on the phone blinks in the window. Have that feeling that comes over me sometimes, the feeling of such desolation that nothing could make it worse. It's never a thought I regret. Usually my mind is so low, so fucking low, that things can't get any worse.

I walk over to the phone. Grace watches me. One new message. I press the button, the crackle of the answering machine fills the room with such a sad sound. Any sound would be sad. The room demands silence.

'Hey...'

Oh, God. The voice jumps happily out into the darkness. Philo. I more or less fall onto the sofa, the crippling punch to the midriff taking the feeling from my legs, from the rest of me.

'Just got in. Thought I'd leave you a message. Another one. I know, you'll be thinking I'm one of those weird...' She laughs. There's a nervous buoyancy about her voice. 'You know... Anyway, it was lovely... gosh, you know that. I'll stop going on. There's some things I need to sort out. I'm involved in this thing, this stupid thing, with... about the churches, bringing the churches back together. David'll be so pissed off if he finds out. Well, that's what I thought. Anyway, I think he might know. He's coming

over shortly. That might be the end of me and the church.'
Pause. I stare at the red light. 'A lot of things might be
coming to an end. Hey, look, I'll see you in a couple of
days, OK. You can talk to me.' She laughs again. 'Just
wanted to say… you know, just called to say… oh, God, I
can't say it after that!' More laughter. 'I love you, Sergeant.
There! Said it. OK, OK, I'm going. See you. Bye!'

Click.

48

Walk back into the office. Still pretty busy for after midnight. Morrow at his desk. Gives me a glance, looks a little longer than is probably polite, nods, head back down.

What's there to see? Dried-in rain, sweat and tears. No jacket.

Straight to Taylor's office. The boss showing no sign of going anywhere. He looks up, a small shake of the head when he sees it's me.

'Your dedication is admirable, Sergeant...'

Close the door behind me, cut him off with the obvious fact that I'm not here to chew the fat. Take my mobile out my pocket. Knowing no other way, I put it on record and held it beside my land line while I replayed the message.

Hearing it the second time wasn't so bad. Had already started putting the walls up. This third time will be a breeze.

'Philo Stewart left me a message the other day, after she got home from my place. I only just listened to it.'

'So, not long before she died?'

I play the recording. Listening to it, but without hearing it. One of those. I know what it says.

He lets it run through, then asks me to play it again. This time I don't even listen. I could recite it, could probably have recited it after the first time I'd heard it. Her voice, soft and funny and insecure and nervous. Her voice, saying words. That's all I hear now.

'David, we presume, is the Reverend Jones down at St Stephen's?'

Nod.

'How would he get to hear about the gang of five? Or

six, if we count the dead vicar.'

'That's a lot of people to keep their mouths shut,' I say. 'Who knows what kind of agendas any of them had?'

'The most obvious one to have told him would've been Mrs Stewart, but that message there suggests otherwise, doesn't it? You met this guy?'

'Spoke to him last Sunday.'

'What d'you think?'

'He reminded me of Hitler.'

He makes some sort of rueful acknowledgement of the analogy, then gets to his feet.

'Bugger it, Sergeant. It places him at the scene of one of the crimes. The guy's a suspect. Let's get on to him.'

Taylor heads to the door. Stops as he gets to it, his fingers poised on the handle. Looks at the floor before he says anything. I know what's coming, head it off at the pass before we get into some shit about how I'm feeling.

'I'm fine,' I say.

'You sure?' he says, looking up.

'Come on. Work to do.'

Then Taylor is out the door, me in his wake.

*

Half an hour later, seven of us sitting in the small operations room beneath that tangle of whiteboards, a bunfight of names and lines and connections. Middle of the night, nobody tired.

Taylor has just entered, having previously given everyone the instructions to get what they could on Reverend Jones and bring it to the table. Pulls out the seat, sits down.

'We've got definite information that places Jones at one of the crime scenes. Enough to get him in here, enough to be able to get his DNA and hope we can also tie him to, at the very least, the scene of Mrs Christie's death. Not enough for court. What else have we got?'

Looks at DI Gostkowski, the first to his right.

'Phone records?'

'Of course,' she says. 'Of the previous four victims, the only one to have called the Reverend Jones was Mrs Stewart, but that makes sense, as she ran the Bible study group at the church. There were eleven calls in the last two months between them. Nothing from any of the other three. Now, this is interesting. There was a call from a mobile phone, the owner of which we have been unable to identify, to Mrs Stewart on the day of her death. This same number also called the Reverend Forsyth several times over the last few weeks.'

'Bingo,' says Taylor, his voice low, the word barely audible. Not looking at her, scribbling in his notebook.

'If we can tie that phone to Jones...' she says. 'All the better, in fact, if we get a warrant to search his house and find the phone itself.'

'That'd be great. Still not enough in itself, of course, but it certainly has value.'

He nods at Morrow. Morrow shakes his head.

'Nothing from the correspondence of Mrs Henderson. She wrote to him, often, but he never replied. Haven't been able to dig up any connections between the others. I'll need more time with regard to Forsyth. Get onto it in the morning.'

Another nod from the boss. Eyes move onto Eileen Harrison. Hey, the gang's all here. Yep, there are seven of us. There's an adjective to go with that, but I can't quite think of it. The Something Seven... No, it's gone.

Shit. Mind is going. Tired. That's all. Tired with the long day, tired with the feeling of cold and damp, tired with the effort of not thinking about the girl and her body rotting in an unmarked grave for the last forty-seven years, and the strange fact that the grave wasn't unmarked, that there was a quote added to the headstone, and how did that happen? And tired, more than anything, or maintaining the denial, from not thinking about the phone message from Philo, of not thinking about what she said at the end, those three words which she said to me, that I never got to say to her, tired from forcing myself to think of that phone message as evidence rather than the heartbreaking, crushing weight that it actually is.

I stare at the table. People talk. This is how it's been for much of this investigation, after all, isn't it? The inquiry has been continuing, and I've been on the periphery. What's my job supposed to be? My overall job? I have the daily duties as part of an investigation, the go and speak to him and look at the next thing and check whatever piece of paperwork. But it should also be on me to have Taylor's back when it comes to overall perspective. Keeping tabs on everything. Complete overview. I'm his right-hand man on that. I really ought to know everything.

And what do I know? Very, very little. Off chasing my own demons, as usual.

Taylor lays his hands loudly on the table, bringing the meeting to a close. Bringing his detective sergeant to attention. Checks his watch. In a Mexican yawn kind of way, so do most of the rest of us. 1.57 a.m.

'Sorry,' he says, although there's no actual trace of apology in his voice, nor need there be. 'Final push, let's just get at this and nail the fucker. The sergeant and I are going over there now to bring him in. This is what we work to. Give it another hour or two, go home, get a few hours sleep, then back here in the morning. We can get a day off when the job's done. Stephanie, get the paperwork on the go for the house search.'

She nods. Taylor gets up and walks from the room, his usual manner, no unnecessary words, no rousing talk. Doesn't need it. Everyone, fortunately, is a lot more switched on than I am.

49

Sitting in the car, the drive no more than the length of Main Street. He's given a couple of uniforms warning that they should be ready to follow in fifteen minutes. We'll call. Doesn't want to turn up too heavy-handed in the first place, although ultimately he might make the judgment to bring the vicar in with the backup.

'We're remembering this guy might have a gun,' I say, halfway along the road, when the thought suddenly occurs to me that the guy might have a gun.

No Bob on the CD player. Bob doesn't play when you're on your way to make an arrest. Maybe on the way back. If it doesn't go badly. Taylor likes to ease the passage of a suspect into police custody with a bit of Dylan.

'Yes.'

'You don't want to—'

'No,' he says. 'The one way to guarantee turning a discussion into a gunfight, is to take a gun.'

'It could be a bit one-sided,' I say. Just paying due diligence to the discussion. Don't really believe that the guy will be a problem either.

'He won't use a gun,' says Taylor.

The manse for St Stephen's is one up the road from the church. Taylor parks outside and we get out the car. Stand still in the early morning. The darkness of 2 a.m. The air is damp, the ground sodden, but it's not currently raining. Quiet, but for the underlying hum of the nearby city, and lone cars on the motorway, down the hill, away on the other side of the river.

The house is dark, no sign of life in the church, except

a night light over a rear entrance.

'There's no family?' says Taylor.

'No.'

Up the garden path, rings the bell, stands back. The quiet beauty of the 2 a.m. bust. So often a dog will start barking at this point, a child will start crying. There will be footsteps on the stairs, locks being thrown, a voice shouting through the door.

Nothing. He looks up at the bedroom window, then rings the bell again.

'Where did you speak to him?' asks Taylor. 'In his office?'

'Yep.'

'Which is in the church?'

Another nod.

'Still at work?'

'Maybe he's one of those Margaret Thatcher types. Only needs two hours of sleep a day.' And even that's taken hanging upside down from a beam in the loft.

Taylor waits another moment or two, and then walks down the road and into the church grounds. Tries the handle of the back door beneath the light. The door's open.

'Somebody's home,' he says, his voice low.

Step lightly into the corridor, close the door behind us. Completely dark inside bar a sliver of light from a barely open door at the end. Having been here before, I know the walls are lined with posters and announcements about the church, drawings from Sunday school, simplistic pictures of Jesus blessing children. The light is coming from his office.

We walk forward, our shoes sounding incredibly loud on the wooden floor. If he's there, he'll hear us coming.

I get to the door first, push it open and walk in, Taylor behind me. Reverend Jones is at his desk, same position in which I previously spoke to him.

'Sergeant,' he says, eyebrow raised. 'I wondered who was calling at such an hour. Seems late to be conducting routine police business.'

Taylor steps forward, holds out his ID.

'DCI Taylor,' he says. 'Can I ask you where you were at six o'clock this evening?'

That's the moment when you intrinsically know if you've got them. Right there. The first hint, out of the blue, that you're on to them. Virtually anyone can prepare for it, but when they don't know it's coming, it takes a real pro to balls it out.

He hesitates. There's the golden moment, the moment when we both think, you fucking, stupid loser, you might as well just give it up right now, and then he waves the hand of deceit to the side and says, 'Here, I think. Yes, yes. Here all along. It's been a long couple of days, what with Mrs Stewart... you know.'

'That must've been hard,' says Taylor, with not an iota of tone in his voice to indicate any empathy with that thought. 'She was the leader of the Bible study group?'

'Of course,' he says.

'When did you see her last?' asks Taylor.

Another hesitation as he pretends to think. As ever, even with someone this calculating, when put on the spot you can see the calculations whirring through his head. How much do the police already know?

If he's got the balls, he has to admit he saw her just before she died. Except, we know he was interviewed by Gostkowski, and said he hadn't seen her since the Sunday. The guy's in a tricky position, but if you're going to commit multiple murder...

'Sunday,' he says. 'At church.'

'I'm going to have to ask you to accompany us to the station,' says Taylor.

'Why?'

'We have a phone message to tie you to the scene of one crime, and possibly a DNA sample to tie you to an—'

'Fuck!'

Whoa. Didn't see that coming. Sure, if you imagine someone is capable of murder, then you've got to imagine that the word fuck might occasionally trip lightly from their lips. But it's not that. It's the cave. The guy caved, right there. He screamed fuck, and he caved.

'Fuck,' he says again, this time less of an ejaculation, more of a resigned statement of despair.

'If you'd like to put anything away, lock anything up, you may do so, but do it quickly and in the knowledge that we will have a warrant to search the premises.'

'Fuck,' says the vicar again, this time with added bite. 'How did you know? Seriously, how the fuck did you know?'

Jesus, for a vicar this guy's language is terrible.

He leans forwards, elbow on the desk, rubs a finger down the middle of his brow. 'Fuck it, man,' he says, then he laughs and sits back. Shaking his head, looking between the two of us. Funny how some people will tough it out as long as possible, and some will just throw in the towel.

However, usually the throw-in-the-towel brigade will have cause to regret, and often repent, their loquaciousness.

Both elbows on the table now, still shaking his head. The look comes into his eyes. The look that says he's going to regain control, of the conversation at least, if not exactly the situation.

'What have you got?' he says.

'I've given you the time to clear up your things,' says Taylor. He looks at me, gives me a nod. I turn my back on the two of them, take out my phone, make the five-second call back to the station to get the patrol car down here.

'Fuck.'

Turn round. This time it's Taylor. The reverend, sure enough, has decided to bring a gun to the discussion.

'Put it down,' says Taylor.

Stare him down, although he's not looking at me. He's interested in the boss. I contemplate charging at him. Do I care if I die?

Jesus, yes. Yes! I do care. Because of Philo. I don't know what that is, but it's because I want to think about her. I want to take her memory home with me. I want to listen to her voice again.

It'll be awkward as fuck, especially if her husband makes some kind of speech, but I want to go to her funeral. I want to remember her.

A gun? Seriously. For God's sake.

'Why?' says Taylor.

Now we're into it. When the guy is coming to the station, you don't want the random confession, you don't want it blurted out like you're in the last two minutes of a TV crime drama and you have to squeeze in all the explanation before the ten o'clock news. The gun on the table is a bit of game changer, however.

'Oh, please, Chief Inspector,' he says. Wonderfully annoyed tone, as if it's absurd that Taylor would ask. 'That arsehole Cartwright and his happy little band of brothers. Jesus. This is my church. MY church! How dare they? They weren't fucking touching it. Fucking Cartwright. That guy was just... he was just a dickhead, with his Daniel obsession and....'

'Why bother trying to fake suicide, when at the same time you were trying to frame Cartwright?' I ask.

On the other hand, might as well get the questions in while he's spilling the beans. Nothing like having a lawyer in the room to shut you up.

He waves the gun. Steady on there, Sundance.

'Aw, crap, I don't know. Keeping my options open, juggling a few balls, that was all. Options. We all need options, and then that idiot Christie walks in on me and I had to put a bullet in his wife's mouth. Jesus.'

'And it was Forsyth who told you about Cartwright's group?'

Jones sneers. A slight shake of the head, a disdainful laugh. Said all he's going to say. A slight twitch. He lifts the gun, puts it in his mouth, pulls the trigger. The noise fills the room. The back of his head explodes, blood and skull and brain matter carpet the wall behind him. His arms drop, his body jerks against the back of the chair, what's left of his head then falls forward and thumps onto the table.

'Bollocks,' mutters Taylor. 'Fucking bollocks.'

50

'What did she mean?' asks Taylor. 'When she said she was leaving you another message?'

3.31 a.m. Wrapping up the crime scene for the night. The vicar's office is awash with our lot. The body has been removed. Taylor is fucked off, and fair enough. Never good when a suspect kills himself in the presence of the police. And no matter the evidence, there will be no end of fuckers who will be happy to assume that we shot him.

Connor has been and gone. He can be relieved, at least, that this whole thing was not down to someone from his blessed congregation. On the other hand, he'll have to handle the fall-out from making a total bell-end of himself over the false arrest of Cartwright. Smooth that one out with all your church buddies, you stupid prick.

'I don't know,' I say. Have been thinking about it myself. And I really don't.

'You look shit, Sergeant.'

'Thanks.'

'Yeah, we all look shit. Listen, I'm going into the office, will work through, get this wrapped up. Maybe aim to work until lunch or so, then I'm going home to crash. You go home now, get some sleep. Be in before I leave and we'll see where we're at.'

'You sure?'

'Of course. Go.'

He turns away from the splatter on the wall, at which we've both been staring transfixed for the past few minutes. I do believe that at any other time he might have suggested that I stay away from alcohol. He knows, however, that that won't be an issue. He puts his hand on my shoulder, the slightest squeeze.

'Hope you can sleep all right. Sorry about the woman.'

*

Early morning. Still dark, still damp. Rain coming on again.

Walk back to the flat. Tired, drained. Am I really going to make it into work for midday? Of course I am. What else is there?

You don't think it's often like this?

There just won't be answers to all the questions. Jesus, everyone's dead. How are they going to give us answers? So we're left guessing. The important thing is that the killing will stop, and that there's someone at whose door the blame is definitely laid.

What do we suppose? That Reverend Jones was trying to frame Cartwright, using an obvious biblical reference with a connection to the guy? Maybe that was all it was. The press can write about it for a while, and the town can gather in huddled groups and gossip. The latter will last much longer than the former.

God knows what will happen to St Stephen's. Well, possibly even God doesn't know. Will they have the balls to go looking for a new minister, or will they fold?

Close the front door, walk through to the sitting room, stand at the window and look down. Spend so much time here when I come in after dark. Nothing to see but an empty street, yet it's beguiling in the deserted middle of the night in a way that it's not during the day.

If St Stephen's folds, who wins? Cartwright. Hmm. Cartwright wins.

No, I don't think there's anywhere to go with that thought. Maybe tomorrow. Maybe tomorrow afternoon, when I've got time to sit down and think things through with a clear head. Yes, Cartwright wins, but how could he have manipulated this situation? How could he have arranged for Reverend Jones to so quickly implode?

No, I'm not thinking about it.

The red light, reflected in the window, is still flashing. I watch it for a moment, then turn. I listened to the message. It shouldn't be flashing any more. It wasn't flashing when I went out earlier.

Someone must have left a message in the middle of the night.

I stand there staring at the phone, getting a peculiar, uneasy feeling. Finally let out a long sigh and walk over to the phone. What am I worried about? Everyone's already dead, aren't they?

Press the button. The machine clicks and buzzes. The recorded message begins. A lot of static, like a call from far away. Another time.

'Thank you.'

Click.

I look down at the phone. The voice of a young girl.

Shivers, a sudden thump of the heart. I turn and look at the room, half-expecting her to be there, but of course she's not. If she had been, she wouldn't have had to leave a message... And she's dead, so how could she be there? She was never there. She always just found her way into my nightmares.

I play the message again. It's gone. There is no message.

I feel so screwed up that I don't know if there ever was a message. I imagine her voice, the voice that had spoken to me so many times, saying those two words. *Thank you.* I can hear her right now, if I concentrate.

What am I thinking?

Go to bed, Sergeant.

Into the bathroom, clean my teeth. Stand staring at myself for a while. Have my clothes dried on me yet? Not quite. Strip off, step into the shower. Hot water, steam quickly filling the room. Five minutes, that's all. Feels like the first warmth for a long time.

Tired.

Out the shower, dry myself off, walk into the bedroom.

Stand there for a moment in the dark and the shadows cast by the streetlights. Look at the bed. I've been avoiding it.

How many nights? Doesn't matter. Will it still smell of her?

Long, tired sigh. Get some sleep, Hutton. Stop thinking.

Pull the covers back. There's a note on the pillow.

Stop, stand there for a few moments, naked and alone, melancholy descending, an avalanche of sadness. This is the other message.

I lift the note, get into bed, pull the covers up and turn on the light. A torn-in-half piece of A4, folded again. A short note, handwriting that I don't recognise because I haven't seen it before, but that I will come to love. Just from these few words.

My Dearest Hutton… it begins. I laugh. Can't help myself. Such a sad laugh. *It might be tough for a while, but I know we'll be together. It's funny. Feels such a perfect thing, almost as though there's nothing we can do about it.*

And I look forward to every single minute. Philo x

I read the note again. And again. By the fourth time I can't see the words for tears. But I know what it says.

51

Connor's office. Taylor and I waiting for the great man to pronounce. Two days later. The day after the bishop blew his brains out Connor wasn't seen much around the office. Out most of the day. Nominally reaching out to the community in an official capacity. More likely, desperately trying to save his own arse. The last thing he wants is a bunch of lawyers and bankers and the sort that frequent the churches here ganging up on him and marching on Pitt Street with pitchforks and lighted torches, demanding his removal.

He's making notes on a file while Taylor and I wait. Can't see what he's writing, but I'd bet it's the equivalent of *rhubarb rhubarb rhubarb*. He's not thinking about his stupid file, he's thinking, *hmm, I wonder how much longer I'll leave them sitting there stewing. Oh dear, I wonder if they are stewing. Maybe they're looking at me with contempt. Maybe they think I'm shit. No, no, that's not it. They're awe-inspired with my capacity to take on so much work, and understand that my life is a desperate push to squeeze everything in. Either that or they think I'm a dick.*

He looks up, closing the folder as he does so. Yes, he closed the folder without even watching what he was doing. The monkey can multi-task.

'Where are we, Chief Inspector?' he asks.

Good morning, gentlemen. It's been a rough few days. I appreciate all your hard work, though, and the long hours you put in. It must've been awful for you to witness the suicide. Obviously I'll be setting up a trauma risk assessment for the two of you on that, and if there's anything else I can do, or that you think you need, don't hesitate to ask.

That's what he really wants to say.

'Paul Cartwright has been more forthcoming on the matter of Reverend Jones, now that he's in the clear. It appears the two of them had a long-standing feud, and even though the situation of the churches was settled, they both still harboured designs on that which they didn't have. Small-town politics, as we knew all along. Cartwright was trying to engineer a takeover of St Stephen's, the vicar... well, who knows? Trying to destroy St Mungo's and have everyone troop along to his place?'

'There was something of the crazed dictator about him,' I chip in. That probably doesn't help. The grown-ups ignore me.

'I spoke to Mr Cartwright,' says Connor. 'He's fine. He's fine.'

He nods vigorously to himself, realising that he's convincing no one. If Cartwright is fine, it can only be because he's extracting his pound of Connor's flesh in one way or another.

'How did Reverend Jones know what Cartwright was doing?' he asks, when he finally stops nodding at how fine every fucker is.

'Don't know,' says Taylor. 'Will keep looking, but my guess is that Forsyth told him. But could have been any one of them, any one of those who ultimately Jones decided to kill. There are a lot of unanswered questions. We'll keep on it, but there are a lot of people dead, so it makes it harder.'

'And what about this girl in the grave?'

Taylor doesn't immediately answer that. He glances at me, which is fair enough. We've wrapped that one up, all the while ignoring the elephant in the room. Connor looks at me, although you can tell he's reluctant to do so.

I'm not usually capable of artifice, and this particular moment proves no different.

'She haunted me,' I say.

'What?'

Taylor gives me a bit of an eyebrow, but no more than that.

'What?' repeats Connor.

I had this uncle. His name was Malcolm. An accountant. Didn't know him that well. He lived up in Inverness, so didn't see him often. Never married, lived on his own. The dude was quite high up in the Masons apparently. So, you know, he probably knew where the Holy Grail's being hidden, that kind of thing. He knew stuff. Thinking about it, he was probably gay, but was of the generation where you hid it. Didn't tell anyone, didn't let it affect his standing in the community.

Told us a story one time. He said that weird shit had started happening in his kitchen. And more than once. Fridge door left wide open overnight. Dirty plates from the sink tossed onto the floor. Cupboards emptied, packets and jars strewn around. At first, of course, he thought someone was breaking in, but then he'd hear it happening, rush into the kitchen, and there was no one there. Decided it was a poltergeist. Spoke to some people, wondered about getting a priest in, some shit like that. Was advised to stand in the middle of the kitchen and tell the spirit to leave. That was all. So he did. That's what he told us. This middle-aged accountant, in his middle-aged accountant's suit, stood in the middle of his kitchen and told an unseen spirit to get the fuck out of his house, because it wasn't wanted.

And it worked.

I think about telling this little anecdote to Connor. To say, there's weird shit out there, man, it's not just me. This is the kind of thing that happens. Don't try to explain it, because you can't. Just take it at face value.

'I came across the fact of Reverend Forsyth's daughter having disappeared under unusual circumstances over four decades ago. She was never found, alive or dead. During the course of the investigation I began to have suspicions about one of the graves at the Old Kirk. I undertook to open the grave, and we found the body of Forsyth's daughter.'

'He killed her,' says Connor, a statement rather than a question.

'Maybe,' I reply, 'but we're unlikely to ever know for sure. She's dead, he's dead, and his ex-wife does not want the heartache of the case being brought up again. She just wants to give her daughter a proper burial.'

'What if the minister was covering up for his wife? What if it was the wife who killed her?' he asks.

He has a fair point.

'I don't think that's the case here, sir,' says Taylor, 'but if you want us to look into it, then we can do.'

Connor stares in that impressive way of his across the table. And we know, of course, that he's not thinking about the merits of re-opening the case, because if he was, he'd be asking more questions. He's thinking about the politics of re-opening the case, thinking about how it will look if Mrs Faraday troops along to the *Daily Record* or the *Mail on Fucking Sunday*.

'I'll think about it,' he says. 'Send me the paperwork.'

We both nod. I, at least, am thinking, if you're waiting for me to upload the fucking paperwork onto your stupid, dumb-ass computer system that you championed so much, then you'll be waiting a long time, buddy. Perhaps that is what he's thinking.

Then, without even looking at what he's doing, this Batman of police officialdom moves the file he's been working on into an out-tray and places another one in front of him. It seems our time here is at an end.

'Gentlemen,' he says.

No, no, really, it's fine, you don't have to thank us for the work. No really, come on, sir, you're embarrassing us. Stop it, now.

We leave. Close the door behind us and walk back towards Taylor's office, although I'm going to peel off before we get there.

'Nice recovery on the ghost story,' he says. 'Maybe next time...'

'Yeah, yeah.'

Make a slight acknowledging hand gesture.

'What have you got on?' he asks.

'Off to see a guy about a thing.'

*

I find my ex-HSBC cleaner at the toilets behind the shops on the lower side of Main Street. There's a yellow board propped up in the doorway. CLEANING IN PROGRESS. He's in a cubicle. There's an overwhelming aroma of bleach. Which is, at least, better than the usual overwhelming smell you get in public toilets.

'Hey,' I say.

'You're fine,' he says without turning. 'Just use one of the other cubicles if you need to.'

'It's the Fuzz,' I say.

He turns, straightens up. He's wearing gloves, has a cloth in his hands.

'Wow,' he says. 'Thought you'd forgotten about me.'

Walks out the cubicle, smiles, makes a small apologetic gesture for not being able to shake hands.

'Sorry, been pretty busy,' I say.

'It's cool,' he says. 'I saw that stuff on the news. You've got to figure that the mass slaughter of church-goers is more important than people writing *you cock* on a wall.'

I smile, look around the walls. The usual collection of insults and toilet-wall wisdom.

'It's been a while since I've had the time to work on this place,' he says. 'Enough trouble keeping it clean.'

I dig the piece of paper out of my pocket and hand it over. He removes his right glove.

'Spoke to this guy at North Lanarkshire. He works with the police on graffiti prevention. Apologised for not having got to work on this previously. Give him a call. He'll get the walls of the toilets, inside and out, done with graffiti-resistant paint. They run a course he said you can go on if you want. Graffiti prevention. He called it a masterclass, but you know, we'll let that one go.'

He laughs.

'What else... There are some CCTV cameras out there, and up at the shops at Hamilton Street. We'll turn them on the entrance to the toilets for a few days. We can't, obviously, catch anyone in the act, but we might get an idea. Some six-year-old walking in with a tin of paint or a collection of marker pens sticking out his back pocket. The guy will also speak to you about people going into the local schools, which is obviously something that works for more than just the beleaguered toilets of the area.'

'I can do that,' he says, nodding.

'You want to go and speak to school children?'

He laughs again.

'It'll get me out the office for a while.'

Bonkers.

'You sort it out with your guy,' I say, pointing at the piece of paper.

He looks at it and shrugs.

'I've spoken to this bloke before.'

'Didn't get anywhere?'

Shake of the head.

'Well, now he's got the Fuzz on his back, I could tell he didn't like it. Give me a shout if you don't get anywhere.'

'Sure.'

OK. That'll do it. The conversation is over, and we're just two guys standing chatting in the public toilet.

'Better crack on,' I say. 'Let me know how you get on. I'll tell you when we're going to do the CCTV thing.'

'Cheers.'

Out the door, back up the short ramp to the precinct.

Stop for a moment and look around. A few shoppers, but not much doing. Not really. This town is dead.

A bright day, crisp, mostly clear skies. Look up at the tower block in front of me, and then over my shoulder.

What happens now?

Well, what usually happens? Life goes on.

Lunchtime. I wonder if I could go and sit in my own personal church for half an hour. Get some peace. Seems kind of weird to think about that now the investigation's over. And Mrs Buttler might not be so welcoming now that we've released Cartwright and found an unexpected corpse buried in her graveyard.

I should probably stay away and find my own peace for a while.

I head back towards the station with no particular thought in mind. Start wondering when the boss might get around to actually suspending me, and I can go off somewhere. North, I think. I'm going to go north.

As I reach the station I notice the coffee shop across the road, check my watch, decide to go in. I can sit in silence and think about looking at the cold northern sea, and I can choose to think about my lost love if I want, and if that's going to prove to be too traumatic, I can think about something else.

The café is quiet for lunchtime, but Sergeant Harrison is there, alone at a table. She smiles as I pass on my way to the counter.

'You all right, Sergeant?' she asks.

'Might be,' I answer. Really, who the fuck knows?

'You want to join me?'

Hmm. Now, I've got my cold northern sea to think about. And the other thing. And anyway, does she really want me to join her or is she just asking out of politeness or some sort of sisterly concern? Although, is that necessarily a bad thing? She's just being nice.

'Sure,' I say. 'Can I get you anything?'

She glances down at her nearly finished baguette and says, 'Americano with milk would be great.'

I head to the sandwich cabinet and grab my cheese and tomato ciabatta with that incredible Italian basil everyone's talking about.

Printed in Great Britain
by Amazon